ORANGE CITY

LEE MATTHEW GOLDBERG

atmosphere press

Published by Atmosphere Press

Cover design by Christina Loraine

Orange City
2020, Lee Matthew Goldberg

atmospherepress.com

"The world breaks everyone and afterward many are strong at the broken places."

-Ernest Hemingway, *A Farewell to Arms*

PART I:

THE SELECTED

1

At six on the dot, the gloved cellular let out a piercing ring. A timer turned on, ticking down with each buzz. E wouldn't have long to remain idle. The entire pod apartment vibrated, and his capsule bed slid open. The white ceiling drew his attention, the walls devoid of color, a minimalist's fantasy—nothing like a home.

Shades of the dream from last night still lingered. His knuckles painted with blood as he beat a shadow. The voice of the shadow belonging to a ten-year-old boy. The boy's cries stabbing E's ears. He shook that dream away.

He removed the intravenous tube that connected him

to his bed and switched off the cooling mist which allowed him to slumber for days. He stretched his old bones, his hair standing up in a state of white shock like it had since he was a young man. Swinging his thick legs over the side of the bed, he yawned at the morning before finally answering his cell.

"I'll be right there," he coughed into the digital eye on his gloved palm.

He removed the glove and pushed a button on the side of the bed. Doors opening along the wall revealed a sliver of a kitchen with a piping pot of subpar and gritty coffee brewing on the counter— the best offered to the Scouts— and two sizzling poached eggs from a suspect source. He scarfed down the eggs and pushed another button to raise the shades along the lone wall facing east. The heart of The City hovered in the near distance, its new buildings staggering on one end like giant colorful stalagmites. Sipping his black coffee, he watched it in motion as he did every morning.

Between the Scouts and the rest of The City lay a half a mile of ice water. The City was made up of many Regions, his situated on the outskirts. Sometimes he wondered what it would be like to fall into those frosty waters and drift off to wherever it might choose to take him, no longer having to shuttle between The City and the faraway Outside World anymore. But instead of a dramatic suicide, he suited up and headed through the tunnel with a suitcase in hand like he had for twenty years. He'd convinced himself long ago that living here was better than rotting in prison like he would've been if they hadn't selected him. At least he was still able to get lost in a bottle of whiskey or feel the sun against his cheek during the few instances it was allowed to peek through the chronic clouds. Even though The City was far from ideal, the Outside World remained definitely worse. It reminded him too often of the man he used to be and of the terrible sins he'd committed. These thoughts returned at the beginning of every week while he geared up for another one, as he wondered if one day the Man in the Eye might give him a promotion and he wouldn't have to be a Scout anymore.

That way, he'd never have to return to the Outside World.

Then, he could possibly be at peace, like all The City's inhabitants wished.

2

As E's taxi pulled up to the Walled Region of The City, the silhouette of the Man in the Eye Tower stood precisely in the same spot as always—immovable. The Man's long arachnid-like arms stretched across the windows, his red eyes scanning every movement below from a hundred stories high. The rest of the buildings were less imposing than the Eye Tower, created with The City's own twinkling glass. The maze of sidewalks below were clean enough to eat off, a stark contrast to the pod apartments in E's Region, stacked beside one another like eggs in a crate, no sidewalks offering a chance for him to walk by a neighbor and mingle.

Passing a row of silent Guards, E fixed his mouth into a smile as he swiped his ID through the machine at the gate. Besides The Finances, The Scouts were the only other citizens allowed inside the Walled Region. The gate opened as two cameras zoomed in until they practically touched his face. The rest of the area, a square about a half-mile long, resembled a ghost town: not even a tumbleweed rolling past. But through the windows he caught a glimpse of The Finances, all required to be chained to their desks, each of them typing in sync with sweat pooling from their foreheads onto the keys.

E spied a rogue Finance, his eyes ringed with purple circles, scurrying into a blue glass building. Brain-fried and pallid, the Finance was downing a fistful of black market Levels while glancing at his watch in fright before stuffing the pill bottle back in his pocket. Clearly late, he'd receive a swift punishment for his tardiness.

In the center beamed the Eye Tower, showing its muscle. For the first ninety-nine stories, an elevator rose through black translucent glass to a windowed office at the top in the shape of an eye. Separate access was required, so E swiped his Scout ID again as two other cameras zoomed in and poked him in the face before massive doors clanged open at the bottom and he stepped inside.

The elevator whooshed up toward the sky, overlooking the entire City. Pockets of Empty Zones, barren wastelands for disobeying citizens, became visible along with the colorful high-rises of the new Downtown area. The Business Region was a blip at the other end, containing everything from the advertising firms, to a publishing house, to The City's own movie studio that financed its one film plus all of the commercials and the porn. The Factory Region spewed smoke rings to the right. By the Wharf, a line of Guards monitored the waters with guns in hand; making sure that no one left or entered without an okay from the Man. The elevator continued to climb up higher into the gray clouds until it all seemed enveloped in a morose haze. E still held his smile, his cheek muscles starting to twitch.

A bell dinged as the elevator reached the top and opened to a metallic entranceway. The door to the Man's office was also shaped like an eye, but closed, resembling a shuteye. An imposing Guard held post in front. Like all the Guards, he had a skintight white mask pulled over his face with holes cut out around the nostril area, replicating the Man's mysterious visage. Past the entranceway was a long silver desk with the Man's relatively new receptionist, Shelby. She had no left eye, the lid sewn shut. E knew the Man required all his secretaries to be missing one eye. Shelby was the fifth during his tenure.

"Morning, Shelby," E said. "How are you doing today?"

"Morning," she responded with a smile, her voice flat and lifeless. She typed something on the keyboard without looking away from the screen. Pushing an intercom button, she spoke into a speaker. "Scout E to see you, sir."

A murmur hissed from the other end.

Shelby pushed a different button under her desk and the eye-shaped door parted. E gave a polite wave, but she was too absorbed in her work and only blinked her one eye in response.

E left his suitcase next to the Guard and walked through the eye. Once inside, the metal doors snapped shut. The spacious office was made up of thousands of small television screens and computers along the walls that monitored all aspects of The City. A life-sized wax statue of Stalin greeted all who entered with a salute. He knew of the dictator from history books when the Outside World was a very different place. E was always surprised about Stalin's small stature; the top of the statue's head barely came up to his own chin. A long table in the center held a mainframe computer and a dozen gloved cellular phones charging on robotic hands. Some of the phones were ringing, completely ignored.

The Man posed by the eye-shaped window. Most of the inhabitants only witnessed this mysterious figure on screens, but the fear he radiated was palpable: gaunt to the point of being grotesque, so emaciated that it seemed as if he could snap in two. He did not eat, only fed intravenously from a bubbling orange liquid attached to his side by a tube. E wasn't sure if it filtered his waste, or was a breakfast that looked like some type of soda. The Man wore the same outfit as always: black suit, white collared shirt and a thin black tie. It was questionable whether the Man had ever changed his clothes, or if he'd lived in this shell of a suit for the past two decades. He often smelled like burning sugar mixed with sour chemicals, and E had to balance holding his breath while speaking so the Man's fumes wouldn't trigger any nausea.

Over the years, the Man had gotten taller and taller through elective surgeries that lengthened his legs until they became distorted. The Man's extended arms were also his obsession and delight—thin-like branches. A few were long enough to reach from one end of the office to the other. His scientists had spent years perfecting these appendages, made from a mixture of aluminum alloy and real muscle and bone along with computer circuitry. Through chips inserted into his tendons, the Man's brain signals were read by electrodes and used to guide these artificial devices. Some of his earlier limbs looked more robotic, but his latest were so lifelike, it was chilling to watch them in motion. E wondered how it looked under the Man's suit: probably all bloody and deformed, a patchwork of humanity; but on the outside, the Man was truly a magnificent creature to behold, both threatening and eerily beautiful, like nothing E had ever witnessed or imagined before.

The Man's few extra hands tapped a staccato beat against the windowpane. He rotated his face a few inches to the left. The mask he wore: a skintight white blur molded to his face. E assumed that he liked remaining an enigma.

"You're late," the Man said, his voice gummy as if he'd been chewing on honey.

A thousand excuses ran through E's brain. None would suffice.

"I apologize, sir."

The Man let out one solitary laugh through the holes in his mask for nostrils. An extended limb slithered past E and punched a few keys on a computer.

"Do you recognize this face?" the Man asked as E turned to a television screen. A young man's headshot: thin face with barely any jaw, eyeglasses, and a forlorn gaze.

"Is that...Graham Weatherend?" E asked in shock.

E had not encountered that face in a long time and his legs went wobbly, the dreams that invaded last night coming back swiftly. He thought back to the year he spent with Graham over a decade ago; the year he was forced to be a monster. Now the boy was all grown up, but the sadness in his eyes remained. He was likely in his late teens now and would want nothing more than to pound E's face to a bloody pulp should the two ever encounter each other again. E remembered how he would go to bed with the boy's blood staining his fists, even after he'd washed them a thousand times. But he was forced to do that. He had no other choice.

"I do recognize him," E said, softly. He tried hard not to show emotion, but it was difficult.

"We couldn't touch him as a juvie, but our boy is nineteen now and has tried to rob a liquor store with a wooden gun. I'll let you guess how that worked out for him. I assumed something like this would happen eventually."

The Man's long arm moved from the computer, brushing against E.

"I assumed one day it would be time for him to come to The City," E replied, as the hairs on the back of his neck stood on end. Graham's computer image stared back, causing him to cringe.

"He's young and malleable now," the Man said. "He'll be indebted to us if we bring him here, easier to fall in line. Who knows if that will be the case in a few years?"

"Won't he recognize my voice?"

One of the Man's hands groped his own chin, pondering.

"Doubtful. It's been so long. We'll insert a Blocker just in case. Anyway, he is looking at a couple of years up in a penitentiary with all his priors. He won't be thinking about anything else but survival."

"Are you sure I'm the right Scout to bring him over–"

The Man's white face spun around. E tried to see something human in the midst of the Man's façade but there was nothing: a hollow face like a puff of smoke.

"You are the only choice!" the Man hissed. He then cleared his throat, calming down. "I trust you, Scout E. You were one of the first we had here. Scouts M, X, K, R and A have either been promoted and live in the Estates now, or passed on. Maybe it's finally time for a promotion for you, too?"

"A position inside The City?" E asked, salivating at the thought. He imagined himself living in the Estates Region with The City's elite. An existence with all the amenities one could ask for, and more importantly, a better shot at never being banished to the Empty Zones.

"If you bring me Weatherend, and he comes without being forced, I will give you what you deserve. Recently, I've had to retire the Creative Director at Warton, Mind & Donovan Advertising and Concepts to the Zones. Terrible business."

"No more Scouting?" E asked, careful with his tone, not wanting to seem too eager or ungrateful for the job he'd been given. The Man sometimes liked to play games to ferret out insubordination.

"I know it wouldn't please you to be a Scout forever," the Man said, sadly.

"It's been an honor," E replied, in his most convincing tone.

"Yes, as it should. I thought of giving you the Creative Director position, since you were once a chemical engineer in the Outside World."

"I don't see how that's connected with advertising."

The Man tapped his intravenous tank with one of his appendages, causing the liquid to bubble.

"Pow!" the Man chuckled, his mouth widening to resemble a black hole.

"I'm still not understanding–"

"Let's say The City is on the forefront of a brand-new vision, one that we want the masses to believe in, but not simply because I tell them."

"Okay..."

"We're years away from getting the tweaks just right. Think about Moods, how long those took to develop, or the Levels being sold on the black market now."

"I've never taken–"

The Man held up one of his many hands. "I am not accusing. I am saying that advertisement firms are the face of The City, the true power. It will only be beneficial for you to work at one. And I will be putting Mr. Weatherend under you there."

"But I would've been his Scout? We can't know each other, that's against the rules." E knew the Scouts were kept separate from the rest of the citizens in a Region because of a sticky situation that had occurred during The City's first few years when a Selected became unhappy with his new home and sought out the Scout that brought him there. The Scout ultimately got his throat slit, so now all interactions were forbidden between the two after the initial drop-off. Since the Scouts spent a good portion of their time in the Outside World, the pod apartments were mostly for them to sleep.

"I made the rules!" the Man said. "And this is what I wish. He'll be blindfolded as always and won't know that you were his Scout. And then once he gets here, I want you to make sure he stays insecure, subordinate, even scared. You will morph into a being he fears...again. This is imperative for what I have planned."

"Yes...absolutely, sir."

The Man's white face spun back around and he chuckled.

"Your head is so far up my ass that you can see out of my mouth. I like that about you, Scout E, I always have."

E had no idea how to respond. He murmured a halfhearted, "Thank you."

"Stalin said that 'Gratitude is a sickness suffered by dogs.' Bring me Weatherend and you'll be out of the pods by next week. You'll be my eyes and ears at Warton, Mind & Donovan. As of late, I've been concerned about the Heads of all the major corporations. Even though I began here as a Head as well, I am so much more now. Sometimes that breeds jealousy, so I want you to be my consigliore. It will be our little secret. You'll report to me if one of them is being insubordinate. How does that sound, my little please-and-thank-you lapdog?"

He reached out to pet Scout E's white hair.

"There, there, little pet. *Moy malen'kiy pitomets.*" [1]

The Man's long pale fingers ran through E's scalp.

"I trust you," the Man said, his fingers gliding down to E's left eye. He closed the lid with a pleased shudder. "You have such a nice eye. If you ever want to give it over to my collection...?"

E exhaled. He never knew whether the Man might pluck out his eye on a whim.

"Yes... I will let you know if I ever decide."

---

[1] *My little pet,* translated from Russian.

"Some were glad to give their eyes over. It is a sign of true devotion. Shelby's was my latest. Gray. Rather rare."

"Yes...rare," E stammered. Sweat formed on his upper lip. "Do you...uhh...have Mr. Weatherend's file, sir?"

The Man woke from his dreamy stupor. He stopped caressing E's eye and pulled up Graham's file on the computer.

E moved back, taking a breath as the printer spit out a glossy copy.

"He's in Dyanama," the Man said, picking up the printed pages. "You will meet with a Scout H for this assignment. She is new and will need to be trained."

"Are there any boundaries?" E asked.

The Man gurgled his laughs.

"You do like them fresh from the Outside World, don't you?"

E looked down at his shoes to avoid eye contact.

"Yes, you certainly do. Like the one who got away...all because you lost your grip."

The Man rested all of his hands on his stomach, satisfied with his dig.

E went to respond, but was at a loss for words. His face turning pale.

"Scout H knows to comply," the Man said. "Just like you did with the former Scout A, and her odd predilections. And if Scout H doesn't, I'll know she's not in it for the long haul, and her contract will be severed."

His fingers caressed E's eye again, one long fingernail circling around the left socket, drawn to it like an addict. E tried not to flinch.

"What does Scout H look like?"

"You'll know when you see her. She'll be wearing a

piece of jewelry with an angel and devil on it as a marker. The penitentiary is in the outskirts of Dyanama. You'll meet her at midnight tonight in a hole of a bar called Bombed Sally's. There's a boat waiting at the Wharf for you now."

"Thank you again, sir. I will succeed."

"*Moy malen'kaya sobachka*," the Man laughed. [2] "This Selected is crucial as I'm sure I made you aware. If you don't succeed, I won't hesitate to toss you into the Zones."

E's mouth dropped, his face flushed with terror.

"I'm glad we're clear," the Man hissed until E finally nodded.

The Man then folded his many hands in front of him and turned back to his eye-shaped window as a sign that the conversation was over.

The eye-shaped door opened, and E slowly backed out until he could only see the Man's faint, arachnid shadow before the door coldly snapped shut.

"Good-bye, Shelby," he said, picking up his suitcase by the imposing Guard, but she only answered by pressing a button to call the elevator. He prepped his wide smile as the doors dinged open.

---

[2] *My little lapdog*, translated from Russian.

3

Once E's boat took off toward the Outside World, The City disappeared from view; all that remained were vast, choppy waters as if it never existed. The Man's scientists had created image projectors long ago that sent out camouflaged holograms to ensure that their haven remained hidden. The City only became visible again once the sensors were crossed. If an unfortunate wandering boat ever smacked into its landmass, its crew would be apprehended by patrolling Guards and brought to the Man for further instruction; but that had never happened before.

Each time E left, he enjoyed watching as The City got sucked into oblivion. For a moment, he wasn't anywhere. Free from the Man's scrutiny, on his own island. A light snow brushed against him, and he let the flakes fall on his tongue. Going back to the Outside World made him anxious, even though he traveled there often. After twenty years, it was still steeped in the past, and he relived the same nightmare every time he pulled up to its shores.

He turned around and headed toward the bow. Squiggles of uninhabitable land, mostly ice formations, materialized in the far distance. He tried not to think of his late wife, like always, but he was powerless against the memories. He wished he could forget her, but that was impossible. She remained frozen in time as the young aerobics instructor he married. Spandex clothes and a blond ponytail that swayed as she walked. He had never felt skin so smooth. He loved the smell of her after a shower, his 'bunny' as he'd call her. He loved her every morning when she'd roll over in bed, run her hands through his thick, black hair, and say, "Wake up, Grumpy."

That all changed when he caught her in bed with another man. She had seemed glad. He recalled the smile on her face, one that he'd never seen before—almost evil.

He punched the guy in the throat, crushing his larynx. She called him every terrible thing that he already knew about himself. He had no idea she was so unhappy. They went at each other. She attacked him. He wasn't trying to hurt her; he was only fighting back. Her nails were sharp and sliced his cheeks. He flung her away from him, toward the window, so hard that his muscles ached after letting her go. She crashed through the glass three stories up. When he staggered over to the shattered window, she lay on the ground below like a broken doll with its limbs all out of whack. He bolted out of the house without seeing if she was alive or dead. He ran for hours until he reached a motel on the outskirts of the next town and hid out there for days in a ball of sweaty fear. One morning, the cops knocked and knocked until they finally blasted the door down. When they found him lying under the bed surrounded by a stream of puke, his hair had already begun to go gray, and he looked like an old, lost man.

He was given twenty-to-life and cried when the jury read the verdict, but he never spent a day in prison. After the trial, they locked him in a cell, but a tall, gaunt man wearing a black suit visited him. This gaunt man referred to himself simply as "The Man". The Man's head was wrapped with bandages like a burn victim, his face unidentifiable. This Man had a badge from some agency he'd never heard of. The Man also had one extra arm, longer than the others. The Man wouldn't answer any questions about the extra arm, but he did have a proposition. Recently, a secret City had been built on an isolated island in an undisclosed location, a place unlike any other. While an unforgivable act of murder had been committed, prison was not necessarily the most useful punishment. The City needed citizens—it needed workers, and it needed them now. Since prisons were becoming overcrowded, the government was looking at different alternatives for a few selected felons. This was a decision that had to be made right away. The Man had no time to wait around. The Man was certain that others who were in a bind would say yes without a second thought, but he came here today because this case caught his eye. A similar thing had happened to the Man in the past, but instead of having his mistake become his undoing, he was given an opportunity, a second chance, a brand-new City to inhabit. This Man believed that everyone deserved that second chance.

"Rise from the ashes," the Man said, extending a pasty hand. "There are a few key moments in life, and this is one of them. Today is your four-leaf clover. Shake to that, Mr. Edwards."

"Is this an angel I see before me?" he responded to the Man, coughing out a laugh. "Or the devil at his most suspicious?"

The Man chuckled as well, causing the bandage tied around his head to slide below his nose. Two blinking, robotic eyes stared back like red laser pointers. The Man's skeletal fingers quickly covered them up with the bandage again.

"There is certainly a thin line between an angel and the devil," the Man said. "But you already know that, don't you? That's why you're here. You've been a relatively good man all these years, but then you *slipped* so easily. Fallen."

The Man hovered, his shadow creeping up the ceiling and devouring the light in the tiny room. His extra arm reached out and collected any guilty tears on his long fingers.

"Come with me, Mr. Edwards," the Man whispered. "You're not the monster they say you are."

"I'm sorry for hurting you, bunny," he mumbled, to the ceiling. "I'm sorry for ever loving you."

"You stay here and you'll remain that monster," the Man hissed. "You come to my City and it all vanishes. You are reborn. But if you choose to come, you will be committed to us forever, never to live fully in the Outside

World again. But this Outside World, never returning to greatness since the War to End All Wars, is no longer hospitable in my eyes anyway."

Mr. Edwards peered up into the Man's bandaged eyes, his own leaking tears, his body convulsing. A contract was placed in front of him. A pen found its way into his hand. He was ready to sign a name that he'd never see again. He knew that he might be making a deal with a so-called devil, but in his thirty-odd years of life, God had never made an offer this good.

So, he signed his life away in blood-red ink, never to be called by his actual name again, hoping that this contract truly meant he was beginning as someone new: a faceless, nameless man who would not be defined by his sins anymore.

Little did he know that those sins would never go away, no matter what faraway world he escaped to.

4

E dropped off his suitcase at the local motel and headed to Bombed Sally's to meet with Scout H. The Man in the Eye never sprung for good digs; it was shoddy motels all the way. Being after midnight, he was running late. A mess when the plane took off, his late wife on his mind more than ever; but after two Dewars, he was finally doing all right. By the time he touched down in Dyanama, he was in a semi-stupor. He slapped his cheeks to wake up and then rented a car.

At Bombed Sally's, a few regulars sat scattered in booths by the pool table. The jukebox played rock music, but it had been turned down, no one here in the mood to dance. A sign at the entrance promised *Dollar Draft Tuesdays, Hope There'll Still Be a Wednesday*. At the bar, an old drunk snoozed into his arm, and a young girl smoked long cigarettes. She was swaying to the music, and he could tell she was slightly inebriated. On her wrist, she had a bracelet with jangling angel and devil charms. She wore a denim mini skirt and a jacket in a lighter denim shade. Her long brown hair slicked back like it had just been washed, pink lipstick making her appear juvenile.

"Scout H?" he asked, pulling up a stool.

She raised her eyebrows with a nod, then offered him a cigarette.

"Only cigars for me," he said.

"You're late. I'm already two drinks in."

She tapped the counter to order another, the angel and devil charms jingling on her bracelet.

"Two of those," E told the bartender.

"It's an amaretto sour."

"Switch the amaretto for whiskey and leave out the sour," he told the bartender. "Sorry I'm late. I was in The City this morning. Long day."

She took a final drag and put out the cigarette without responding. Scout H had an innocent face, but her eyes were sharp, judgmental.

"Have you been to The City yet?" he asked her. The bartender brought over their drinks and E left a ten.

"No."

"I've been there twenty years."

"Should I bow?"

He waited to see if she was joking, but she gave him nothing. Her pink lips tightened into a frown. He figured she hadn't warmed up to the reality of leaving the Outside World yet.

"I'm sorry, did I say something to offend you?"

She sighed, lighting another cigarette.

"I'm just...trying to rationalize all of this."

He stared at her long fingers, the nail polish chipped and girlish.

"You don't have to be afraid to come," he said. "The Scouts' apartments are quite sufficient. They're finally building a new Downtown area too, with tons of entertainment, and there is opportunity to move up from Scouting. The whole City is really..."

"Really what?"

"It's a good time to come is all," he said, swallowing hard. He chugged the glass of whiskey, savoring the burning sensation as it dripped down his throat. "And better than any prison sentence you'd be given here."

"I haven't committed any crime."

"Come again?"

"I've never even been arrested before."

He scratched his head, baffled. The only citizens who had been Selected before were those about to be sentenced, their position in The City reflecting the level of crime they committed.

"I'm not going to The City either," she said, shrugging her shoulders.

E was stunned, trying not to show his confusion. He looked around the dive bar as if someone could be watching them, and then felt foolish for doing so. Often, he forgot that in the Outside World the Man's cameras could no longer monitor. He leaned in close and whispered, "You have to live in The City. It's a requirement–"

"Not for me. I'm allowed to stay here in Dyanama...for now. It's in my contract. One day I will have to come, but the Man said he doesn't want me there yet."

E chugged the rest of his third whiskey of the day. He wondered if he'd drank too much and if this conversation was all part of an inebriated hallucination.

"I have a child," Scout H said, into her amaretto sour. She then knocked it back.

This was news to E as well because the Man had also only sought out people who were unattached. Those with no one in their lives who'd try to track them down.

"You're so young," was all he could say.

"What does that have to do with anything?"

"Nothing...no...it's just that you are."

"Well, I have a child. That's the reality."

She tapped the counter for another drink. E got the bartender's attention for another one as well.

"What's her name?"

"Amelia," she said, as if she hated the name, the word bitter on her tongue.

"That's a very pretty name."

"Yeah, pretty, sure. She was born with Tetra-Amelia Syndrome. You don't know what that is."

"No."

"I was coming down from the epidural. She was a really difficult birth. I lost a lot of blood, and I almost lost her. The doctor told me her syndrome before I even saw her. We didn't have any money or insurance so I had only been to clinics that didn't even notice a problem. The name Amelia...seemed right. I was so doped up. I pictured her as a little girl doing cartwheels in our back lawn."

The drinks arrived and Scout H took a break from speaking to nurse hers. There was no emotion on her face. A robot relayed this story.

"What is Tetra-Amelia Syndrome?"

Scout H exhaled a plume of smoke in his face. She didn't look like a young girl anymore, but someone trapped in a wrong body. The angel and devil charms clinked as she chewed at a fingernail.

"It means she has no limbs. No arms, no legs. She has some facial issues too...a cleft palate, but nothing too serious there. Most babies like her die stillborn, or shortly after, but she's...lucky I guess."

"I'm so sorry."

"I don't need your pity."

"No, no you don't." He sipped at his whiskey, pondering what she had told him. The Man had the ability to change The City's rules at any time. It had happened before and it was happening again. He rationalized that her daughter's missing appendages were the reason for this newfound deal the Man had offered, even if he hadn't exactly figured out why yet.

"So the Man has promised you limbs?" he asked, casually, as if he already knew the answer. "Is that why you agreed to work for him?"

"What a detective you are."

"I've seen what his scientists have done recently. Completely lifelike limbs connected to his brain with full control and everything."

"Look, I signed the contract. I've already been sold. I don't need your pitch, too."

"And you get to stay with your daughter here?"

"Before we begin any procedures, I need to wait until

she's close to fully formed, at least a teenager. In the meantime, I'll be shuttling back and forth at his beck and call."

"Aren't we all?" E winked, really feeling the liquor now. He found her story touching, her body attractive. He'd always been drawn to those from the Outside World, since there was something more complete about them.

"A Scout just like you showed up at my door a couple of months ago and said his boss had seen my case in the papers," she continued. "I was looking for donations. I'm a waitress and medical bills are expensive. Amelia's father had taken one look at her the day she was born, called her a mutant, and I never saw him again. And the way the new government treats anyone with disabilities, it's a disgrace."

"That's tragic," E said, fumbling to cup his hand over hers. She didn't take it away.

"Anyway," she said, "this other Scout told me that 'there were a few key moments in life and this is one of them'. And that 'today was my four-leaf clover'."

E nodded with a smirk; a speech he knew all too well.

"So are the twenty questions over?" she asked, starting to slur her words. "Can I finish my drink and go to bed already?"

"Let me walk you back to the motel," he said, soothing, his hand on the back of her neck now.

"I'm fine." She slammed her glass and spun off the stool, tottering on high heel boots. She wobbled and then held onto the bar for support.

"Don't be silly," he said, his arm around her waist. "I'm supposed to look after you."

She coughed into her hand and wiped some dribble

from her lips.

"Is that right?"

"That's how the Man wants it."

He took a step with her in his grasp. She was looking the other way, as if the distance called her to run far from this ludicrous deal. Outside the night air was crisp and real. The air in The City was always stuffy, like being stuck on an airplane. He breathed in the Outside World through his nostrils, a hint of pine floating by.

They stumbled back toward the motel, its neon lights flickering through the trees. Not another soul around. She rested her head against his shoulder and fumbled through her purse. She found her key, but he took it away.

"What're you doing?" she murmured, and he removed his own key instead. They kept stumbling along until they reached his room at the back of the motel that faced a parking lot and a solitary lamppost. Cicadas buzzed through the air.

"Come inside," he whispered in her ear, his tongue catching her earlobe.

"I'm so tired."

"Then you'll just lie down for a moment. I want to make sure that you don't get sick."

Scout H looked at him as if she was aware of what he'd planned but had lost all ability to care anymore. He remembered giving the same look to Scout A, years back, when A led him into her motel room and proceeded to have sex with him while making tiny cuts along his body with a switchblade, each wound lessening the ones that ate her heart, or so she said. Not long ago, he read in The City's paper about a woman in the Estates who'd killed herself by a thousand cuts to her body and knew, sadly, it was her.

The motel door flung open, the room smelling dusty and used. He guided Scout H over to the bed and removed her shirt. The moon was out, almost full. It danced in through the heavy curtains, illuminating her white back and the tattoos of an angel and a devil on each shoulder blade.

"You're a confused one, aren't you, Scout H?" he asked, swaying with his tongue in her ear. She'd sold herself to the Man like all the rest. She closed her eyes. "My bunny," he continued, with a lump in his throat.

"Go numb, H," she whispered out loud. "Go numb."

5

The next morning, Scout H appeared at E's motel room in a professional skirt, a blazer, and high heels. E still lay in bed, fondling at his dreams from last night and the memories of who he wanted her to be. At the door, she smoked a long cigarette and wore huge sunglasses, looking like a completely different woman than the girl he met yesterday.

"You certainly make a habit out of running late," she mumbled. He felt the sheets, half-dreaming and expecting her to be in bed with him. He squinted at the morning sun as it came barreling into the room.

"When did you leave?"

"I'll be out in the parking lot," she said. "Hurry up, because I was told I'd be briefed before we confront the Selected."

He rubbed his eyes and then she was gone from the doorframe. Groaning, he rose from bed and meandered into the bathroom to splash water on his face and swill some mouthwash. He put on his suit, glancing at the same old man he always did in the mirror. When he stepped outside, she was finishing her cigarette by the rental car, flicking the butt into the surrounding trees.

In the car, she refused to remove her sunglasses or say a word. He was thinking about his dead wife so much last night that at times she was the one prowling beneath him. Even now the silence between them rang eerily familiar.

"I hope it was enjoyable for you," E said.

"It was serviceable."

Her cold tone caused a knot to form in his stomach.

"Oh. I know that the Man recommends copulation as a way of releasing any tension before acquiring a Selected."

"I *know* what the Man recommends."

"The same thing happened with the Scout who trained me–"

"You told me this already."

"I wouldn't have wanted you be uncomfortable–"

"I wasn't. This conversation is unnecessary. As are any emotions you're starting to display."

"Oh. Well. Okay then."

"I think it's about time you briefed me already," she said as their car headed onto the highway. They spent the rest of the ride in silence.

At the penitentiary, E brought out his special ID badge. Given only to Scouts, it granted access into certain jails and prisons across the land. He had always been assigned the ones in the middle territories, possibly as a punishment by the Man to keep him near his past. He was never allowed to discuss his job with any of his peers, but noticed that some of them would return to The City with the types of tans he could only envision getting in a place like Califa. He tried not to be jealous of them, knowing that Califa was probably their own version of hell for a different reason.

He showed his ID badge to the front guard, a black card hanging from his neck with a picture of him from two decades ago. Never had he had a problem being allowed inside before, but he always feared each time would be his last and whoever was in charge above the Man would decide to lock him up for good. Uncertain how exactly the prisons were connected to The City, he always wondered which sought out the other first.

Graham was brought out of his cell and left in a separate room, blindfolded and handcuffed. Normally, after a Scout delivered a Selected, their relationship would be severed, but E would have to get used to seeing Graham around. He'd be Graham's new boss. He had no idea how he'd be able to handle that. All these recent changes in the rules had muddled his mind, so he watched Graham through the tiny window in the door, not ready to turn the knob and face reality yet.

"The Man prefers to wait a few days after incarceration," E said to Scout H, who smoked beside him. "Reality begins to settle in and a prisoner grows desperate enough to listen to anyone who might help."

"Why aren't we going in yet?" she asked, but he ignored her. He was thinking instead about when Graham was placed in his care shortly after the boy's parents died. The Man's only demand was to beat the boy daily, to break him down until he was barely a person anymore. E knew that the Man wanted the boy treated this way for a reason, but he was never told precisely why. He was simply forced to carry out a madman's wishes, like always.

E looked down at his hands. Since his dream the other night, he saw faint traces of blood across his own knuckles. It was as if his mind envisioned this future reunion on the horizon and understood its importance, started to equip E for the task at hand. The boy was a crucial part of the Man's plans, and now it would be taking shape. Time to put on his game face, the mask they all must wear to avoid being expunged. He shook away any torturous visions and burst through the door.

Graham jumped in his chair, his head whipping from side-to-side.

"Thanks for the warning," Scout H said, as she followed E inside.

"Who's there?" Graham asked. "What do you want?"

E slammed the door. Graham's breathing had already accelerated. He appeared thin, like when he was younger, his clothes hanging loosely from his body, cheeks pale, his skin washed-out, glasses over the blindfold sloping down his nose. The kind of person who blends into the walls. A meek individual destined to be picked on, discarded, forgotten. It baffled E that Graham could hold such magnitude in the Man's eyes, but it had never been easy to understand why the Man did what he did. Maybe that was the key to the Man's brilliance, leading The City without any way to undermine him because there was no guide to his actions. And yet, this boy, this wet noodle, would one day reveal his crucial purpose.

E cleared his throat to begin and slightly altered the tone of his voice.

"Mr. Weatherend, we are here to offer you a proposition–"

"Why...why am I blindfolded?" Graham asked meekly, as if he didn't want to cause any trouble.

"For your own safety."

"I don't understand," Graham said, his voice cracking as tiny tears leaked through the blindfold. "What's going on?"

E couldn't help but think how young Graham still was. He remembered back to when he was that age, getting his chemical engineering degree, a serious young man who bordered on obsessed. Then he was drafted to the War to End All Wars and came home fractured until The City scooped him up and chewed up whatever remained. Now all of his former life seemed carved out of another man's mind.

"You're looking at a couple of years behind bars, Mr. Weatherend," E started to say.

"It was a wooden gun I painted black," Graham pleaded. "I never set out to hurt anyone, I just needed a couple of bucks–"

"Zero-tolerance policy. Everyone in the liquor store thought it was real. You scared a lot of people."

Graham fully broke down now. His face flushed red and he was sobbing. E wondered how much he'd played a part in turning this boy into a sniveling pile of nothing. He wouldn't be surprised if the kid was wetting his pants, but he had to stop feeling bad. Going against the Man's orders now would only bring more trouble.

"I can't go to jail...I can't," Graham whined, squirming in his chair.

"What if I told you that you didn't have to?" E said, his tone calmer now, welcoming. He nodded at Scout H to pay attention.

"What do you mean?" Graham asked. "Please remove the blindfold so I can see you. I need to *see*..."

"Mr. Weatherend, please calm down and listen. We're not here to hurt you. If you don't like what we say, you can dismiss us. Now take a deep breath with me. Okay?"

Graham nodded. Scout H sucked at a fresh cigarette and crossed her arms in apparent boredom.

"Your case caught the eye of my superior," E continued. "When he was a young guy like you, he got in trouble for a similar thing."

Graham's expression changed, his mouth wide open. E could tell he was listening closely now.

"You are not a monster," E said. "Everyone deserves a second chance."

"Are you letting me out?" Graham asked, his voice rising in octaves. "I promise I will be good. I'll follow the law, I'll do whatever."

"You'll do whatever?" E raised an eyebrow at Scout H.

"Yes, whatever, sir. Anything. I promise."

"There are a few key moments in life and this is one of them, Mr. Weatherend. Today is your four-leaf clover."

"How...does this work?" Graham stammered, a sense of hopefulness in his tone. "What...what do I have to do?"

"There's a secret City far from here that only a few

Selected people know about, not even a part of the territories. This City is establishing itself and there are jobs that need to be filled. There's an entry-level position at an advertising agency that has been picked out for you."

"Advertising?" he asked in disbelief. "I don't know anything about that."

"That's not a problem. We believe it's an industry that you will prosper in."

"Yes, I would do anything. I'll work hard."

"I don't doubt that. I've been looking over your file. We know you've had a difficult past, Mr. Weatherend. The tragic death of your parents at an early age, being in-and-out of foster care, having no real family. You've been living as an itinerant for the last two years."

Graham didn't respond. His head drooped and his shoulders sunk.

"In this City, Mr. Weatherend, none of that matters. Your entire past can be obliterated if you want. It doesn't have to follow you. You can be whoever you want to be. Born again."

"There must be a catch."

"Well, the catch is that you must commit to us. Once you agree, you cannot leave The City—ever. But I assure you that there'll be no reason to. You will be given a generous Stipend and an apartment that is all yours. In my profession, I am required to leave now and again, but I would honestly rather stay in The City permanently because most of what I see in the Outside World, I don't like. Things have been built up some by the new leadership, since the War to End All Wars, but it's never truly returned to what it once was."

E took out the contract, a pen, and a set of keys.

"I'm removing your handcuffs for a moment so you can sign the contract. Can I trust that you will behave?"

"I will."

E released the handcuffs. Graham rubbed his raw wrists until E placed the pen in Graham's hand and guided him over to the contract.

"I can't see what I'm signing," Graham said, with a thin smile. It was the first time that E had ever seen a smile on the boy's face.

"We're not here to fool you, Mr. Weatherend. This is opportunity knocking at its loudest."

Graham finally signed, causing E to give a thumbs up to Scout H.

"You may also change your name if you want, Mr. Weatherend. Many do. It's symbolic of your rebirth and–"

"No," Graham said. "I don't want to be difficult, but that's my name. It's what my...parents chose for me."

"Yes, yes, of course. Now if you permit me, I must handcuff you again."

Graham nodded and held out his arms. The cuffs went back on and E led him out of the room. Somewhere deep down, E's tiny conscience screamed for Graham to run.

But that conscience got squashed as always.

After filling out the necessary paperwork, E put Graham in the back seat of the rental car and shut the door. Scout H went to get in the passenger side but he stopped her.

"What?" she said, avoiding eye contact and looking into the flat distance.

"I wanted to say good-bye while we had a moment to

ourselves. We'll be leaving you with the car once we get to the airport. I didn't think it would be the right time then."

Scout H shrugged her shoulders. "Good-bye."

"Wait, I really want to apologize. Sometimes when I come back here, I remember the person I used to be, and I fall back into his patterns. If anything I did was strange..."

"Stop."

"I'm not supposed to return to the Outside World again, but if we were able to see each other? I think I would like to see you more. You remind me–"

"If I were you, I would work on developing a spine, Scout E."

"This is my last Scouting assignment."

"All the more reason. You have a job to do related to the Selected. We all will eventually. Get your head in the game."

E's hands were shaking. The last time he touched Graham a decade ago, he had shattered the boy's collarbone. He had a specific job then, and when he spoke up about it to the Man, that job was taken away and he was demoted to being a Scout again, a hair away from being permanently sent to the Zones for questioning the Man's authority. If this new position required him to be a monster again to the boy, he'd have no other choice but to comply.

"Can we go now?" Scout H asked, annoyed.

"Okay. Listen, I hope she'll be all right," E said, talking really fast before his conscience would be silenced for good. "Your little girl. That she gets all the limbs she needs. That all of this will be worth it."

Sunglasses still masked Scout H's eyes, her lips pressed together so firmly.

"Thank you, but it's not needed. No emotions, right? That's what the Man wants. You'd be smart to follow."

She opened up the passenger door, slid inside, and slammed it shut.

He tapped his fingers against the glass, wanting to say more, but there was nothing left inside of him.

The boat ride back to The City was fraught with chopping waves. Graham puked over the edge more than once, but E had an iron stomach. It wasn't until they closed in on its coordinates that he started to feel a troubling gurgle. His mouth opened and he let out a stream of vomit so intense that the blood vessels in his eyes burst. He looked up and imagined his hidden prison: The City's twinkling behemoth skyscrapers, the Eye Tower beaming a spray of light toward the night waters. He began to cry like a child. This would be the last time he'd ever leave this place, the next reprieve being his burial.

The docks along the Wharf reined in the boat as they passed through the image projectors and The City appeared once again. The line of Guards lowered their weapons in sync. The Welcomers waited with clipboards and plastered smiles. E shook Graham's hand good-bye and hopped back on land, walking away at a slow pace so he could watch over his shoulder as the Welcomers removed Graham's blindfold. The kid was in awe upon first glance, like everyone when The City appeared new and idyllic, before the claustrophobia set in, before the veneer lifted, before the only escape was during shuteye. A dead wife was still alive, his hair hadn't turned white yet, and this place was someone else's reality, someone more deserving of castigation.

After this assignment, he would need two full days in his pod bed, enough for his dreams, hopefully better dreams, to delude him into numbness before his cellular glove rang with the Man on the other end and a new life waiting.

He could only wish that it would eventually allow him to be at peace, free from the chains of his past. But tucked deep inside was a festering ball of doubt; the same one he'd had ever since the first time his own blindfold was lifted, and a secret, bewitching City materialized on the horizon.

PART II:

DON'T LET LIFE PASS YOU BY, DRINK UP!

1

Graham Weatherend stared at the ad in Archipelago Station. A girl on a beach bringing an orange Pow! Soda to her lips with the slogan: *DON'T LET LIFE PASS YOU BY, DRINK UP!* In a City overcrowded with advertisements, this one captured his attention more than any other. The girl smiled like she was personally smiling for him. A thirst overwhelmed his dry throat despite the Rise-And-Shine coffee he gulped on the walk over from his apartment on Boxed Lane. He swallowed hard as the saliva struggled to trickle down and imagined the soda's sweet fizz on his tongue. The girl's toothy grin kept sucking him in, and momentarily, he was lying on a beach with a Pow! in his hand, completely at peace, while the girl sipped on orange forever.

A gust of freezing wind blew through the tunnel as the fantasy faded and the X train's lights glistened along the track and crept toward the herd of waiting passengers. An elbow jammed into the small of his back, carrying him with the crowd into the opening doors, nose-to-nose with a similar-looking stranger. Both wore suits slightly too big for their thin frames and had glasses and short hair styled with a severe part; but the stranger was older, more worn-down. The stranger's eyes had no life in them, just red veins and a numbed glaze. A smile looked like an effort, a foreign gesture. The stranger exhaled a cloud of foul breath, like he hadn't brushed his teeth in a while. Graham made sure to give his mouth a good minty rinse that morning, but for how long? After another ten years in this City, he might stop caring entirely.

The closing doors offered a final glimpse of the girl in the Pow! Soda ad; a dream of her syrupy orange lips against his own, but then the train whipped into the tunnel, the girl vanished, and he and the stranger collided.

The blackened glass monstrosity of Warton, Mind & Donovan Advertising and Concepts loomed at the corner of Excelsior Avenue and Imperial Street, taller than all the other surrounding buildings. Graham usually liked to be early, sometimes only the cleaning staff and him welcoming dark mornings together. The hum of the vacuum usually culled him out of sleep, but today he was like all the other ants, racing to make it by nine. These ants zoomed in every direction. Whistling for cabs with fear that they were late. Barking into electric gloves. Shoving bear claws in their mouths as they navigated through the maze of rush hour.

At the corner, Graham had to wait behind the crowd entering Warton, Mind & Donovan. An Empty Zone lingered down an alleyway, a pocket of nothingness with brainless, Sloth-addicted outcasts knocking into one another from the frozen winds. Most of them were missing at least one limb. Graham was certain that his company had been built near one of these Zones to inspire fear in its employees as they waited single-file to enter each morning. Its threat kept him at his desk into all hours of the night, praying that he'd be seen as a viable contribution and not expendable.

He closed his eyes to picture the girl from the Pow! ad. It'd been a long time since he could relax and the thought of her dancing along the waves made him warm. He hadn't felt warm since he'd left the Outside World, the temperature of The City always kept chillier than average, the threat of a snowfall sometimes switched on from its endless clouds. A trickle of a smile emerged on his lips, but soon vanished. The Outside World also represented a place he'd never like to return, even in his mind. While the weather might have been pleasant, his life there had been tumultuous. Parents dead when he was a boy, a cruel blur of a foster guardian, the War to End All Wars making jobs scarce, living on the streets, robbing that fateful store with a wooden gun, which brought him here. If he really thought about it, he'd never experienced a true warmth.

A co-worker nudged him from behind. He nodded to the impatient co-worker and scurried toward the entrance, the Pow! girl forgotten.

Once inside, he rushed to the elevator and stuck his briefcase in the door as it was about to close. The door opened and he uncomfortably wedged himself in. Everyone watched the numbers. On the other side of the packed elevator stood the new office intern Marlena Havanderson, pocket-sized and perky with a cute button nose; clearly optimistic about the day because this City was still fresh to her. Unlike everyone else, she didn't watch the numbers. She glanced his way with her deer-like eyes, spaced unusually far apart from one another, and gave a tiny wave, but he didn't acknowledge or return the wave. With a busy day ahead of him, distraction could mean catastrophe. His sweaty hands clutched his briefcase as he watched the numbers go higher in silence.

When the doors opened at the Creative Department on the 31st floor, Graham was pushed out amongst the suits and skirts bustling in every which way. The office's interior followed The City's minimalist, ultra-modern aesthetic. Metallic gray walls gave a feel of being trapped in a submarine. Bright fluorescent lights wrapped around the entranceways while the windows were tinted black. Rows of cubicles had been encased in glass so nothing would be hidden. Cell phone chargers shaped like mannequin hands were equipped on each desk and scattered across the walls. Tiny cameras embedded in the marbled floors monitored and replayed all the employees' moves, a requirement in the workplaces. Ambient music floated from speakers in the ceilings, there to keep the employees calm and focused. The office stayed tuned to the one existing radio station, and every twenty minutes a commercial came across the airwaves.

Wet-No-More. Even in a downpour, our umbrellas will keep you Wet-No-More.

Graham hummed along to the commercial's tune and caught Marlena glancing at him again before she headed in the opposite direction.

Another elevator opened and his co-worker Mick McKillroy flew out. Big and burly, Mick remained the eternal frat boy: just a few wisps of hair left at age thirty-five and dents in his face that told the story of an acne-scarred childhood. The buttons on his suit strained and begged to pop due to a hanging gut. Mick was gluttonous in every way: food, drink, drugs, and carnal pleasures, while Graham had chosen the opposite path here.

Mick usually said hello by giving Graham a powerful slap on his back, causing Graham to practically fall over.

"Whoa, watch it there, bud," Mick said.

Graham straightened himself, smoothed down his suit, and fixed his tie. He did not like his appearance to be altered, or to appear ruffled. An air of professionalism was the only thing he believed he had to offer. He mumbled hello out of the corner of his mouth as they continued down the hallway.

Translucent screens of the company's clients adorned the walls: vacuums, candy bars, watches, whiskeys, and its latest acquisition, a computer manufacturer called Imbedded, which inserted its flat computers into tables and desks as a means for saving space.

"Insane weekend," Mick informed him. "Did one of those machine-fingers group things. Cost a ton of Stipends. It was totally twisted, like a dozen of us, women and men, ranging from twenties to sixties. I'm telling ya, I'm becoming a sucker for the freaky shit. It's gotten to the point where normal is just bland."

Graham nodded along, knowing Mick's penchant for anything unusual, sometimes dangerously so. Tales of masturbatory asphyxiation. Rolling the dice by eating blowfish at the restaurant Killer Dishes once a week. Seeking out amputees indebted to The City for their lifelike mechanical limbs who could bend in unimaginable ways, or according to Mick, were able to elicit tremendous amounts of pleasure with their new machine fingers. To Graham it was all overindulgence, too much time off from work, and a trap that could get him replaced and left to rot in a Zone.

As they walked down the hallway, Graham and Mick passed a trio of guys. These men younger than them—hungrier, less disillusioned, and therefore, a threat. The trio was caught up in a joke about something that brought tears to their eyes. Mick threw a fake punch at them.

"Hey! The douchebag convention is in town."

The trio of guys continued laughing and fake punched back at Mick.

"Dude!" one of them shouted.

"Dude..." Mick replied, as they shadowboxed each other. One of the guys, Shep, was high on Levels already, the best way to achieve heightened clarity, to focus, focus, focus. He seemed to be at a functional Level 2, but untamed impulsivity was sometimes an unfortunate side effect of the black-market drug. Shep twisted his body toward Graham, his fists swinging so fast that he might lose control. Violence was something Graham tried to steer clear of, so he recoiled with a shudder, blinking rapidly and picking at his cuticles. The trio grew silent and gaping. The word *feeble* reflected in their eyes; their silence broken by cruel laughter.

Graham closed his eyes to shut them out, taken back to a chronic dream that haunted him as a child instead. Sometimes the sound of excess laughter brought this dream forward. He envisioned two men with white coats dragging him into a cold white room, their faces marred with wrinkles, speaking in an unintelligible language before erupting into laughter. They pressed him down onto a table and shoved a long device into his ear until it felt like it punctured his brain. Each time he had this dream, no one came to help or protect him. No one ever would.

The trio strolled away, slapping each other's backs with howls that still rung in Graham's ears, but all he wanted to do was forget about them and his nightmares and avoid any more distractions. Mick looked at him with pity.

"You have to learn to chill, buddy."

"I have a lot of work to do," Graham replied, taking a deep breath until his nerves calmed. "Those guys just like to mess around. I can't afford to let it affect me right now."

"So...one of those amputees with the machine-fingers," Mick began, squeezing Graham's shoulder, "had abnormally ginormous areolas that were super red like pepperonis... A little spicy too, come to think about it."

Graham was unwilling to let out a grin because Mick came off as a clown. Sometimes the clown cheered him up, but this morning, he was more weighted down than usual, a dread rumbling through his belly.

"C'mon! That was funny. Your buddy Mick is a funny guy. What did you do this weekend, Mr. Sense of Humor?"

Graham chewed on his lip.

"I was here."

"All weekend?"

"Yes," Graham replied, annoyed that Mick flourished at his job without putting in overnights or weekends. Back in the Outside World, Mick had actually been an ad man, until he and a few other co-workers got caught lining their pockets in an accounting fraud scandal.

"The Suck-Up Vacuum ad campaign is overdue," Graham said, freaking out. "The client isn't pleased with any of the proposals. I'm showing what I have to the boss today, and I don't think he's going to be happy."

"The boss is never happy."

Graham stopped walking and lowered his voice to a whisper. The entire office seemed to have gone mute around them.

"I've dried up," he said, practically mouthing the words for fear of being heard.

"We all get blocked," Mick replied, his voice loud and sharp.

The suits and skirts still bustled by, no one paying any attention to Graham and his weak jaw, practically non-existent lips, and a cheap suit that hadn't been fitted properly. He chewed on his lip some more until he tasted a droplet of blood.

"I've been visualizing this void lately," he said. "Sometimes when I'm sleeping, even when I'm awake. It's waiting to swallow me. Leave me jobless, penniless, thrown in the Zones, addicted to Sloths."

"That's some very fucked up shit," Mick said. "There's morbid, and then there's a whole other league of morbid, and that is you."

A co-worker swished by; bright red on her lips, her

cheeks rosy with rouge. She gave Mick a grin. Her hips swayed from side-to-side as she continued along her way.

"God, I love the smell of toner and Felicia to start my week off right," Mick said, leaving the conversation as he often did while Graham frowned at Mick's jocular slapstick. Mick started to walk away, but then turned around and snapped his fingers.

"Why don't you come to the Downtown tonight and we'll hit the Citrus Club?"

"Tonight?" Graham asked, as the co-worker disappeared around the corner.

"I know it's a school night, but when was the last time you even talked to a girl like Felicia out of the office? Let alone had one in your bed."

The marbled ink patterns in the floor absorbed Graham's focus. Admittedly, it had been awhile. In fact, he could hardly remember ever sharing his bed since he came to The City.

"There's inspiration beyond the glass walls of your cubicle," Mick said. "It's just a box that's stifling you."

The thrill of an uninhibited night in the Downtown with infinite sensory overloads. Part of him craved a night off from his reticence, but Graham knew his limitations all too well and the crippling discomfort that came along when he left his box.

"It's not that I don't want to," he said, half truthful and half melodramatic. "I'm overloaded right now. I don't think the boss will like the changes I've made. Advertising jobs in this City are so sought after, second only to The Finances. I mean, they are literally chained to their desks during the day, but at night, their Stipends could buy anything they desire. Everyone's holding knives over all of our backs. You're not petrified every day?"

"Jesus Christ. You've rehearsed that speech to yourself so often that you've deluded yourself into believing it. That's what keeps you locked away in that cubicle while...life is passing you by."

A chill crawled up the base of Graham's spine.

"What did you say?"

The girl in the Pow! ad popped into his mind again along with the slogan: *DON'T LET LIFE PASS YOU BY, DRINK UP!* His palms started to sweat, almost losing his grip on his briefcase.

"Look at me," Mick said. "I'm a schlub of all schlubs, but I grab life by the *cojones*. I attack it each day without consequence, even living in a place like this. I make the most of my penance. I know how to get big fucking accounts instead of losing them to Kellner & Woods, and none of my lovers expect much from me, so when I deliver, they just melt. I become more than my advertisement," he continued, indicating his portly frame. "That's what all the best advertisements succeed in doing."

"I'm not you, Mick. I'm exactly how I'm perceived from a first impression–"

"But it's never about the first impression. It's what gets someone to look back, again and again. Our job is to manipulate people into using their Stipends on what they don't really need. And it works. They blow their loads on all the garbage we produce, just to give them something to do. That's the beauty of working the ad game here. No one really *needs* any of what we're selling, but they *want* it. Make them *want* you. You're not delivering with your campaigns because you don't believe in your power."

Graham hadn't been listening, caught up in his own

point, certain that the way he'd chosen to live his life here was crucial for survival. He was terrified of disintegrating like he'd seen with so many others, faces that only appeared now in murky train tunnels, or in the Zones as they reached out with whichever limbs they still had, grasping for something, anything. Graham had nightmares he became one of them, waking up with his heart on fire and shaking into morning.

"I enjoy my box," he said, nodding to convince himself. "That box is security. It is four walls I can count on, four walls that won't let me down."

"Fine, but tonight you take a chance, and tomorrow you can leave an *I Told You So* Post-It on my desk if I'm wrong. They have this orange concoction at Citrus Club made with psychedelic Powder around the rim. Guaranteed to get your mind spinning. C'mon, man, a little living won't kill you."

Mick formed his hand into the shape of a gun and fired.

"Hope it works out with the boss today. Either we'll be celebrating or frantically brainstorming, but either way it's time to stop hugging that wall, wallflower."

Mick blew at the pretend smoke steaming off his fingers and then holstered his pretend gun.

2

At his cubicle, Graham neatly lined up a row of Level 1s and placed them one-by-one on his tongue. He hid the pill bottle deep in his pocket just to make sure any suspicious eyes wouldn't notice and rat him out. He'd picked up a stash in the park by his apartment so he could be on his toes for his boss today. His boss, who sometimes reminded him of that foster guardian he had as a boy in what almost seemed like a different life. This guardian had a similar raspy boom to his voice and cigar smoke on his breath. He'd beat Graham so hard that the blood would collect in Graham's eyes and force them shut until he'd be stuck in a dripping, foul darkness. He rationalized that anyone with authority could reanimate this monster and that his PTSD would never leave, even years and miles away from it all in this mirage called The City.

Graham shook away as much of the past as he could and swished the Levels with some water, squeezing his eyes shut with each swallow. He blinked and everything became visually sharper, colors more pronounced and vibrant. A massive headache had been forming earlier, nothing alarming since he'd gotten them since childhood, and they usually only lasted a few minutes. They always began in his right eardrum before shooting up into his cranium. He counted to ten slowly until the throbbing subsided. When he opened his eyes, his mega-organized cubicle materialized. No personal touches or pictures except for printed mantras neatly framed and laminated throughout the space.

- Every man is really two men – the man he is and the man he wants to be.

- Advertising is based on one thing: Happiness.

- You are the product. You are feeling something. You are OK. That is what sells.

"I am ok," he mumbled, massaging his throat as the pills spilled down.

On his desk, a six-pack of orange Pow! Sodas. A note attached read: *Our new client. Drink up! Come up to my office ASAP!!! – E.*

"Graham!"

He jumped in his seat, causing the note to pirouette to the floor. His boss E leaned against the doorframe with a signature look on his face, like he was permanently chewing a cigar.

"Get in my office," E said, his voice sounding like he'd been gargling with rocks. He loomed over Graham, his face turning an unnerving red as Graham sunk down in his chair. E always used his stature to threaten: grinding his teeth, ready to chew his subordinates up.

"I...just got in," Graham managed to say, looking into E's eyes and hoping to find a glimmer of humanity. Most of the time pure rage was all he saw, but on a few occasions those eyes softened as if E had tired playing the villain, or maybe that was simply wishful thinking on Graham's part.

E pointed at his watch, his eyes hardening again as his bi-polar switch flicked back on.

"Your fucking generation," he spit. "A bunch of pussy-whipped, do-nothings. At your age, I'd already been shot in the ass on the battlefield. Twice. Once in each cheek. What can you say?"

Graham never knew how to deal with E. Agreeing with what he said would make him look indecisive. Disagreeing was just foolish.

"I...nothing, I've never..."

Flashes of his former guardian exploded in his mind. Bloody knuckles. Eyes swollen and sealed. He hated to even allow that terrible man to keep affecting him, but once those memories got triggered there'd be no escape from the horror he experienced. Despite the Levels doing their damnedest to curb an episode like this, E's intimidating face had an uncanny way of always bringing him right back.

E sighed, shaking his head. "Where are we with the Suck-Up campaign?"

"Right, Suck-Up," Graham said, as a tiny amount of

puke crept up his throat. He managed to calm himself. "I...was here all weekend getting this together...sir."

He opened his briefcase and handed a mock-ad to E. On it, a cartoon vacuum sucked up dirt with a smile. The slogan read: *Because it's not always bad to be a 'Suck-Up'.*

"What do you think I'm going to say about this?"

"Excuse me, sir?"

"Do we not give you enough here? You have an apartment in Boxed Lane. You get breakfast, lunch, and even dinner tickets from our cafeteria, plus a decent Stipend."

"Yes...no, it's more than enough."

E let out a tiny chuckle that sounded like a deflated tire.

"All of that for you to basically create toilet paper."

"I...don't follow."

"Toilet paper, you cipher, because the most that I can do with this drivel is wipe my ass with it!"

He balled up the mock-ad and pitched it at Graham's face. Graham took it like he always did, steeling himself for the abuse to follow. E got quiet, this insane man becoming scarier when not yelling. He tiptoed around Graham as if he was waiting for the precise time to pounce.

"I've been summoned from above," E said, practically glowing in awe of his accomplishment. "The eighty-first floor. Warton, Mind, and Donovan themselves. It turns out that Pow! Soda is primed for a complete overhaul, and it's all my baby, my little bundle of joy that's gonna move me up from thirty-one and hopefully get me closer to becoming one of the Heads of the company someday, and an apartment in the Estates."

"Oh...well, that's...very good news," Graham replied,

unaware where this was going and treading carefully. The orange girl in the Pow! ad brought out a tiny grin. “I’ve seen Pow! ads all over.”

“Of course you have and they’ve been...reasonably well done. Kellner and Woods represented them for years, but the hot news is that both Kellner and Woods have flung themselves off the top of their company’s tower last night.”

“They’re dead?”

“Very much so. Apparently, they were siphoning a ton of the company’s money into their own pockets and the Man was not happy. About to send them to the Zones. Anyway, the whole company is being shut down, which means we’re running the ad show solo in this City, and I am determined to reap the benefits.”

“That’s some news to hear.”

“You don’t know what I’ve sacrificed to get this opportunity,” he said, those eyes softening again and a twinge of regret in the base of his voice.

“I’m sure you’ll do an outstanding job in charge of the campaign.”

“God, you’re pathetic,” he said, back to being the old, menacing E. Hot breath spewed out of his boss’s nostrils. “You know what you get from brown-nosing? You get shit on your nose and nothing else!”

Graham stepped back as the room pivoted. His past still lingered all too closely—the guardian who’d breathe over him in the middle of the night after he thought the abuse ended. He blinked as the Levels tugged on the receptors of his brain, doing their job by getting him to focus.

The ambient music coming from the speakers above

switched to a jingle for New-U.

New-U make-up makes you up all new! It's time, it's time for a brand New-U!

"I'm sorry, sir," Graham said, taking a deep breath. "I spoke out of line. I can start researching the old Pow! Soda campaigns if you want. Do you have an idea about the new direction they want to go in yet?"

E narrowed his eyes and leaned in as if hard of hearing.

"Pow! is being primed to become the beverage choice for sodas in The City. Now I've come to your little hole of a cubicle because the file we have on you lists an unstable childhood, no real parents raising you, blah, blah, blah, so I assumed you'd have a sweet tooth, an unnatural attraction to anything juvenile."

"A sweet tooth? Not particularly."

"You'll go down to the Pow! plant today to test out some brand-new sodas. They're refiguring everything right now. I don't need your brain for this campaign. I'm not looking for your pedestrian ideas. You will be the dumb schmo that will tell me what these new sodas taste like in comparison to the old ones, and that's about all I need from you on this."

"Oh," Graham said. "O-o-okay, sir. Sure. I can do that. I *know* I can."

"The ones on your desk are what's out on the market now. Take enough of the new prototypes home with you."

E went to leave, but stopped.

"I've yet to be wowed by you, Weatherend. You know, your last report from the Elders was less than stellar."

Graham lowered his head.

"With a snap of my fingers, I could put in a

recommendation to the Man and have you living in a shanty in some E.Z. You want to spend your days with one arm grilling rats over fires?"

"I'm sorry, sir."

"Don't be sorry, just start drinking," E sighed, and again his eyes softened, but not long enough to put Graham at ease.

E motioned for Graham to pick up a can. Graham tried to calm his nervous hands. He hated that he only appeared weak to everyone here, but didn't know how to be anything else.

"Down the hatch like a good old boy."

Graham cracked open the tab and took a sip, practically gagging.

"Like piss in a can, right? Let's hope they improved on that."

Graham could sense E scrutinizing each sip and fought to hold it together instead of curling up into a ball and rocking his tears away. He had spent his entire week's Stipend on Levels to avoid his frazzled nerves, but they didn't seem to be helping much. So, he continued gulping the Pow! down as E's grin got wider and a bubbling war erupted in his stomach.

3

The company comped a taxi for Graham, and he sped through Empty Zones to the Factory Region by the Wharf at the other end of The City. He passed by those threats of shanties that appeared to be made out of cardboard. Trashcans full of fire made the area look like an apocalyptic wasteland. People peering through boarded up slots, tears frozen in dirty lines. Stubs for limbs attempting to reach toward his window. Eyes begging to be put out of their misery. Those Selected to come to The City and now were being punished worse than in the Outside World.

A former Finance wandered through the wreckage in

a tattered double-breasted suit. The color had been sucked out of his face, leaving it pale and murky, his teeth loose and jagged from chewing on Sloths, the only nourishment the Man sent. There had been whispers that these people were being used as test subjects in underground labs, but for what, no one knew. It was easier and less dangerous to look the other way than to probe. Smoke in the air curled from the trashcans on fire, so Graham rolled up his cab's windows.

Off in the distance, the Eye Tower and the silhouette of the Man watched all. Graham recalled a legend whispered about through The City where long-ago things had been different. He'd heard that a group of people had once created this place as a utopia for those who needed to be Rehabilitated, but only a few elderly citizens really remember what it was like. The Man was the last of the creators and the one who constructed The City's laws. He had abolished any type of government in his demented dictatorship. The pervading thought from everyone that he was an eccentric billionaire, but his motives remained suspect. The citizens knew that this place must prosper—idleness close to sin—but no one was sure if their second chance at a life was due to a charitable gesture, or an excuse to place them under a giant thumb. To inspire fear right before someone got banished to the Zones, the Man spoke to his citizens in an unintelligible language blasting from loudspeakers.

To further maintain the Man's ominous presence, a light always beamed from the Eye Tower, even in the dead of the night. The Man stood in the center resembling a pupil for the windowed eye, forever observing, his long limbs stretched out and appearing from afar like bloodshot veins. Sometimes Graham wondered what it'd be like to have power and influence like this mystifying figure with his City full of marionettes, but other times he wouldn't wish that fate on his worst enemy. He knew he'd never have what it took to be a leader, accepting his role as an obedient drone.

The taxi turned a corner and skimmed along the Wharf. A thin film of ice from the cold front that rarely seemed to go away covered the water. Large, gray industrial buildings spewed smoke, one after the next. The Factory Region ran for about a mile and housed all the Sponsors. All the citizens knew about these Sponsors was that they invested in The City. The largest sponsor, Lifelike Limbs, was placed prominently in the center, a domed factory with a sole window stretching across its surface in the shape of a long leg. The second largest Sponsor was Pharma Plant, which produced Sloths and other pills. Pow! Soda sat sandwiched between New-U, a one-of-a-kind makeup conglomerate, and Wet-No-More, an umbrella manufacturer.

Inside the factory, the production of Pow! Sodas put on a show. A large roll of aluminum sheeting fed through a machine. A press punched out round pieces and bent them into cups. The cups went into a hot air dryer, coated with varnish. The cans were printed with an orange Pow! label and sent into an oven to harden. Stacks of cans then got placed in a pulley to be shipped out. Mesmerized, Graham became lost in the clacks and clangs of the machine until his name got called from an overhead speaker and he was told to wait in Boardroom #13.

Minutes went by in the solitary boardroom. He sat at an oval table twiddling his thumbs. Four walls without windows surrounded him, each painted a drab brown. Posters adorned the walls with Pow! cans in place of people during historical events: the moon landing, raising the flag of Iwo Jima, a Pow! Soda can at a podium with a cartoon bubble saying "I Have a Dream".

A maintenance man entered with cartons of Pow! on a pulley. Grossly overweight with an unkempt beard and a soiled baseball cap, the lines on the man's palms caked with dirt. Four separate cartons were brought out. Orange. Lime Green. Raspberry-Blue Blue. Cherry Red. The maintenance man plunked them down.

"These are all for me?" Graham asked, counting in his mind about a hundred different cans.

"Yeah, all for you. Dey said to start with orange."

"Orange? Who said?"

The man pointed up to the ceiling with his thumb.

"Dey said."

Graham's studio apartment on Blank Street was located in Boxed Lane, a middle-class residential region that had cookie-cutter tinted glass apartments and a movie theater showing The City's only film called *Robot or Die*. It was about a future where Earth had become uninhabitable, the only survivors being humans who'd been able to turn into robots. Boxed Lane also had The City's only park, besides the exclusive one in the Estates. Graham hardly ever went to the park, not being much of an outdoors person. In another life, he imagined getting a dog and rolling down hills, taking picnics there with friends and even a girlfriend, popping champagne corks and sitting on blankets under the clouds, but not in this life. In this life, the park remained only safe during the daytime and became a haven for scoring black market Levels and other barbiturates at night. Dealers emerged from the shadows promising "clarity, clarity, clarity." Graham knew them well because, like a vampire, he rarely saw the daytime. He shuttled back and forth underground in the dark and stammered home with bloodshot eyes and a crook in his spine long after most had already gone to bed.

His apartment gleamed immaculate and sparse: bare white walls punctuated by a few paintings resembling Rorschach blobs, all in black and white, always appearing to him as something different. He enjoyed staring at them and letting his mind float away. The rest of the apartment consisted of a bed in the corner sectioned off by a Japanese shoji screen that he'd paid way too much of a week's Stipend for, and a coffee table with a copy of *The Rules of The City*, like every household must have displayed.

When he returned home that day, he placed the orange carton of Pow! Sodas on the circular dining room table in his foyer and then slid the rest under the table. He popped a TV dinner in the microwave, never being much of a cook or having the drive to learn. The microwave beeped, and he transferred the dinner onto a plate. He sat down at the table with a napkin in his lap and a glass of ice. He thought how every night of his last ten years here had been the same. Others went out in the Downtown, formed fleeting relationships, since most were too damaged to live with a steady partner, yet he feared a loss of focus if he veered from his routine. There were much worse fates that could befall him here, many lost in the Zones who would never return, the fear keeping him compliant, mundane; an emotionless robot who lived only to work. Ten years later and all he had to show for it was a slight receding hairline and frown lines.

He grabbed a can of orange Pow! from the carton. The brand name was written in swirls with a defining exclamation point.

"An intern should be dealing with this," he said aloud, as if anyone was there to listen. "E has always thought I'm nothing."

He poured the neon orange soda into the iced glass. The bubbles tickled his nose as he went to take a sip. He anticipated its piss-like tartness, which was how it'd tasted before. Because of that, he took the tiniest of sips, one or two bubbles fizzing on his tongue. His eyes squeezed shut in anticipation of the terrible flavor, but instead, something very different occurred. His tongue curious for more, unquenched. This time he went in for a mouthful and found himself unable to stop. The taste revelatory, all consuming, the sweet orange mixing with the firecracker bubbles exploding in his mouth. He knocked his head back and continued to guzzle it down until it dribbled from the sides of his mouth and he was pouring more, and more, and more, endlessly. His breathing became heavy, demonic; his eyes bulging and lost in a dream. The room soon turned hazy and undefined, the Rorschach-like blobs morphing into various shapes like clouds on a windy day, oozing all over him. He lunged for another can. Popped it open. Fulfilled the same ritual, his chin and neck sticky with orange, his tongue lapping up the nectar around his lips. He'd never desired something as much as this soda, a yearning in his veins, the night alive in his veins, powering him up. He turned into a throbbing entity now, all impulse and want, full but thirsty at the same time, hands quivering with delight, his small mouth finally upturned into a real smile, into the realm of satisfaction, his heart beating-beating-beating like he was truly living and breathing, gulping life for the very first time.

Before he knew it, empty cans sat at his feet. He paced around the apartment. His spine more erect than ever, he felt taller, more assured and with a passionate need to do something, to do everything, to achieve, and love, and lust, and stretch outside of his body. He passed by a lamp and it seemed to glow orange, the overhead track lights flickered orange as well. The halogen in the corner beamed orange waves to the ceiling, and it all seemed delicious and sizzling and captivating. He closed his eyes and saw orange instead of darkness in his closed lids; he opened them and became covered in orange hues. He found himself in front of the full-length mirror on his bathroom door and just stared, looking at his smile as if he'd never seen it before, confused but exhilarated at the same time. He made it bigger and bigger until he felt the strain, until it burned, but he didn't stop, wouldn't stop, couldn't stop, until he finally stretched outside of himself and left the man he used to be in a pool on the floor, emerging free.

"Citrus Club," he nodded. The distorted image in the mirror nodded as well before they both walked back over to the dining room table for one last fizz-fueled binge.

4

The Downtown was full of vibrant colors. Nobody actually lived there, since it was a place for entertainment, so everything stayed open twenty-four hours and had been built with bright glass: glimmering reds and shining greens mingling with cool blues and hot oranges hues. The desired effect was for the area to appear like a cutting-edge beacon beyond the Zones where the cold front was shut off and oxygen got pumped in the air to keep everyone as awake and alive as possible. Dens of any kind of outrageous depravity one can imagine existed here too. Powder Dungeons for sadomasochistic psychedelics.

Legalized gambling in joints that resembled speakeasies. Strips for drag racing marked by burned tires and the occasional lost limb. Men and women prostitutes in darkened, life-sized glass tubes with computerized menus of everything they'd allow. Ear-splitting electronic music halls loud enough to literally stop you from thinking until you were consumed by the throbbing beats. Laughing Gas Lounges for those unable to laugh on their own anymore. Millions of different ways for everyone to spend all of their Stipends and release whatever had been pent up inside.

Graham zoomed there in a cab that cost him over a hundred Stipends, since he lived on the other side of The City. After passing through Empty Zones, the Downtown's colored glass structures glinted in the night like a prism. Its energy made him tingle and he rolled down his windows to let it all pour in. The colored glass buildings were twinkling and delightful, candy for his eyes. Translucent screens of commercials hovered in the air above, schilling products. A digital forty-foot geisha hawking her Cream of the Orient lotion, her face powder-white with a come-hither wink in her giant eye. Near her, an ad with two life-sized bees, post-coital, puffing on Smoke 'Em cigarettes in bed and buzzing that *Smoke 'Ems were the bees' knees*. Graham's creative team spent weeks on that one, and he was in awe that when the people of the Downtown looked up into the night, they were influenced by something he'd sacrificed many days to bring to life.

The cab sped until it hit Excess Street and the heart of the Downtown. A woman lay in a giant martini glass on the roof of a bar, beckoning for him to come inside. Nearby, a line of people in masks waited to get into Anonymous, a club that required you leave your identity at the door so that you could be whoever you wanted to be. People swirled around in the streets, lit up or drunk, but happy and smiling, their cares left behind in other Regions. Two girls on the arm of a fat man got in the way of the traffic, all of them caught up in maniacal laughter. A businessman puked up a flood next to them but still danced away to the music in his head. A couple wrapped around a lamppost, thrusting into one another. A little person covered in Powder crooned to the stars like a beagle, his voice hoarse and lost in the clamor. In the distance, the roar of drag racing and twisted crashes mixed with cries and cheers. So much to take in, and it all rapidly clicked by.

On Fervor Street, the cab stopped and Graham stepped out into the cold air, the frozen mist settling on his face. The Citrus Club across the street glowed orange and pumped dance music. The patrons waiting outside were decked out in different types of orange, and he could barely contain his enthusiasm to get inside and mix with all that color. The street between him and the club blinked red as the cars whizzed by until it finally blinked green and Graham could finally cross.

No sign of Mick inside Citrus Club, but Graham didn't feel awkward being alone like he normally would. This new sensation, electrified by the night's possibilities, had him believing he was charismatic enough to have whatever he wished. He was comforted by the surroundings: the walls and floor in various oranges, the lights luminous and orange, too. A hallucinatory quality to it all, a hesitation that with the slightest stirring it could just disappear—the last thing he wanted.

Powder filled the air, a euphoric drug crushed into

dust and dyed orange tonight. The club-goers blew it from their fingertips. As Graham walked through, it settled on his eyelashes and made his eyes pop wide-open and exhilarated. He moved through the club on fire, ablaze with passion and desiring everyone and everything around him. He ordered a screwdriver and made his way to the dance floor. The music pulsed and his body twisted and turned effortlessly. He'd never been the type of guy to dance, but the music rumbled inside of him tonight and he flowed.

He knocked back his stinging drink, drunk already, and when he looked up, a girl in an orange dress with an orange drink in her hand was staring him down. The alcohol he'd consumed, strong and coated with Powder on the rim, created the sensation of swimming. The girl stood too far away for him to see her face clearly, just a blur on top of a body that swished over. Her orange dress hugged every curve with every step. She sparkled and he couldn't help but to want her. He'd never wanted anyone as bad and urgently before, longing to pursue her until she was his. He took off his glasses and cleaned them, but her face remained a haze.

"Get you another?" she asked, with a soothing purr to her tone as she pointed at his empty glass.

"Sure," he grinned, wide and eager like the Cheshire cat.

"Lonely sailor tonight?" the girl in orange asked, lighting a cigarette until she morphed into a cloud of smoke. Her voice so throaty and alluring that he wanted to crawl inside the cave of her mouth and spelunk.

"Looks like."

"I noticed you," she purred again, weaving with the

music, an orange swirl. "From all the way across the club. I only saw you in a sea of oblivion, sailor."

He weaved with her until they fell in sync; sweat spilling off their bodies, her orange dress almost in his grasp.

"Oh yeah?"

She breathed sweet smoke. He moved closer until they practically touched.

"Did you notice me, too, sailor?"

"Oh yeah," he nodded, his head bobbing so hard that it could just snap right off. He reached for her orange dress, and she spun around. He reached out again, grasping at the lonely air.

"And what did you think?"

She touched herself all over, hands blending with her orange ambiance. Absorbed, Graham began panting: a drooling, out of control mess.

"You are so orange," he said.

A Powdery orange tear fell from his eyelash.

She chuckled. "I get that all the time."

"I'm sure you do." He extended his hand, wanting to touch her any way he could. "I'm Graham."

"Well, Graham...let's just say I'm *here* and leave it at that."

She placed her orange drink in the hand he held out.

"That's all I get for a name?"

"That's not all you'll be getting," she said, leaning her blurred face against his shoulder as they moved to the beat.

Later that night, back at Graham's apartment,

darkness surrounded except for a beam of moonlight leaking in through the window. Graham lay on his bed in his boxers as the girl in orange pranced over. She undid the straps of her orange dress with a shimmy, and it fell to the floor. She picked it up and hung it over the bedpost. She took off her bra and threw it over her shoulder before sliding down her underwear and twisting around while she lit a cigarette. A tattoo of an angel had been etched on one shoulder blade with a devil on the other. Both so clear: the devil red with piercing eyes, the angel cherub-like, innocent and scared. She finished her cigarette and let the smoke settle into his pores, her face still a blur as she crawled on top of him.

He became unhinged with her. Lips sucking and biting every inch of her body. She squirmed and squealed, all energy and sweet smoky breath as he devoured but didn't let up. He wanted to consume her; to never lose this passionate being that he had become and live in a realm of unending pleasure. He disappeared inside of her, and instantly was ready to go again. Again and again and again, the world spinning as her blurred face hovered below and her knockout orange dress danced on the bedpost from a breeze blowing in.

The alarm clock blared at 8:00 a.m. Graham's eyes shot open. He embraced the sheets, but they were empty. He rose, groggy and hungover. Her orange dress still hung from the bedpost. He climbed out of bed and headed into the bathroom. He yanked back the shower curtain, but no one was there. Walking back over to the bedpost, he felt the orange dress between his fingers, visibly confused.

With a pounding headache, he meandered through his living room into the kitchen as if some magnetic charge pulled him, but there was no sign of the girl. There must be a logical explanation for her leaving without her dress. Maybe she had a spare in her purse? The night had been too wonderful to pepper it with doubts this morning so he went his refrigerator, mostly empty except for ten orange Pow! Sodas sitting on the top shelf. He grabbed a can, popped it open, and chugged it down as if he hadn't had a sip of anything in days. He did the same with three more Pow! cans, popping the tabs and chugging like a machine; a machine that could chug all it wanted and still never feel quenched. He drank more and more until his heart raced so fast that it began to hurt and he had to leave for fear of being late to work. He chalked up the ill feeling from being dehydrated by too much alcohol last night. He jumped into his suit and finally jetted out of the apartment. As the front door swung closed, he looked back longingly at the refrigerator that cooled his desires, his beautiful orangey bubbles, which he already, desperately, missed.

The improvements made to the brand were really that good.

5

With a hop in his step, Graham made his way toward the elevators at Warton, Mind & Donovan. A little fidgety, sure, but most would interpret it as being wired for the day. They'd assume a trail of Rise-And-Shine receipts shoved into his pockets and an aroma of espressos coating his words, but the orange Pow!s had lingered on his taste buds. He'd never had a reckless and uninhibited night like last night, becoming someone else, someone better, and he wanted to hold onto this new persona for as long as possible because he felt so energized walking down these halls. It had to be from his encounter at the Citrus Club.

He couldn't imagine losing this brand-new euphoria bubbling inside of him. In the elevator, he waited alone, rolling his tongue around to squeeze out the sublime traces of the morning, of that orange girl and the ghost she'd become.

A clacking of high heels fired into the marble floor.

"Hold it!"

A lovely manicured hand appeared between the closing doors. When the doors opened, a woman came inside, her hair cut short and pulled back with emphasis into a professional ponytail. She wore a heavy peacoat buttoned up to her neck and sheer stockings, her outfit plain except for orange high heels and a swash of orange eye shadow dusting her eyes. He became immediately drawn to every bit of orange on her. With each glance, she came off as distant, standing as far away as possible—the type of person who relished her personal space. He'd never seen her before, which meant she must have been from the Outside World. Because of that, he became even more curious about her and the flashes of orange she wore from head-to-toe.

"Push thirty-one for me," she said, fixing her hair to combat any rogue strands.

"Already did. That's my floor, too."

He nodded at her, comfortable and reassuring, a hint of flirtation and charm in the base of his voice that he never knew he possessed. She smiled politely and then watched the numbers. Her cheekbones were sharp enough to cut him if he moved in for a kiss, but he couldn't help thinking it might be worth it. The orange girl from last night had transformed him into a being focused on desire.

"You work at Warton, Mind & Donovan?" he asked, as

the elevator beeped away. He didn't want to watch the numbers in silence as usual; he wanted to explore this woman and everything about her, enthralled by her blinking orange eyelids.

"First day."

Her tone all business, she slid one foot along the back of her leg, the tip of the orange high heel pinpointing the source of her itch.

"I've been here almost a decade," he said, normally feeling old with a statement like that. Not today, though; today he felt as young as when he first arrived. The woman looked away from the numbers, somewhat impressed. "I'm Graham."

The elevator reached the thirty-first floor and the doors opened. Their solitary moment together had been broken, the whirl of the office pouring in. He had to raise his voice as they stepped outside.

"Human Resources is down the hall."

"Thank you. I'm Gayle." She shook his hand, her touch cold but intriguing. "I'll be seeing you."

She started to head the other way, but things were still unfinished. The conversation needed to be stretched a little more.

"It's not a bad place to work," he said. "Decent Stipends and all."

There was a freshness to her that he craved, a presence The City would eventually squelch. Whatever brought her here, it still represented potential, bound to fade as the years blended.

She turned around, closing her eyes for a second as two orange orbs flashed at him from the eyeshadow she wore. His legs went all loose, and he puckered his mouth in thirst. She opened her eyes again and tossed off a "Good to know, Graham," before swiveling around and clacking away with those orange heels against the marbled floor. *Clack. Clack. Clack.*

He didn't know why, but he pictured himself being that marbled floor with her clacking all over him, her orange soles gliding up his torso before slipping inside his eager mouth to gulp down.

Life's not dim with Lifelike Limbs. Try our appendages on a whim!

Graham tapped his pen to the commercial on the radio during a meeting, his gaze locked on the fluorescent lights flickering a muted orange glow. The commercial ended as the ambient music switched on. The rest of the boardroom was windowless and painted black with white scoop chairs surrounding the circular table and a few paintings that resembled erosions in the walls. A dozen other employees, including Mick, were present. All had a shade of orange in at least one article of clothing: tie, blouse, headband, all except Graham, but instead of seeming odd, it was welcoming. Along with the fluorescent lights, their orange clothing glowed, and it enveloped him, made him want to fling off his suit and howl, bursting with energy like a shaken soda.

At the head of the table, E gave a presentation wearing a bright orange bowtie: all eyes trained on him. E definitely relished this power each morning, but for a change, Graham didn't see him as imposing.

"Guess the secret?" E asked, gritting his teeth in anticipation.

Everyone looked at one another, unsure what the boss was getting at.

E held up a large cardboard ad that depicted a can of Pow! Soda, the words GUESS THE SECRET? written on one side of the can with the logo Pow! spelled out across the other.

Everyone looked at each other again, nodding.

"An extra second is all you need to grab someone. Ask a question and they'll want the answer. You've already hooked them, right?"

E crushed something imaginary in his fist.

"Andy!" he barked. Andy chirped in his seat, caught off guard. "Show them what we got."

Andy popped up from his seat with an orange handkerchief sticking out of his front pocket and a stack of mock-ads that he handed out. Graham traced a finger over the large orange question mark passed to him. All his other co-workers had different colored question marks over black backgrounds.

"Keep them guessing, people, and they'll come in droves. We burned the midnight oil over this one."

Josephine raised her hand. She wore an orange blouse with rouge on her cheeks to match.

"So, what's the secret?" she asked.

E dismissed her with a frown.

"Pow! isn't telling. That's the point. For now, we're hyping up this thrill of the unknown." E paced back and forth, tapping his chin. "Actually, Josephine, despite your usual buffoonery, you're pretty much on the mark with your question."

Josephine smirked at her co-workers, unaware that it was not a true compliment.

"This is what we want everyone to be asking. What is the secret? Well...take a sip and try to figure it out for yourself. They've added a new ingredient and their brand doesn't taste like battery acid anymore."

A few people chuckled around the table.

"Isn't that right, Graham?"

Lost in the curve of the orange question mark, Graham didn't hear his boss until he was asked a second time.

"Graham!" E smacked the table and then regained his composure. "What would you say they taste like?"

One of Graham's eyes remained absorbed by the orange question mark, but the other one stared at E. He rolled his tongue around in his mouth again, remembering. Everyone leaned forward in anticipation.

"Like...sipping on passion."

Everyone turned to E for approval.

"Sipping on passion," E said, chewing on the phrase. E stepped toward Graham, but Graham didn't slink away. For once, he was entirely confident about his ideas. Pure passion that lingered. How it truly tasted.

"Yesssssssss," E said. His words had a slither to them. "That's a shade of fucking brilliant. Maybe even a future slogan."

Now that the boss had given his input, everyone around the table began to agree. All were nodding at Graham, the star of this meeting who'd never been a star before; but all Graham noticed was the orange in their clothing, as if it hung on invisible bodies. And he was happy, not just from the compliments and the encouragement from his boss, but because of the orange in the room, because of the passion circulating in his blood.

A wad of paper bounced off his left cheek. He picked up the paper and opened it. The note read: *What is brown and hides in an attic?* He flipped the note over, checking for an addressee. E had gone back over to the head of the table, ending the meeting with some final words. Everyone stayed, listening, making sure not to alter their glazed stares.

From the other end of the table, Mick tossed another wad of paper. Graham zeroed in on the orange polka-dotted tie his friend wore. He shrugged his shoulders and opened the second note, which read: *The diarrhea of Anne Frank.* Graham considered the punch line and then let out a laugh with such power that it echoed off the walls. Everyone stared at him now, but he couldn't stop purging with laughter. And it wasn't even that funny. In his mind, he rationalized that Mick's crude humor shouldn't cause him to behave in this way, that he'd never even laughed this hard at anything before, but now his throat was closing up from a swell of laughter going down the wrong pipe. Sweat spewed from his face. Choking on guffaws that mixed with the bile at the back of his throat. His co-workers offered him water, but he didn't want water. Water wouldn't help.

"What should we do, sir?" one of them asked.

"Oh, my word!"

"Someone help him. Make him drink water."

He was not paying attention to the mania in the room. A carton of orange Pow! sat in the middle of the table. He nodded at the Pow! frantically, his face beet red. And when, cool as a cucumber, E finally cracked open a can and slid it down the table, Graham felt safe, pouring it down as the co-workers all patted his back. He managed to apologize, and they told him "it's ok," that "everything's ok." With each sip, he became more assured that nothing would ever cause him to lose control like that again.

The last drop fizzled on his tongue along with a gasp, and E called the meeting by clapping his hands.

6

The cafeteria at Warton, Mind & Donovan had been built with the intent to curb long lunches. The walls metallic, harsh, and devoid of paintings and other flourishes. A strip of concave windows offered views of only Zones. Everything automated. You keyed in your desired meal from the imbedded computer at your desk, and it'd be ready for you piping hot by the time you entered. Any additions could be made from tiny imbedded computers built into the tables, which also started beeping in a shrill, plaguing tone if you sat for longer than half an hour. If there were higher-ups eating around you, it certainly didn't look good to linger.

Graham stood in front of a Pow! Soda machine that had been installed. Usually, all food and drink came from the giant automat that spanned one wall of the cafeteria. He balanced a tray with one hand and slipped two Stipends into the machine that appeared to whisper the word Pow! as it spat out two frosty orange cans. He rotated one in his hand as his mind traveled back to that orange dress rocking on his bedpost from the wind, the fabric delicate between his fingers, a lump of yearning in his throat. He placed both cans on his tray and walked over to a table by the windows where Mick shoveled down his lunch. The table had been positioned so it appeared as if the people dining were hovering over a Zone, dark and vacant, stretching out into the distance.

"When did the cafeteria get a Pow! machine?" Graham asked, sitting down.

Mick sucked on his cheek.

"E didn't say anything?" Mick asked. "It's for you, actually. So you can try out the new prototypes while at work."

"They installed it just for me?"

"Well, anyone can drink them, but yeah. Don't pretend you didn't notice how much the boss man blew his load when you came up with the 'sipping on passion' slogan."

"That was two hours ago. They got the machine here already?"

"E works fast."

"Anyway, I got you a Pow! too," Graham said, passing one over. Mick pat his beer belly instead.

"I'm good. Been trying to watch the old guttarooni. More for you, I guess."

Graham agreed with that statement, wanting both sodas anyway, forgetting entirely about his strange and maniacal laughter in the boardroom. His stomach had been gurgling from the few he'd already had today. He opened one. A delicious perspiration lined the can that made his lips quake.

Andy and Josephine were eating at the table close by, dead silent. Just the sound of their chewing could be heard until the imbedded computer in their table beeped loudly. The entire cafeteria swiveled over as Andy and Josephine rose without finishing their meals and scurried away. Once they'd left their seats, the beeping stopped.

"Rats," Mick said. "The both of them. Rushing back to their cages to spin on their wheels for more cheese."

"How are you any different?" Graham asked, but he was focused on the can in his hand. An extension of his body.

Mick gave a sly grin. "I have an exit strategy planned and an even bigger hunk of cheese waiting on the horizon."

Once Graham took an indulging sip, his only concern was the orange river spilling down his throat; Mick might as well be at another table. Before he knew it, he already finished one Pow! and was onto the next one, his eyes aglow.

"You're acting different," Mick said.

Graham exhaled, coming back down to reality. The room spun and then righted itself again. He shrugged and wiped his mouth with his sleeve.

"Did you get laid last night?"

"What?" Graham blushed and avoided the question by eating his food. In the past, he'd always been a careful eater, delicate chews, mouth closed. Throughout most of his life he was never taught proper table manners. Canned food was dumped in bowls like he was a dog; but fragments of memories from early childhood still existed. His mother, her face hazy but her voice soothing, telling him to remember that a fork went on the left because both 'fork' and 'left' had four letters while a 'spoon' and a 'knife' went on the 'right' side because they all had five letters. Since there wasn't much he remembered about her, he'd held onto those table manners because they were important to her, an essence of character; but now a few sodas into the day, he attacked the sandwich on his plate like a Neanderthal until its contents were strewn all over his face.

"You know, you never showed up to the Citrus Club last night," Graham mumbled, with mayonnaise oozing from the corner of his mouth. He finished the sandwich with one last shove, using his sleeve to clean his face.

"Like you were there."

"I was. And you weren't."

"You want a napkin?" Mick held one out, but Graham shook his head. "And I *was* at Citrus Club. I struck out there the entire night."

"How did I not see you?"

"That's a...mystery," Mick said, picking up an orange from his tray and rolling it in his hands. "So, tell me about this lucky lady."

Graham became caught up in the movement of the orange gliding from one of Mick's fat hands to the other.

"I never got her name," Graham said, his belly full of butterflies and desire. "If I had to pick her out of a line-up, I couldn't do that either."

He remembered falling into that blurry face as she prowled beneath him with her back arched and a wink from the angel and devil tattoos.

Mick nodded approvingly. “Anonymous. I can get into that. Bodies banging. Nothing more.”

“She was gone when I woke up, though,” Graham said, antsy in his seat now, his fingers tapping, tapping, tapping. “But...she forgot her dress.”

“Well, that either means she wanted to get the hell out of there, or leave a part of herself behind.”

Graham stopped tapping; the sodas had settled in his stomach, his body a boat being rocked at sea. Through the concave window, he wondered if she was out there, wandering through The City’s streets in just her undergarments. She could’ve left behind a shred of last night so he’d become fixated and search relentlessly for a body to match that abandoned dress.

“Honestly, the whole night was strange. Like I dreamed it all–”

“That’s screwy all right.”

Mick rolled the orange he’d been manhandling over to Graham’s tray.

“Here. Take.”

“You don’t want it?” Graham asked, but he already brought it to lips, his teeth bared and ready.

“Nah, it’s your healthy snack.”

Graham dug into the orange, rind in his fingernails. Sweet acid and pulp dribbled from his lips. He devoured it like he devoured the girl in the orange dress until it vanished just like her, only the peel remaining as a memento. Mick scooped up the peel in his hand as an offering.

"Here. Finish it all."

"Eat the peel?" Graham asked, sticky and panting. He glanced over at the table that Andy and Josephine had vacated. A lady with thinning hair had sat down and looked up from her book: *Awakened Dreams: A Guide to Awakening in Your Sleep and in Your Life.* Unable to avert his gaze, he stared at the book as she stared back at him until Mick finally spoke again.

"Sure, eat the peel," Mick said. "One man's waste is another man's paradise."

Graham placed the peel on his tongue, his taste buds gliding over the texture of its bumpy surface before he started chewing it up in a frenzy.

"How do you feel?" Mick asked.

"I feel–" Graham began, the taste tart and bitter on his tongue, unsure what he was even going to say. The tiny imbedded computer in their table started beeping.

"Let's get Tequila Sunrises tonight at the Citrus Club," Mick yelled over the beeps, as he cleaned up the table. "For real this time. Eight o'clock at the bar."

The two placed their trays into a flume-like chute by the automat that sucked the garbage up into oblivion. Graham chewed the last remnants of the orange peel, the hairs on his arm standing on end. He was still caught in a dueling stare with the lady with thinning hair, but more concerned with her book, as the words *Awakened Dreams* floated off of the book's jacket and followed him and Mick out of the cafeteria.

Graham continued to float down the long hallway toward his cubicle. Lunch had settled nicely and he was deliriously content. Each step of his walk would normally be heavy with the weight of his past, but today he could barely feel the ground beneath him. He was excited to get back to his cubicle to create other slogans. The void that usually sucked up any good ideas was closing. He wouldn't be inconsequential, or just a cog on a spoke, but revolutionary. 'Sipping on passion' would be the beginning of a flood.

Josephine passed by with a wave in her orange blouse. For a moment, he couldn't remember anything he was thinking. All he wanted to focus on was that orange blouse. His heartbeat accelerated, loud enough for him to hear each thump. Right behind Josephine came Andy with an orange handkerchief stuffed in his front pocket. Graham's muscles started to twitch. Lastly, that douchebag Shep, who'd caused him to flinch yesterday, turned around the corner with orange cufflinks glimmering in the fluorescent light, but Graham didn't flinch this time. Feeling invincible, he checked Shep with his shoulder, hard enough to make the guy wonder if it was done on purpose, and then he continued down the hallway, even more content than before.

At the far end, Marlena the intern came into view. A skintight orange dress hugged her body that seemed to call his name as her long legs stepped toward him—*Graham, Graham, Graham, Graham*. He slowed down time for a beat to observe. Marlena, from Floraldala, whose tan hadn't gone away with the endless winter in this City, whose skin tone was practically the color of her dress as if a never-ending beach was her backyard. People here had a tendency to act like shells of what they once were. They avoided their pasts in any way possible by retreating within themselves, or becoming lost in work, or by the excess highs of the Downtown. They'd escaped from whatever tragedy had brought them over and then settled in The City's overpowering seclusion, remaining shreds of who they used to be, half of them a simulacrum, and therefore a façade. But Marlena was different. Sunny and pure. All of her limbs appeared to be real, and it didn't seem like she was the type of person that committed a crime in the Outside World. What other reasons could have brought her here?

With orange lipstick on, she gave him the warmest smile he'd ever seen and he got hard instantly. The blood ran to his dick so fast it made him shiver. She didn't seem to notice, or maybe it didn't bother her. She kept smiling. So, boldness growing, he moved in closer to taste the sunshine on her lips, but she spoke before he had the chance.

"Marlena is orange," she said, and he did a double take. "Crash."

For a split second, he pondered what she said—which made no sense. The delicious fantasy had crumbled. His brain froze, and there was a tic in his eye as he was pulled out of this dream. His mind traveled to a time when he was a child in the backseat of an out of control car. A storm was raging outside as the car careened off a bridge. The feeling of helplessness was so raw, so real, so consuming. The car plunged into deep waters and then he found himself thrown back into the present, stumbling and leaning against the wall for support. He didn't know where he was: alive, or still getting pulled under the water.

Marlena's dress called to him again—*Graham, Graham*. She continued toward the other end of the hallway as if she hadn't said anything out of the ordinary, as if her orange words, her orange clothes, and this orange world that had surrounded him for the last day was an absolute reality. He followed her swishing legs, his heartbeat resuming to normal. The shock of almost drowning became fragmented and undefined now, like he wanted it to be, like he'd hoped it would have become after all these years by coming here, since it was the true crime he deserved to be punished for.

7

"Here's your can!" Mick said, slamming an orange Pow! on the desk as Graham snapped back into focus. "You left it in the cafeteria."

Graham was unsure how long he'd been spacing out, thanking Mick for bringing the drink. He couldn't even remember walking back to his cubicle. He was so thirsty that his lips had become dry and cracked, and his saliva tasted like a thousand needles pricking his throat. He thought he had drunk both Pow! Sodas from the cafeteria's vending machine, but he cracked another one open anyway and chugged until it was finished and Mick left.

On his desk sat the mock-ad of the orange question mark. GUESS THE SECRET? He had work to do but couldn't take his eyes off the ad, attracted to the question mark. It became more than an inanimate object, fully living and breathing. His finger traced its curve, caressing the dot until it morphed into an orange sun hanging in the distance. He recalled a memory so old it barely felt like his own anymore. Running through cornfields somewhere in Middle Amercyana, his feet moist and the earth squishy. Giggling as his dad caught up and tickled him to the ground. His dad just a drifting shadow; his mother cast in shade as well. They were headed to the lake for the day to feed the ducks, which had settled back into the water now, zigzagging away toward that melting orange sun. He didn't remember any of the conversations from that day so it appeared like a silent film; but he did recall that it was the last time he knew what it felt like to be loved. The shadow of his dad stopped tickling him and met up with his mother as they watched the sun sink. They locked their shadow fingers together, and she leaned against his shoulder. The sun fizzled out into the cornfields as his parents blended with the darkness until they were gone forever, puffs of vanishing smolder.

When he looked up for any last traces of them, he realized he was back in The City. The glass walls of his cubicle surrounded him and the mock-ad sat in his hands. Minutes had blended into hours and he'd fondled the question mark so much that the orange had begun to fade and only white fingernail scratches remained.

Outside his cubicle, the copy machine whirred and took him out of his trance. He was so thirsty again he could barely open his mouth. His spine stung from sitting hunched over. The noise of the copy machine became oppressive, nails on a chalkboard, and he craved stillness: the comforting radiance of the orange question mark. Now that its color had faded, his energy had also depleted; his passion subsided. He grabbed the last orange Pow! on his desk and headed out of the cubicle.

Down the hallway, the copy machine blinked green. A woman stood in front of the copier with her back to him. She wore a dress with orange and green horizontal stripes, looking like a giant centipede. He cracked open the can, startling her. Just the smell of the soda's sugary aroma made him excited again, eager to trace her orange stripes infinite times over. The woman turned around with a stack of documents in one hand and the other hand holding her heart. It was the woman he'd met earlier this morning in the elevator. Her dress was different than he remembered, but he hadn't forgotten those orange high heels.

"I didn't see you."

"Sorry, I didn't mean to sneak up on you."

The woman responded with a half grin. They shared a moment of awkward silence. She blinked, and he was still mesmerized by her orange eye shadow. He took a sip of soda. The colors on her dress seemed to be at war with one another, but if he concentrated on the orange weaving around her body; then she was a muse. Her name leaped into his mind.

"Gayle, right?"

"Yes. Gayle Hanley." She spoke in a monotone but seemed pleased that he remembered. "And you're Graham."

The copier outlined them both in green, but he remained focused on her orange swirls. He took another sip, more alive with each swallow.

"How are you liking it here so far?" he asked those swirls.

"Oh, it's good." She shifted her weight to cradle the heavy stack of documents. "You know, a lot to learn at once."

She was nervous about something, possibly first day jitters.

"What did they hire you for?" he asked.

"I was Selected to be an analyst for Pow! Sodas. To supervise and give input on the new campaign."

"I work in Creative. I'm a part of the Pow! campaign, too. Actually, as a tester of the new prototypes."

"I'm sure we'll see a lot of each other then," she replied. The other end of her mouth finally curled up and finished her smile. Her lip muscles quivered, as if it was something she was unfamiliar with doing.

In the elevator this morning, he didn't really get a good look at her face. The orange high heels and shadow dusting her eyes were a distraction. But looking up from her dress now, he realized she was beautiful enough to be an actress on the big screen. High cheekbones and a long, graceful neck. Thin lips and sleek hair, not a strand out of place. He wondered if he'd seen her before today; at least, her presence felt familiar. He didn't know if she was being flirtatious or not (he'd never been good at gauging intentions), or if it was just her way of masking nerves; but he was certain his new philosophy should be to never second-guess, to embrace each moment rather than shrink.

"Have you been in The City long?" he asked, stepping closer until he could smell the citrusy perfume emanating from her neck. "Have I seen you around?"

Her eyes searched the ground, the orange blush staring at him now.

"No. I'm new here. I was living in Califa."

"Califa? Far away."

He'd never been to Califa, only skirting around the sad middle of Amercyana in the Outside World before he came here. All indistinguishable now, rolling through adolescence from one nowhere town to the next.

"So far away, but this is home now," she said, humorless again as she tugged at a hangnail with her teeth. She pointed at the can in his hand. "I see you've started your research."

He glanced at the can, its tin shell now like an extension of him.

"I like to get into my work."

"You'd be surprised at how far dedication can take you."

Graham took another sip. Before he knew it, he'd drunk half the can.

"Someone's thirsty."

He lowered the can, but his hand started to shake. Unable to resist its sugary flavor, he brought it back to his mouth until he sucked out the final drops.

"So how many have you had today?" Gayle asked, watching him with what appeared to be a frightened allure.

"A couple. I don't know."

His smile waned as he thought about it.

"I guess I could count the empty cans in my recycling

bin."

They headed into his cubicle where he picked up his recycling bin and removed eight orange cans placed on his desk. He doubled back, certain that he only had maybe three or four at the most. Sweat beaded at his temples.

"You're really into that Pow! aren't you?" she asked. "And all orange, too?"

"I've had more than that today," he said, his voice barely above a whisper. "At my apartment, the board meeting, the cafeteria...."

He looked to her as if she could explain, his lips starting to tremble.

"Is that normal for you, Graham?"

The tone in her voice shifted, more direct and less concerned than before. The analyst emerged and her nervous energy that he figured was first day jitters had been left in the hallway.

"Do you think that's strange?" he asked her, but was really asking himself. "I've never been given this much responsibility with a campaign. The boss has never regarded my input, so I want to make sure I'm putting everything I can into testing out..."

He tried to remember each Pow! he drank, but he was consumed again by the flow of orange stripes on her dress. He followed them around and around until he was left staring at the stack of documents in her hands. The paper on top blank.

"Are all those documents blank?" he asked.

Flustered, she dropped the pile to the floor. The pages scattered and each document was in fact completely blank. She quickly gathered them up.

"Yeah...the copier...it's broken."

Fear wrestled in her eyes. One strand of hair had been dislodged from the gelled helmet she'd created, and she appeared like an entirely different woman. He was about to question her again when Mick barreled into the cubicle.

"Hey, Graham-O!" Mick shouted.

Gayle stood, clutching the blank documents to her chest, fidgety and eyeing the hallway.

"Didn't realize you were busy, bud."

"No, go ahead," Gayle said, taking long strides to get out of his cubicle. "I'll...see you around, Graham. I have to get back to work."

She mumbled her last words, already at the hallway before she finished. Her heels clomped away and grew fainter which each step.

He was confused about why she'd be making copies of blank documents, but the cans on his desk diverted his attention. He checked each one for any last drops of soda until the odd interaction he had with Gayle dissolved. One can had some swill at the bottom that tasted flat. It was not enough; he needed more.

Graham tossed the cans on his desk back into the recycling bin, unsettled and panting, his forehead soaked with sweat.

"What did you come in here for, Mick?"

"Huh? Oh yeah...I dunno, totally forgot. If my dick wasn't screwed on, right?"

Graham's heart beat so fast it made him wince. Sweat dripped into his mouth, tasting like salty orange Pow!.

"I don't feel so hot," he said, as a war brewed in his stomach. "Actually, I feel really hot."

He wiped sweat from his brow that sizzled on his fingertips.

"Ah, too bad, bud. A night out should make you better. So, Lime Lounge at eight?"

"Lime Lounge?" Graham asked, perplexed. "I thought you said Citrus Club–"

"Nah, Citrus Club is passé. Lime Lounge is the spot."

A huge gas bubble rolled through Graham's stomach. He locked his arms around his rumbling belly. The sweat on his forehead had covered his eyes and practically fused them shut. He wanted Mick out of his cubicle so he could splash some water on his face.

"Fine, Mick. Lime Lounge. Whatever. Eight. I'll see you there."

He pushed past Mick and left his cubicle. The employee lounge was bathed in fluorescent orange light and called out to him from down the hall. Once inside, he turned the sink on full blast and dipped his head into the stream of water. His heartbeat slowed and he no longer needed to explode. He wet a paper towel, turned off the faucet, and dabbed the back of his head. Convinced himself this was just a panic attack, which could be relieved with a few Levels.

Marlena the intern came inside, her deer-like eyes glancing his way. His anxiety dissipated when he saw her orange dress and tangerine clutch purse. He blinked, taken back to the morning when he felt the silky-smooth fabric of the orange dress hanging from his bedpost. He wanted to feel Marlena between his fingers, too. The need for a Pow! had been replaced by her orange glamour, and his stomach settled down.

"Mr. Weatherend, you're soaked," she said, stepping over a puddle.

He brushed aside his wet bangs.

"Yeah. Looks like." He tried to brush it off. "Was a little anxious and needed to cool down. Please, call me Graham."

Genuinely concerned, she handed him some paper towels.

"It's stressful here, isn't it?" she whispered, touching him on the elbow.

"Yes. Thank you."

"Do you need any Levels? I think I might even have some threes in my purse?"

She rooted through her tangerine clutch.

"No, no," he said, concentrating on that tangerine purse, wanting to touch its orangey glow. "Please don't worry. I'm fine. So, tell me. How is your internship going?"

"Good, I guess. I mean...it's weird, like, being in an office every day. And just this City, it's..."

"It's what?" he asked, craving the outsider's perspective that he's lost.

"I mean, I've been at the University of Floraldala on a campus for the last four years. My whole reality is skewed, ya know?"

"I never lived on a campus before. I never even went to college. Few get that chance."

"Get out."

"No...I...just came here."

He closed his eyes and the terrible anxious feeling returned, longing to burst out of his skin. When he opened his eyes, her orange aura was there to welcome him. She radiated, and now he was bursting to be comforted by the softness of her orange dress. This whole day he'd found himself going from zero to a million in just seconds.

"I'm gonna find you some Levels, Graham."

She placed her tangerine purse on the table and sat, bobbing her foot as she searched for Levels. He stared at that bobbing foot until he got sucked back into the past. She'd sat across from him two weeks ago during an entrance interview in a metallic room without windows; bobbing her foot like crazy in the same way.

In addition to the two of them at this interview, two older men, the Elders, were scribbling notes at his side. He asked Marlena the basic questions that an interviewer had to ask, but the Elders were there to monitor him. They popped up on random days once a month at all the companies to catch an employee off guard, to study and report on how integral one was to the company's success. Both were covered with so many wrinkles that their eyes and mouths were barely visible. They looked like twins. Their facial expressions never altered, and therefore Graham didn't know if his questions were intelligent or not. All he knew was that this girl in front of him was excited about coming to The City, recruited by the Man himself. She was eager to learn, and explore, and step outside of her boundaries, which made him sad because he couldn't remember the last time he'd thought similarly, or if he'd ever felt that way.

"Why advertising?" he had asked her. The Elders scribbled frantically. She crossed one tan leg over the other and didn't answer immediately. She took her time, awarded him with a smile.

"The great writer Oliver Wendell Holmes said that a 'man's mind, once stretched by a new idea, never regains its original dimensions'. Advertising is the best forum I can think of to spread your ideas as messages by connecting to a product and making people feel like they need that product, that they need your words, that it gives them the comfort they're searching for."

"And why come to this City of all places?" he asked.

"The City gave me back something I lost a long time ago, but that's not the only reason. I like Floraldala, but I've graduated from school and too much sun can poison one's brain. I'm ready to have my mind stretched in this new place where I'll be challenged and where I won't be able to use the good weather as an excuse to slack off anymore."

She seemed wiser to Graham than her twenty-one years would have one believe.

"So, is that why you have such a nice tan?" he asked. "Barely anyone here has nice tans anymore." He heard the words come out of his mouth but disbelieved that he actually said them. The Elders scribbled faster, their pens slicing at the pads on their laps, but Graham shut off all other sounds as she continued talking, radiating hope, and soon he was adrift in the dance of her moving lips.

"Is there anything else you can tell us, Ms. Havanderson, to distinguish yourself from the other applicants?" he asked.

She bit her lip seductively.

"I give amazing head."

"Excuse me, what did you say?"

She didn't respond to his question, just kept bobbing her foot. He tried to wrap his mind around what he'd heard and then found himself blinking uncontrollably as he was flung back into the present.

Now Marlena stood before him holding out three little pills.

"Um, what did you say?" he asked.

"I said the Levels should clear up your head."

He was certain he'd mixed up parts of her interview with daydreams. He couldn't have asked about her tan, that was nonsense. He'd remained the model of professionalism he prided himself on. Only today had her tan plagued his mind with its orange luster.

He popped the Levels in his mouth and swallowed two of them, but the third got lodged in his throat. His face turned bright red. All of a sudden, he couldn't breathe, completely losing control.

"Omigod, you're choking!"

He flailed his arms around, wheezing. Marlena ran behind him, placed her hands around his waist, and thrusted him against her.

"Help," he gurgled. Even in the face of possible death, she felt so good with her warm breath on his neck that he became erect in her arms, the sensation of truly living and slowly dying surging through him.

She lifted him off his feet and thrusted again.

"Gaaaaacckkkk."

As she lifted him again, one of his winged-tipped shoes fell off. With one final thrust, the rogue Level shot out of his mouth and he lost all control by coming in his pants. She released him with a yelp. Both were frozen with no idea what to do or say. Marlena went to speak, but he pushed past her and bolted out of the lounge before he could see her reaction. Co-workers flew by him in a blur as he ran with a panic-stricken look on his face.

When he reached his cubicle, out of breath and turned to ooze, two lime green Pow!s sat on his desk dripping with condensation. He fought the impulse to drink one. He told his brain to chill and figure out what was going on, to take stock of these last twenty-four hours, but his hands didn't listen to his brain anymore.

The nuclear-green fizz got sucked out of the can as he basked in the green Xerox light that crept up the hallway. Orange became a thing of the past, and all he wanted was everything green instead. He couldn't explain why his cravings had switched so easily, but this new color was a part of him now, in his veins. Its signals already had been sent to his brain, and he knew it was too late to fight, nothing but a victim to its charm. Fall into green's vibrant tartness, its reassuring, cooling warmth. Everything balanced now. Fresh and harmonious. Slowly, the mortification of what happened in the employee lounge faded and he was a new man again.

Glug, glug, glug. Repeat.

Burp all problems away.

8

Graham's cab got stuck in traffic because of the crowd Downtown so he paid the fare and headed over to Lime Lounge on foot. The rain had been switched on to wash the vomit-soaked streets, and he practically wiped out as he rushed over. When he arrived, a nuclear-green carpet led up to the lounge's door shaped like a large lime. Green lights pulsed from inside its glass walls. Graham waited in the long entry line, sipping from a lime Pow!.

The people on line were mostly Finances: the only ones in The City who really had money, since they controlled it. Once released from their chains, they often decided what the new hot spot would be, but because of the limited amount of establishments in the Downtown, places didn't have to wait too long to be dubbed hot again.

A bouncer with a neck nearly the size of Graham's torso let in all the pallid Finances and the modelesque girls hanging on their arms. Graham never used to be impressed with The Finances, not even sure what their day-to-day jobs consisted of, whereas he spent his time creating, actually producing something; but today, as he chugged his last drop of lime Pow!, he felt insanely jealous of them. Their Stipends never depleted. They got to live in the Estates. He'd never been jealous like this before, but as the last lime sip slithered down his throat, he desired their lives so much it burned.

After a half an hour, he was let inside a cubed space with transparent glass ceilings and floors. Green lasers flashed in every direction. People sat around tables sucking down Gas from oxygen tanks used as centerpieces, their eyes practically bleeding from laughing so hard. Jarring electronic music bleeped from the speakers, but no one was dancing. They sat and sucked and laughed maniacally.

Mick waited alone at a table with a Gin Rickey, an array of cut limes around the rim. He wore a bright neon green tie.

"Graham-O! You're late. I'm already laced, catch up."

He nabbed a waitress passing by. She had green highlights in her black hair.

"Two more Rickeys. And kill it with limes."

She nodded with a snap of her neon green gum and a laugh before heading toward the bar.

"That's for you and you," Mick said, firing at Graham

with his index fingers.

Graham couldn't stop thinking about what happened between him and Marlena in the employee lounge. He'd never experienced a full loss of control like that, picturing her repulsed reaction and wishing it had happened to Mick instead. Mick, who acted like he had this City all figured out. Even the waitress with the green highlights seemed amused by Mick while Graham didn't even know if he'd ever be able to face Marlena again.

"I think I need a drink," he said. "I think I need two."

"You always need two. Not *you* in particular, but *you* in general. This City takes a double."

"If I told you what happened to me this afternoon, you wouldn't believe it."

"Try me." Mick picked up the oxygen mask attached to the tank on the table. "A little Gas? I've paid for ten breaths. I've been jonesing for some hilarity."

"No, I'm good."

Mick sucked in a lungful of Gas and let out a string of rat-a-tat laughs.

"All right, I'm ready," he said.

"Do you know that new intern Marlena?"

Graham pulled at his collar, feeling hot, his throat incredibly dry. He wished the waitress would bring over his drinks already.

"Well, it was ridiculous," he continued. "I mean...I was choking on a Level, and while she was giving me the Heimlich, I...came in my pants."

"HAHAHHAHAHHAHAHHAHAHHAA!"

Graham crossed his arms while Mick pounded the table until the waitress came over.

"Oh, honey, slow down with that Gas there," she

snapped. She placed the Rickeys in front of Graham. "And you look like you could use a breath or two." She held up the oxygen mask over Graham's mouth, but he jerked away. "Suit yourself, Stick-in-the-Mud."

"Go ahead, doll," Mick said, wiping his eyes and still laughing hysterically. "Take a breath instead of a tip."

She shrugged her shoulders and inhaled, giggling like a little kid after a Halloween candy pig out. The green lasers illuminated her glowing teeth. Looking around Lime Lounge, Graham was envious of everyone because they all appeared so easily pleasured. He longed for a minute inside their minds and a break from his own because he couldn't stop picturing Marlena, shocked and disgusted as she told E everything that had happened; then E would unleash his wrath and get Graham kicked out into a Zone.

"You don't see the consequences?" he yelled. "I could lose my job!"

"Impossible. She's an intern. She's not gonna want to make any waves."

"She could think it's sexual harassment, go to E–"

"You're being paranoid."

Had he been acting abnormally paranoid? He'd always been a little on edge walking down the halls of Warton, Mind & Donovan because of the tiny cameras in the floors monitoring his every move. He understood that the company hated insubordination, that all companies here were hell bent on weeding out any employee who would poison it from within. But this paranoia was different. Yesterday, he was soaring, invincible; today, he'd turned into a sniveling mess, resenting everyone around him.

His mind drifted again as the limes around his drink caught his attention. Paranoia got thrown out the window as he took in his green-tinted surroundings. His thoughts became clear enough to assemble together a question that had been nagging him since he'd left the employee lounge.

"Do you ever feel like you're not in complete control of your brain?" he asked, leaning in closer to Mick as if the hysterical crowd listened to every word. "That you could be corrupted?"

"Don't know what you mean," Mick said, eyeing him carefully.

"Earlier today, I had this overwhelming sense of passion, not for anything in particular, but...for life, and it was unfamiliar."

"That's why I come to the Downtown. Nonstop nights of fulfilled desire."

"But the Downtown has a control over you. You need to keep coming back to lose that feeling of malaise, right?"

Mick let out another peal of laughter. He knocked on the metal oxygen tank, testing to see what was left.

"Sure, your Gas tank is bound to run low and you need a filler up. We're helpless consumers, Graham, forever sucking more and more from that big teat."

"God, I'm...so thirsty," Graham said, barely able to speak because of his dry throat. Both of his Lime Rickeys were empty. "Am I cracking up?" he asked, but he didn't recognize the voice as his own. It came from deep within, struggling to get out, still present.

Mick took another breath of Gas and responded with roars.

"Nah, you're just overworked. The less you're cooped up in your box, the less you can pick at your mind and question, question, question. Those questions will drive you insane. You gotta come to the Downtown more, like me, and just be. Say, this'll cheer you up. I got a treat for you, bud."

Mick indicated at his sleeves, showing nothing up the right one and nothing up the left. He waved his hands around like a magician and pulled a lime Pow! out of the left one.

Drool collected in Graham's mouth. He cracked open the can and wanted to empty it in one large swig; but since it was the only one he had for the time being, he sipped cautiously.

"I gotta go. Enjoy the Pow!," Mick said. "I'm meeting up with another one of those machine-finger amputees. This one's hand got in the way of a chainsaw before they came to this City. Pity for them, dynamite for me."

"You're ditching me?" Graham asked. As the bubbles dripped into his belly, he wondered why he couldn't be the one having a date with a machine-fingers, why Mick was always charmed.

"You were late, Graham, and the night and my dick are getting old."

Mick tossed a twenty Stipend on the table. Graham picked it up, engrossed with the green in his hands.

"Why don't you call that girl you just hooked up with and take her out for another drink?" Mick asked. "The one who left her dress on your bedpost. She sounds like a lime."

"A what?"

"I said she sounds like a peach. You really gotta get out of this fog you've been in."

Mick buttoned up his coat and took a last breath of Gas for the road.

"Check you later."

An overwhelming ping of envy coursed through Graham again as he finished his Pow!. Mick was always the superior one, doling out advice, and viewing him with pity, but Graham couldn't stop thinking about reversing those roles. One day he might have the upper hand, and Mick would be crouched on the floor, begging.

"No one can be charmed forever," Graham said to himself as he squeezed the empty Pow! can until it was crushed entirely.

In the middle of the night, Graham remained at Lime Lounge, his table covered with sucked limes, longing to spend time anywhere but back at his apartment. The crowd had thinned out and no one was laughing anymore. The green lasers still flashed, but the bar changed over the course of the night, or at least how it appeared. The walls dripped a nuclear-throbbing green, and the few Finances and their remaining dates were decked out in green as well.

At the bar, a lonely girl in a green dress with green high heels sipped an appletini. Her face a blur, like the girl from Citrus Club, except for the inviting green eyes that matched her dress. Graham wobbled to his feet and headed in her direction, unsure of what he'd say or do. She bobbed her foot and then used the tip of her green high heel to scratch the back of one of her never-ending legs.

Mick appeared from out of nowhere and reached her first. He grinned until his jowls strained and they began touching each other in a mechanical way, her blurry face leaving kisses on Mick's cheeks as she scratched his back with her long green fingernails. All Graham could do was boil with jealousy, clenching his fists until his knuckles glared white and blood pooled from biting his lip so hard.

Graham blinked and he was back in Boxed Lane, unsure how he even got there. He stepped into his pitch-black living room, but sounds were coming from his alcove bedroom. He searched for the light switch but there was none, feeling his way through the dark, the sounds closing in on him.

In the bedroom, the moonlight creeping in through the blinds was a putrid green. Mick and the girl groped each other on his bed, both naked except she wore her green high heels. His fat body having sex with her from behind. With each growl, the angel and the devil tattoos on her back slapped against his torso.

Graham let out a tormented scream, but neither Mick nor the girl paid any attention. He stalked them with the intent of causing Mick immeasurable pain. He wanted to wrap his hands around his friend's fat throat and choke him for taking his girl and rubbing it in his face. The moonlight's greenish tint blinded Graham as he moved toward the bed, and the blinds snapped shut until they were all left in a debilitating darkness with only their screams to locate one another.

Graham woke in a fit. He sat up, rubbed his head, and put his face in his hands, his head heavy like a medicine ball. He could taste a dry trickle of blood on his bottom lip. He placed his feet on the floor and almost tripped over the dark green high heels lying beside his bed. Hungover, he meandered into the kitchen, oblivious, the light of the morning an evil plague and all of their screams still faintly ringing in his ears. Why had Mick even been in his apartment with the girl when he had his own? Opening the refrigerator, three lime Pow! Sodas sat on the top shelf. He considered the sodas, hesitating, but couldn't help himself, cracking open each one and seething as the sweet venom trickled down.

9

The note on Graham's desk later that morning read: *See me immediately and bring taste descriptions*! – E.

With a lime Pow! in his hand, he headed into E's office. Like always, he was taken aback by its grandeur. Tall, arching ceilings and tinted green windows overlooked the Business Region and its struggling ants below. Sparkling silver walls with imbedded computers displayed various commercials and ads. A few black leather sofas were in one corner, along with a personal bathroom and a stocked mini-bar. Graham couldn't help but simmer with resentment at his boss's daily paradise.

E sat behind his massive desk munching from a bowl of prunes. A framed picture of Joseph Stalin hung next to him, staring Graham down.

"You want?" E asked.

"Want what?"

E held out the bowl of prunes but Graham shook his head. E shrugged and then tucked a *City Gazette* under his arm before going into the bathroom. Graham overheard a few groans and took the opportunity to observe the imbedded computers showing stills of classic films from long, long ago like *The Seven Year Itch*, *The Right Stuff*, and *Pulp Fiction*, but the actors had been replaced with Pow! Soda cans.

The toilet flushed and E shuffled out.

"Those were some of the old Pow! ads. Cute, but cute isn't going line my pockets with Stipends at the end of the day."

"No, sir."

E removed a cigar out of his pocket, cut and lit it, and blew the taunting smoke at Graham.

"So, tell me what the limes are like. Let's see if your 'sipping on passion' was a fluke."

Graham would need some time to get used to this new personable E. Even now, E was patting him on the back instead of smacking him on the head. He knew that at any point his boss could switch back to being terrorizing.

He took another sip of the lime Pow! and rolled the soda around his mouth: the astringency most perceptible on his inner cheeks while the fizz burned the back of his throat. He pursed his lips and inhaled through them before chewing the soda vigorously and then swallowing. He hadn't spent any time beforehand considering lime Pow!'s taste, but a slogan floated off his tongue seamlessly.

"Sour never tasted so sweet."

E crossed his arms and puffed at the ceiling, pondering the slogan.

"Do you feel special, Graham?"

"Not...especially."

"You are more special than you know," E said, quietly. He then cleared his throat as if he realized he said something out loud that he shouldn't have. "And uh...a smart man, too. I was just telling Mr. Stalin that earlier."

It was odd for E to fumble with his words since usually he was so commanding. Graham shook his head at this arrogant man who didn't deserve a magnificent view from his office tower, who'd left behind a trail of used and abused employees for far too long.

"Brilliant man, that Stalin," E continued, straining for a thought. "The...cult of personality he created by having villages and towns named after him. *That's* the kind of branding to emulate."

"I never thought of him in that way."

E blew another gust of cigar smoke Graham's way. Graham tried not to let his mind wander, but he briefly receded into his past of bruises mixed with that smoldering cigar smell.

"Looking a bit thirsty there, kid," E said, as he handed him a Pow! from the mini bar.

Graham cracked open the can and started chugging.

"Stalin was famous for a lot, though," E said, his tone more serious now. "Warton, Mind & Donovan's Great Purge was inspired by the one he birthed."

Graham stopped drinking. He knew of the company's Great Purge all too well; those were not words that any employee wanted to hear. The Elders would present their bi-annual report of any employees poisoning the company with their ineffectuality. Sweat broke out on his forehead as he inhaled a deep breath.

"I've certainly gone back-and-forth in the past between sending you to the Zones," E said, pacing back-and-forth, his oversized feet pounding into the marble floor. He refrained from speaking for a while so the impact of his words could hang in the air.

"Now that we're running the ad game solo, we've become The City's heart," E continued. "We'll decide the trends, what will make it tick. We'll be expected to keep things fresh. To weed out the weak and shape the dedicated."

The word "weak" bounced off the walls in whispers. Graham spun his head around, trying to find the source of those whispers. E blew another smoke cloud and resumed talking, but the green tinted windows and the ants below absorbed Graham's focus, as if they were the ones whispering: all of them hovering on the edges of the Zones and easily teetering toward a life that could be stripped away.

"Am I being replaced, sir?" Graham asked, pissed off rather than groveling, jealous of everyone with the ability to snatch his existence from under him.

E let out a laugh that showed his fangs.

"Replaced? Kid, I'm saying that you're just what we need right now." He took a puff, becoming the *good cop* once again. "I might as well kick the rest of Creative to The Zones and pick, pick, pick at your inventive mind."

E blew a final stream of smoke and stubbed out the cigar.

"Speaking of minds, how is yours doing?"

"Come again?" Graham said, rubbing his skull that had started to throb uncomfortably.

"It seems like you've found a way to...tap into ingenious ideas that have...certainly eluded you before."

"I...can't explain it," Graham said, wondering if there could be something else behind these outpourings of slogans besides his simple brain.

"Well, mostly your old boss is just checking up. Knocking on your head to make sure everything's rattling around like it should."

"I am...fine," Graham gulped, but the words were shaky as they escaped from his lips. E's eyes were locked on the Pow! can as Graham comforted himself with a final metallic sip.

Walking toward his cubicle, all of Graham's co-workers appeared out of focus, just green blobs whizzing by at a super speed.

"I am fine, I am fine, I am fine," he murmured. The lime's tartness still stung his taste buds. His steps were weighted with longing.

Four lime Pow!s waited on the desk in his cubicle. His stomach gurgled and he swiped one, a shred of him realizing the ridiculousness of this new *want* that seemed to have taken over, but the majority of him craved its tartness, which superseded all logic.

Mick lurched in like an oaf, his hand extended for a high five. He wore a light green suit.

"Graham-O! What's the word?"

Graham didn't respond to Mick's high five attempt as

each succulent sip drew him further back into last night's mind-fuck. The girl in green—who he craved as much as a Pow!—and Mick taking her from behind in Graham's own bed as her green high heels dangled over the edge of the bed. The putrid moonlight and their demented moans.

Was it all a dream, or had reality naturally become more incredulous? He didn't know which would scare him more.

The girl's skin was so consuming, her blurry face an enigma he needed to solve. If she was a dream, then was anything real here? For all he knew, the last ten years in this place could have been a façade, a moment of REM.

You had sex with the faceless girl! Graham thought, as he glared at Mick. His eye began to twitch with such speed that it hurt.

"Dude, your eye is twitching real bad," the oaf said.

"I'm aware of that."

"You gotta get more sleep, man. Let's get lunch."

Graham followed him down the hall like a drone, his eye a separate vibrating entity. Mick lumbered in front, loud and obnoxious to all the greenly dressed co-workers passing by. They embraced Mick, but barely acknowledged Graham, and Graham fumed, begging for the attention, the admiration. Mick was the star as always, and Graham wanted to take a knife and plunge it into Mick's back, twisting it around for fucking the faceless girl.

In the cafeteria, the beeping imbedded computers gave him a headache. He was simmering as he waited on line, keying in his choices. Only hungry for greens: lettuce, kale, broccoli, celery, and a pesto vinaigrette. He went to pick up his tray at the end of the line.

The lady with thinning hair who he saw here yesterday

waited for her lunch as well. She cradled her *Awakened Dreams* book as if it was a newborn child. She nodded shyly, pale fingers running through her sparse strands of hair. She wore an emerald-colored dress and green teardrop earrings. The automat spat out a sad yogurt and a spoon. She placed the book on the counter, pushing it closer to him, so she could pick up the yogurt.

"I don't like what they're doing," she said, as their eyes met briefly and then she looked back down toward her book, as if telling it goodbye.

"What who's doing?" he asked.

She met Graham's eyes again before picking up her spoon and flitting away. The book remained, but he didn't chase her down to give it back; he stayed still until she blended in with the rest of the cafeteria. The automat shot out his greens, and he slid the small pocket book into his suit pocket.

Mick had already scarfed down half of his green lunch as Graham sat, replaying the lady's words over and over in his head. He chewed on his lip, wondering if someone out there really was playing with his mind, if he wasn't just going crazy. Since he'd been having odd dreams, he pressed the book down in his pocket so Mick wouldn't ask any unnecessary questions. Even though he was insanely curious to dive into its pages, it wasn't the right time. If no one saw him take the book then that would be enough of a success for now.

The overhead speakers switched on, and the Man began speaking in an unintelligible language. He was angry, his voice guttural and foreboding as if he was admonishing his City. The people in the cafeteria covered their ears from the volume being turned so loud. Some made the sign of the cross or squeezed their eyes shut. The Man let out his final demand and then hissed into the speakers before going silent. The speakers switched off, and an imbedded computer by the concave windows beeped. It was coming from the table where the lady with thinning hair ate. All the other workers sighed in relief. The lady looked around in confusion before she rose on shaky knees and had no other choice but to leave. He could vaguely make out the Elders waiting for her at the archway entrance. She walked toward them so slowly that she was practically standing still.

"Better start getting to those greens," Mick said, with lettuce spilling from his mouth, ignoring what took place. He slid a lime Pow! over to Graham. "This was the last lime in the machine."

Graham's tongue tried to form the words to say that he was good, that he didn't need another, but he'd already lunged for the Pow!, glad to focus on it rather than wonder what was happening to the lady. He had her book, all that mattered. Showing any contempt or concern could cause the speakers to switch on again and seal his own fate; he'd seen it before.

"So, what did you do after the Lime Lounge?" Mick asked. Graham took a large gulp of the Pow!, his eye resuming its chronic twitch.

"What did you do?" he growled, between more gulps.

"I got some Selected to jerk me senseless," Mick smirked.

"Yeah right, did they have a face?" Graham asked, the words flying out of his mouth.

"A face? What is wrong with you?"

"She is *mine*!" he said, visualizing Mick with the girl

from his dreams and wanting to rage. "Get it?"

Graham knocked back the rest of the Pow!, and Mick's green suit became electrifying, all encompassing. Suddenly it was the only color in the room, the only thing he cared about once again.

"What are you talking about? You don't even know the Selected," Mick said, but Graham only heard it as mumbles from a far-off place. He'd delved into a world of green, swimming through a river of envy. He clutched the knife at the table, ready to stab, ready to take back what was rightfully his.

"Your eye is twitching again," Mick said. "I'm getting you some dessert."

Graham heard those words, but they were coming from so far away, a wall of green separated him from what was concrete. Green filtered through his blood, flooding his brain until Mick stepped through the wall with a blue-raspberry Pow! and two plates of blue Jell-O. Graham reached through the primordial green, the blue can cold and numbing his hand. He wanted a lime Pow!, but this would have to do for the moment. He knocked it back in three large swallows, enamored with the new flavor, the extra sweetness of the blue raspberry making his lips pucker. His green world got sucked up into the vents along the cafeteria's ceiling. Mick sat across from him now wearing a blue tie in contrast with his suit. Graham hadn't noticed that blue tie before. For sure, he'd been dressed all in green.

"Here you go, my friend," Mick said, passing him the blue Jell-O. Graham picked up a spoon. He stared at the blue Jell-O, demoralized, but Mick coaxed him to take a bite, so he did. He finished one serving and swiped another, the sweetness melding with the blue-raspberry's kick as a tear, solitary and also blue, zigzagged down his cheek, caught between his lips.

He eased his grip on the knife, since now he only wanted to use it on himself.

10

Graham moved through the hallways like he was walking underwater, a chilling hopelessness to each step as if he anticipated melting into the marbled floors and disappearing entirely. His eyes were outlined with violet circles and tears formed. Co-workers passed by in blues: navies and midnights, aquamarines and royals. As each one glided past, he broke down even more. Something twisted churned inside of him at the whim of a puppeteer in tin can form, but with each sip he felt better, truly better; only in its absence his heart sunk. He gripped the *Awakened Dreams* book in his pocket, the only possible salvation, promising to help get to the root of this emerging insanity.

Outside of his cubicle, Gayle made copies in an aqua-colored power suit. The Xerox machine flashed blue against the walls. Her hair was styled up in a bun and pulled back so tight that a lightning-shaped vein on her left temple throbbed uncontrollably.

"Hi, Graham," she said, sounding professional as ever. The video cameras clicked underneath his feet. He had a million questions, but his mind was waterlogged. His body excavated. All that remained was a soaking sadness.

"Can I...talk to you?" he asked. The whir of the camera under him, zooming in. The Xerox still flashing blue.

"We are talking," she reminded him, nonchalantly.

He took two steps toward her and leaned in to speak close to her ear. "Privately."

She seemed caught off guard but maintained her composure. He almost confided everything that had been happening, but noticed an iciness about her. He'd always appeared cold and withdrawn too, not letting his guard down for anyone. A part of him wished that maybe they could chip away at each other.

"I have a fiancée," she said, indicating at the sparkling blue diamond on her ring finger.

"I didn't...no that's not it, I'm not–"

He wiped his moist eyes with the hope that she'd be sympathetic. She went back to making copies as if he wasn't crumbling.

"Lean over the copier," she whispered, out of the corner of her mouth.

"What?"

"Over the copier," she said, slower, and then hunched

over the screen until her face became inundated in blue.

"Why?" he asked. An uneasiness rumbled through his belly, but he welcomed it because only emptiness had resided there before.

"We'll be out of the range from the cameras."

He leaned on the copier with his elbows, squinting from the harsh blue light.

"What's...happening to me?" he choked, the words dangling from his lips, the desire to put them back in his mouth for fear of her answer.

"Stop asking questions," she ordered.

"What do you mean?"

His eyes pleaded with her.

"I've learned really quickly here that you shouldn't ask too many questions." Her tone scarily serious. "Please, Graham."

Her voice became hushed, so he inched close enough to smell the mint candy on her tongue. She pulled away, checking her hair to make sure that every strand was in place and returned to making copies.

"Are all your pages blank again?"

She didn't answer, her green eyes trained on the documents. He grabbed her arm out of desperation and she gave a little yelp.

"Why are all your pages blank?" he asked again, getting angry. But all he produced were bumbling tears. "What does that mean?"

A ringing sound came from her pocket. She removed a light blue glove and placed it on her hand.

"Okay, okay. I will," she said, into her gloved palm. "I'm sorry," she then told Graham, gathering up her documents. "I have to go. Just...just, please, Graham."

If he grabbed onto her and wouldn't let go, she'd have to tell him something, anything. Maybe it was because she was from far away so he believed that she'd be different than everyone else here, that he could trust her.

She slid from his grasp and picked up her pace with the documents close to her chest. Her dark-blue high heels clacked down the hallway and gave him a vague sense of déjà vu until she disappeared around a corridor.

He watched the empty hallway, broken.

After a few seconds, Marlena turned the corner in an ocean-blue blouse and matching skirt as if she were timed to do so. Or maybe that was just his creeping paranoia. He tensed up as she approached. The unfortunate incident in the employee lounge still sat like a stone in his stomach.

"Hi, Graham."

He couldn't tell if she was disgusted and only acting polite.

"Marlena." He avoided her eyes. "I feel like I should..."

He stopped, woozy from the glare of the blue Xerox light that still flashed. The tears built from deep inside and rushed to escape his body. He could use some fizz on his tongue.

"Listen, what happened the other day–" he continued, fighting hard to keep those tears at bay.

"Oh, Graham, no." She touched his hand delicately. Warmer than anyone else who'd ever touched him, as he hoped she could save him like this every day. "Really, it's fine, it's no big deal."

"You don't have to say that."

Her sweet doe-like eyes showed no judgments. "I know I don't, but I mean it. Really. It's the stress here, it makes us behave–"

"I've been losing it–" he started.

"You're shaking, Graham."

"Am I?" he asked. "Thank you."

"For what?"

"For being so warm."

She patted his hand, her warmth flowing through him and the chills subsided. She let him hold onto her for a moment. No one had ever acted so kind since he'd arrived in The City. He'd experienced lust, but never fondness, thoughtfulness. There was a connection between them. Something...real, like he'd felt before in the Outside World when he was a teenager in a foster home and shared a room with a girl named Jubilee. He'd been away from the cruel foster parent's home for a while then, but he was shy around the other kids, kept to himself. Jubilee's parents died in the War to End All Wars; she had no other family. She'd been abused too, a grape-like stain of a bruise on her collarbone. One night she showed him a lightening bug she caught in a Mason jar. Their bedroom was dark because the foster house didn't have electricity but the bug became their nightlight. She asked if she could crawl into his bed, and he was thankful because there was no heat and he often went to sleep shivering. They held onto one another with the illuminated jar between them and slept like that for months, relying on each other's body heat. One day when he woke up, she was gone and he was cold again. She'd been sold as help to an elite family; this often happened to teenage girls there. No one else moved into his room so his bed remained frozen. She was one of the last kind people he remembered. And now, he felt cared for again by Marlena, who he barely knew but he could tell was kind and broken, too.

His heart swelled, but then he heard the cameras whirring beneath them. Marlena slipped her hand away and let it rest against her blue satin hip while the world turned cold again.

"When was the last time you were really able to, like, relax, Graham?"

He ran his fingers through his hair. Was there ever a time? He couldn't even recall.

"Why don't we get a drink after work?" she asked.

"A drink?"

"Maybe two?"

"Are you sure that you want to be with me after–"

"Guys have behaved worse. Here and in the Outside World. You're all aliens."

"Aliens?"

"I mean jerks, but I know you aren't, Graham. Look, there's this place in the Downtown called Blue Moon," she said. "Off McGlinty Street. How about at six? I'll buy."

Her ocean-blue blouse fluttered from the air conditioning, and an immense calm settled over him.

"Oh, okay. I could really use an ear," he admitted, wanting to trust someone, still hoping that the entire City wasn't against him.

She cupped her hand around her right ear with a smile.

"It's all yours."

He stared at her ear: the flicks of sapphire hanging from her lobes, the intriguing question mark curl of her pinna. He imagined whispering secrets into it: what brought him across oceans to this City and what he thought might be happening to him now, which he was too afraid to say out loud.

He could only hope she'd listen and keep it hidden inside that beautiful pink canal, then take his hand in her warm one as they figured out what to do, together.

Blue Moon was a lounge drenched in a cool blue light. The walls were made of water encased in glass, giving the feeling of being submerged. The atmosphere was muted in comparison to Lime Lounge and Citrus Club. People talked in hushed tones, and the music playing on the moon-shaped speakers dangling from the ceiling was from Miles Davis' "Kind of Blue". As Graham entered, his stomach bubbled from the six-pack of blue-raspberry Pow!s he'd spent the afternoon polishing off. He passed by a sad couple, their lips covered with dark blue Powder, resembling cadavers who were brought back to life but wished they'd stayed dead.

"Graham," he heard someone call his name, and turned away from the sad couple. Marlena waved him over from a table in the back. She wore her hair up and had a cigarette burning between her fingers. She stood to kiss him on the cheek and then they both sat.

"You ever been to Hawaiiatha, Graham?"

"Hawaiiatha? No."

"You're about to."

He imagined the two of them leaving behind lines of footprints along a tropical beach.

A waitress came by. She had tear tattoos trickling from her left eye.

"Two Blue Hawaiiathas, Raquel," Marlena said.

How had she already ingratiated herself into The City in such a short amount of time, while after ten years, barely anyone knew him? He fidgeted and then sadness set in when he realized she probably noticed his discomfort and thought him pitiable.

"So, this might sound...strange, Graham, but I really wasn't bothered about what happened between us yesterday."

She smoked her cigarette, seemingly unfazed by his spastic fidgeting.

He coughed into his fist. "I thought you'd be disgusted. I've been beating myself up for losing control like that. It was out of character for me. In fact, these last few days everything I've done has been out of character."

"Well, who's to say how we're supposed to act all of the time? It's claustrophobic not to color outside the lines every once in a while."

"But that's not me," he said, louder than he expected to. Since his lunch in the cafeteria earlier today, he'd felt so fragile. "I like my rituals. I like things safe."

"Do you, like, believe in opposites?" she asked, and he questioned if she was even listening to him, if there was anyone out there who would just listen while he sorted things out.

"What do you mean, opposites?"

"Well, like somewhere in another galaxy there's another you and that you does everything that the you here could never do. That other you is everything you want to be but can't."

She became more excited as she talked: There was a sublime thrill of getting wrapped up in her rush. No one in this City ever got truly excited. They lived with false thrills because they knew this was the last stop. There would never be anything else.

"I was a different person back in the Outside World," she said, looking down at her hands as if she was angry with them; but then she fell back into her perky personality and was all sweetness and flips of her hair.

"But I can be anything here. We're all newborns when we step off that boat; it's limitless."

"Is it?"

"How could it not be? The Outside World is gone, along with everything in it. I am not an invalid here. I don't have to be worthless and neither do you."

Her tone was fierce, and he figured that he was probably like that as well ten years ago, when the ocean stretched out before him and a new glassy skyline twinkled in the night. He began to well up, and Marlena became a blur of blue. The Scouts that brought him here had hoodwinked him. Deep down everyone in this purgatory knew they've been conned, but they were all too scared to make a peep.

Marlena blew a smoke cloud, and he wiped his tears away to see her clearly again.

"So, Graham," she said, "I really am intrigued by you. Even though it might be taboo, I'm letting you know that."

The tear-tattooed waitress came by and dropped off the Blue Hawaiiathas.

"These are delicious," Marlena said, taking a long sip.

"I'm so much older than you," he said, thinking about all his wasted years.

"I love people who've lived. There's wisdom behind your eyes."

She took his hand, ran her fingers over his palm, traced his lifeline.

"There's history in your lines."

He sipped the Blue Hawaiiatha as his chills died down and the sadness seemed to spew out of his pores.

"Good drink?" she asked, and before he knew it, the drink was already gone, and a faint trace of raspberry bubbles lingered at the back of his throat.

"Pow!?" he asked, his eyes lighting up.

"Oh, yeah, that's how they make Blue Hawaiiathas at this place. Gives it that extra kick."

"It's great." He allowed her finger to trace every last line on his palm.

A posse of drunks began belting out the song "Blue Moon" in tone-deaf howls.

Marlena and Graham looked at each other as if they were the only normal ones in a sea of lunacy.

"I think it's time to split, old man," Marlena laughed. "Show me your pad."

Her tone soothed, like a blue wave licking at his bare toes. He'd give into her, to allow some jubilation in the midst of this funk. So, the two of them rose and headed out into the blue-mooned night.

11

From his kitchen, Graham watched Marlena swaying in place as she observed his Rorschach-inspired black and white paintings. A blue shawl dangled from her shoulders.

"What can I get you?" he asked, poking his head out.

"Just a glass of ice with a splash of water."

He joined her in the living room with a blue-raspberry Pow! and a glass of ice.

"I love how mysterious these paintings are," she said, accepting the glass. "You're not so into color, are you?"

"I find it distracting. The ice is all you want?"

She took out a mini bottle of Blue Curacao from her

purse and poured it into the glass.

"I'm good now," she said, taking a slow blue sip.

"You always come prepared like that?"

"I got that from my mother. You mind if I smoke?"

He shook his head.

"She always had a bottle on her. I was even told that she did when she was pregnant with me. That's why my eyes were so far apart. A touch of fetal alcohol syndrome."

She blinked as if embarrassed by those deer-like eyes, but Graham liked her unusual features. It was one of the first things he'd noticed about her. She lit a cigarette and spit out the smoke in annoyance.

"It's what killed her, too," she said, as if she could care less.

Upon hearing the word *killed,* his mind flashed to the sensation of plummeting toward the ocean in a car; but he shook away the memory before it could do any more harm.

"I'm sorry," he said, rubbing his temples.

"What are you gonna do? Welcome to the zoo. Our generation, we're all children of the scarred, what they went through, the horrors they witnessed. They weren't fit to raise us."

"She was in the War to End All Wars?"

"A decoder. My father, on the front lines, died early on. I have no memory of him. But she never really returned, ya know? The flashbacks, the night terrors, I was a reminder of him, too. My arms, she always said I had his arms; well, until she found a way to not have them remind her of him..."

Marlena had already become melancholy like Graham after just a few weeks here. But maybe everyone was already so downhearted that they'd be the same if they remained in the Outside World.

"But you went to college?" he asked. "You had a sense of normal?"

She tugged at her lip with her tooth. "We found alternative ways to get me there. Made the best of bad situations, right?"

Beautiful tears slunk down into her lips. She didn't wipe them away but took his hand and led him to the couch.

"Come sit with me," she said, tired.

He sat next to her, opened his Pow! Soda, and sipped and sipped.

"When was the last time you had someone in your bed, Graham?"

He thought of the woman with the dark-green high heels from last night. Her face remained a blur as the angel and devil tattoos on her shoulder blades illuminated from the moonlight leaking in. He had no idea if she was an actuality or just a teasing dream.

"I don't get out much to meet people," he told her truthfully.

"You met me."

She removed her blue shawl and eased into the crook of his arm. Her lips tasted like cigarettes, and he kissed her cheeks to taste her tears as well. She moved his hand onto her breast.

"Take off my blouse."

He pulled the blouse off.

"Now my bra."

He fumbled with her bra as she scrunched up her face.

"Rip it then. Just...get it off of me!"

She unclasped it and then unbuckled his belt and put her hand down his pants. He was ready for her, for something real. He clasped her breast, but it was cold, unlike the warm hands groping his dick, so he recoiled in shock.

"What is it? What's wrong?"

"No, nothing."

He went soft in her grasp. She removed her hand from his pants and looked at it with scorn as if it was to blame for his dysfunction. He lunged for the blue-raspberry Pow!.

"I'm thirsty," he said, gulping down his liquid security blanket.

"It's okay, Graham."

"Is it?" Two blue lines dribbled from his lips. He finished the can and sat back, catching his breath.

"Do you like me?" she asked, quietly. "I thought from what happened in the employee lounge–"

He started crying again, unable to stop.

"Did I do something?" she asked.

He started panicking because his tears wouldn't let up. He'd lost control of his emotions again and all he could think of was to run into the kitchen for another Pow! to make it better. He shouldn't have to rely on a quick fix, but he was jittering too much to care.

"I'm falling apart."

She slid back next to him and got rid of the empty Pow! from his hand.

"We can take it slow. Really."

"Can you hold me right now?" he asked, feeling that if she said no, he'd just fling himself out of the window into the night.

"Hold you?"

"I just...need that," he said. "Tonight. All night. Please."

"Let's go lie down."

From his bed, she sauntered in front of the window. A light rain pitter-pattered against the glass. She slid down her blue underwear until she was naked for the entire City to see. She lay down next him and they spooned. He was still crying the exhausted cry of a lost soul. She stroked his arm soothingly.

"It's fine," she whispered.

He wiped away his tears with her hair and hugged her body as if he was holding on for dear life. The sound of their exhales filled the room.

In the dark dreamland he'd entered, the rain fell in staccato clumps as the old powder blue Chevy rolled through the dusk. Hoarfrost iced the roads, and Graham's hands were blue from the cold. They were the hands of a child, sticky from chocolate Pudding Pops. He was buckled in, not too well, so he was able to squirm around. The moon waxed crescent, mostly hidden because of a soupy fog. His father complained that the windshield wipers weren't working. His mother wanted to slow down but his father talked of "making good time". Graham didn't know where they were headed or why they needed to get there so bad. He couldn't visualize his parents faces either, only the backs of their heads clear. His father's thick neck, which was always a little red and smelled of aftershave, and his mother's pretty brown hair, which sat perfectly on her shoulders, smooth enough to fall asleep upon. Their voices had been lost as well; replaced by actors he'd seen on shows, different cadences as the years stretched on and the night's horror began to feel like something he'd watched on TV, with a commercial afterward to cut through its incessant reality.

The rain now hit from all sides and frightened and excited him at the same time. He rolled down his window as an iced mist sprayed against his face. He wiggled out of his seatbelt, then popped up behind his father's seat and threw those sticky hands over his father's eyes. What possessed him to do this, he'd never know. Maybe it seemed like a fun thing to do, or that his parents were arguing and he wanted to distract them. It was a moment he'd always return to, searching for that baffling reason, but the reason never came. What was clear in his nightmares was the way his father jerked the wheel so severely, flinging Graham into the side window. He hit his head, but he kept holding on, his tiny fingernails now digging into his father's eyes as the car burst through the barriers along a bridge and plunged into the soupy air. Time slowed to a crawl, the car hanging in the fog as if the moon held it by a string. His mother, never a woman to raise her voice, was now yelling so loud, yelling with venom in her voice so he yelled too, his fingers sticky with blood, before the blue waters opened up and swallowed them whole.

The car plunged deeper and deeper until the world above turned black, but upon impact, Graham was flung out of the side window he'd rolled down and floated to the dark surface. The painful rain welcomed him as he emerged, gulping air and drifting in and out of consciousness, the current carrying his quivering body until morning fishermen plucked out the chilled boy whose tears had clung to his cheeks hours ago and whose mouth gaped open in a silent, permanent scream.

The rain beat against the window angrily. The moon hovered so closely it seemed like it was trying to get inside. Graham woke up in a damp sweat, holding onto memories of those fishermen from long ago that had pulled him out of the churning waters; but he was back in The City, his mouth dry and his tongue made of sand. He swallowed hard to calm his thumping heart and swiveled over to grab the blue-raspberry Pow! on his nightstand.

Marlena sat at the edge of the bed, masked in cerulean shadows. She cried softly as she watched the rain outside. Her naked back faced him, but her arms were missing, like a warped Venus De Milo brought to life. The nubs where her arms used to be were pink and gnarled like a squid's mouth. On his bed lay those arms, thin and dead in the moon's gleam, looking like discarded afterthoughts. Marlena stared at the arms as if she had no idea what to do with them, or how to possibly put herself back together. Graham wanted to gather her shattered pieces and make her feel whole again, but he didn't know what to say. Her touch had been so warm because it was never real. He lay back down so she'd think he was asleep and unaware of her secret, but since her eyes were so far apart, he believed she could see him without turning. She cried like he'd cried since yesterday, refusing to stop.

His eyes then snapped shut. He eased back into the whims of dreamlands. Before he drifted off, his last thought was whether she was really an amputee, or if that was just another fabrication of his distorted mind.

Graham found himself at Blue Moon, submerged in water up to his chest. Fish swam around the barflies. A girl sat at the bar in a shimmering blue blouse with legs dangling into the water. She filled her empty shot glass with tears. Her face blurry as usual, but this time she had blue eyes and no arms as well. He had a sense that what seemed like reality in the past had always been a dream. There was never a girl with warring angel and devil tattoos. He had created her entirely out of loneliness, and now the faceless girl at the bar resembled the real, shattered one lying in his bed, tangled up in her limbs while he dreamed of an underwater watering hole.

In this delusion, he waded through the clear water, wanting to kiss her gnarled nubs until the taste of her injuries stayed on his tongue in an attempt to quench his own malaise. He had a feeling in his gut that she had something important to tell him, but she finished crying into her shot glass and dove in before he could reach her, wriggling out of her clothes and swimming toward the exit. He dipped down to find her, scuttling through the legs of other patrons. He wanted to tell her that he'd always be there to reattach her arms, like she'd been there for him. He swam up to the blue dress she left floating in the middle of the bar as her armless body glided away. There were no tattoos on her back; she was uncorrupted. He reached out to touch that purity, a moment of wonderful in a place where everything was a sham, but she was already gone.

A school of fish zipped by and cleared away her glass of tears. He balled her blue dress up in his fist and let in a huge breath as the water and the fish rushed into his lungs until he was drowning, drowning, dead.

"Fishes," Graham said, waking up tangled in the sheets.

Marlena stood at the foot of the bed holding onto the bedpost for support and slipping on her blue blouse.

"It's fish. Not fishes," she said.

He opened up his fist to reveal her balled-up blue blouse.

"What?"

She fumbled with her blue high heels.

"Usually the plural of fish is also fish. Like with sheep." She gestured to the garment he was holding. "I think you have something of mine."

"I'm sorry about last night," he said, handing her the blouse.

She tucked a strand of hair behind her ear. He stared hard at her fingers, trying to decipher how real they were.

"You were out cold," she said, putting on the rest of her clothes left in a heap by his bed. "Don't worry, I didn't take offense."

"I was dreaming of you all night."

She looked up in shock. He'd never noticed how blue her eyes were. There was a nervous twitch to her mouth, too. He'd clearly made her uncomfortable and said something he shouldn't have.

"I should go. I...have to swing by my place and change before work."

He could pull her back into bed and tell her about the mysterious girl who'd followed him from dream-to-dream and how last night Marlena was that girl. But it was awkward between them this morning. He wished it would go away. He was afraid of her reaction so he grabbed the blue Pow! on his nightstand instead. Their eyes caught each other as he froze with the can to his lips. It appeared as if there was more she wanted to tell him, but she didn't say anything. She kissed him on the cheek, her lips seeming distant, as if she realized she'd done something wrong by coming to his apartment, as if she needed to confess a slew of secrets, but was petrified.

"I'll see you at work, Graham."

She was out the door before he could tell her goodbye. He lay back and clutched the Pow!, craving a sip. He turned the can upside down—there was nothing left. He became a mess of tears all over again.

"Sheeps," he said, sinking into the covers and shutting out the world until the alarm clock blared and he was forced to face the day.

The X train chugged through the tunnel. As it slowed, a pair of eyes hovered by Graham's window. The people who'd been shuttled to the Zones sometimes wound up fleeing to the tunnels. There'd been whispers of uprisings in hidden caves, but mostly it was rumors. These Rejects only came to the tunnels to avoid being monitored, to hide away from the rest of The City and themselves as well. Graham turned away from their eyes.

As the train picked up speed, the lights blacked out, and when they went back on, everyone in the car became veiled in blue. Graham shook out the last few drops of blue Pow! onto his tongue. He hated the need for the soda, but felt way worse without it, truly blue and melancholy. The instant the can touched his lips, however, the bubbles coursed through his body and he basked in a moment of serenity. He needed to cut back on the sodas, but the withdrawal would be overwhelming; he was unsure if he was strong enough.

That morning, Marlena seemed like she was on the cusp of saying something when he reached for his Pow!. She had to know more than she was letting on, and there had to be a reason she appeared in his dreams last night instead of his normal blurry muse. The next time he dreamed, he'd make sure that she wouldn't swim away before he'd be able to confront the truth. The *Awakened Dreams* book that the lady gave him would help; it had to.

He took out the book and read the words: *An awakened dream, also known as a conscious dream, is a dream in which the sleeper is aware that they are dreaming. When the dreamer is lucid, they can actively participate in and often manipulate the imaginary experience in the dream environment.*

The book gave meticulous instructions on how to achieve this state. He spent the rest of his commute committing them to memory. After he reached his stop, he finished it, more focused and sure of himself than he had been in days. He felt good as the blue-raspberry Pow! settled in his stomach. Tonight, when his head hit the pillow, he'd attempt to get back in control of his life by demanding some answers.

He just had to make it through the day.

12

Graham's co-workers sped by in a blue-blurred haze as he lumbered through the halls at a drugged-out pace. After his long commute, he needed another Pow! desperately and each step felt like he'd taken a thousand. In his cubicle, one last blue Pow! sat at his desk. He popped open the can as Mick rushed in, fixing the knot of his turquoise tie.

"Hey, bud-a-roo, what's up?"

"What does is look like?" Graham indicted to his tear-stained face. The serene Graham from earlier in the train car had become a memory, like he'd feared would happen.

"Looks like you're getting an early morning start on those blue-raspberry Pow!s. E wanted me to come and see if you had any brainstorms for new slogans."

Graham chugged the rest of the Pow!, but the tears kept coming.

"Are you going to keep pretending? I look like I'm about to have a breakdown!"

Mick leaned in close and carefully watched the camera buzzing under their feet.

"Listen, pal, the workplace is not the time for personal traumas. We'll go to Red Rum in the Downtown after work, you'll calm–"

"Do you know what's happening to me?" Graham asked, but he realized Mick likely wouldn't say anything even if he knew what was going on. Sure enough, his shady friend responded by reaching into his pocket and pulling out a cherry Pow!.

"Here," Mick said, "a change for your palate."

Graham didn't take the cherry Pow! right way. He let Mick sweat it out. His buddy's eyes glanced again and again at the cameras below, as if he wanted to make sure that he was playing his role in this perverse game correctly. They were all in on it, every single one of them; no one could be trusted, only himself. They were all waiting to see how he'd dance.

Gayle sashayed in wearing a red dress and holding her stack of blank documents as if on cue. She scrunched up her face in an expression that oozed pity, rested a hand with painted red fingernails on his shoulder.

"Are you all right?" she asked, but his bloodshot eyes were enough of an answer. The sorrow lingered in the back of his throat, in the pit of his stomach, flooding his mind. He'd do anything to make it go away, anything to see them all clearly again and not through a wall of gloom.

"He's fine," Mick said, with a sigh. He nudged Graham with the cherry Pow! "Go on, you...look thirsty."

Graham swiped the cherry Pow!, cracked it open, and swallowed the red fizz down in a few large gulps. He'd drink what he was supposed to. He'd dance exactly how they want him to, for now, so the cameras wouldn't catch a moment of defiance.

The bubbles sloshed around. His tears had dried up and were replaced with the wicked grin of someone who'd become truly deranged. Gayle slinked away from his cackles. Her dress was so red that he wanted to put his fist right through so someone else could finally feel the pain he'd been carrying around since this madness began.

Fueled by the new flavor of Pow!, he imagined his glass cubicle stained with all of their traitorous blood.

The taxi going to Red Rum swept by the Zones. Graham peered out as dusk loomed on the horizon and a gleam of frozen sunshine pierced through the ruins. The people of the Zones huddled up together for warmth and climbed into their cardboard hovels, ready for a dinner of Sloths. Some wandered around aimlessly as though wondering how they got here and unable to accept their realities. Usually the newest detainees had the hardest time letting go of The City. They'd worked so hard for however long they'd been here, and it was strange to be idle. One woman seemed more lost than anyone else. She roamed past trashcans on fire wearing a disheveled green dress and green teardrop earrings. Her hair looked so thin on her scalp that it was practically non-existent. Graham rolled down the window, drawn to her.

He clutched the *Awakened Dreams* book in his pocket and realized it was the lady with thinning hair from the cafeteria the other day. How could she had fallen so quickly? He wondered if the Elders had chucked her to the Empty Zones because of what she gave him. She was the only one to try and help and now she was paying for her insubordination. He wanted to fling open the cab door and take her with him, to wash the grime from her pallid face and thank her for her sacrifice.

For a second, they saw one another. She reached out for acknowledgment, and he realized she was missing a hand. Had she always had a prosthetic? He rolled up the window. Anyone could be watching them. He couldn't help her, not even make eye contact any longer. Despite his debilitated mind, he knew he had to play it smart or he'd wind up like her.

Dance along, dance along, he thought. *And then strike when they least expect it*. Strike them down along with everything else about The City that had contained his spirit for too long.

He finished another cherry Pow! and then crushed the can so hard, it split apart and blood seeped down his wrist. He cleaned up the blood with a flick of his tongue until he had the dark red smile of a predator who'd recently been feasting.

13

Abandoned streets and condemned buildings existed at the far end of the Downtown except for the lone restaurant Red Rum, a beacon in the midst of nothingness. The cold front had been switched off again, the air humid like after a rainstorm. The taxi's headlights crawled over dark streets until red neon lights popped up as a warning just before where The City spilled into the ocean. In the distance, the rest of the Downtown was a smear of colored lights and muted clamor. Red Rum sat at the edge of the cliff, the night waters below black as molasses.

At the curb, three girls in red velvet dresses welcomed

Graham as he stepped out of the cab. Demonic red contacts flashed in their eyes. He couldn't think clearly as they took him by the arm with their red gloved hands and led him into Red Rum, its entrance like a gaping mouth. A red carpet in the shape of a snake's tongue flowed from its doors. The girls showed off fresh scars on their arms. They told him he wouldn't be let inside unless he was wounded, and the one with the darkest red lips dug her fingernails into his flesh. He howled but enjoyed the pain and knew he would enjoy it more if he were the one causing them to bleed.

The bouncer inspected Graham's fresh wound and let him inside. The carpeted snake's tongue weaved through a long hallway. Angry wails blared from overhead speakers, sounds of torture. Ruffled scarlet curtains covered the tall windows. Thin wax candles as tall as him flickered fiery red flames. The walls appeared sticky as if they were painted with blood. A fetid smell hung oppressively in the air, the place becoming hotter and stuffier as he wandered farther from the entrance.

The hallway led into a circular, grand room. The wax candles spanned its circumference, and the patrons were all lit in reddened shadows. Mick sat at a table, hunched over two viscous Bloody Marys and wearing a red bowtie. At the sight of Mick, Graham had a festering urge to thrust one of the glasses into his friend's neck to slice open his throat, but he was ready for this emotional shift. He simply had to find a way to outsmart whatever was attempting to take over. He felt himself reaching for a tasty murder weapon, but then put his hands in his pocket before he did anything rash.

"*Pour vous*," Mick said, sliding a Bloody Mary across

the table as Graham sat. He sipped the drink, leaving a red moustache on his face before finally wiping it away.

"Why so silent, bud-a-roo?"

Mick's red bowtie caused Graham's anger to swell. He slammed his fist on the table.

"Why do you always give me these moronic nicknames?"

"Whoa, buddy, who lit your ass on fire?"

Graham averted his attention from Mick's red bowtie to Red Rum. The walls dripped red as well and the sight of that only made him angrier. He simmered in his seat and shut his eyes. It didn't help since he still only saw red.

"It's the colors," he mumbled. "It's only getting worse."

"You okay?" Mick asked, sitting back and maintaining a safe distance.

"I feel like a time bomb. Tick, tick, ticking away."

"Did that girl not call you back? The one who left her dress–"

"She doesn't exist. She never did. She was always just a dream."

Graham's voice rose to an uncomfortable level. People looked over, whispered and pointed. Sweat dripped down his neck from the heat and he ground his teeth together, tasting thin bone shards on his tongue.

"Why me?" he asked his friend. If he didn't get an answer, he'd punch Mick in his red nose.

"How could she not be real if she left her dress behind? Think about it. You're just bugging out and not giving yourself enough credit. You scored big that night."

"I'm onto them," Graham said, whispering.

Mick's eyes widened. Graham let his words linger in the air.

"What's that, buddy?" Mick finally responded, his jocular tone disappearing.

"Whoever has been fucking with me. This has to end tonight and you can tell them that."

"Who exactly do you think I'm going to tell?"

"Fuck you," Graham said. "You've been their pusher, their stoolie. Always a different colored soda in your fat fuck hands to screw with my mind. What did they pay you? Were they able to secure you a lifetime supply of Levels?"

"I have no clue what you're talking about." He pointed a finger in Graham's face, dropped his voice to a whisper. "Don't let them see you like this."

"Who? Who should I be afraid of? Are the Elders lurking in the shadows? Is E so desperate for a perfect slogan that he's willing to sacrifice my sanity? Does this even go all the way up to Warton, Mind, and Donovan? Have they chosen my brain to see how far it could be stretched before it explodes? Or even the Man? Why?"

He slammed his fist into the table again causing it to wobble. Mick's Bloody Mary crashed to the floor. A thin, old waiter stomped over and cleaned up the glass while glaring at Graham. Mick nodded for a replacement drink. The music on the speakers became louder, throbbing in Graham's ears, its desperate squeals echoing through the room. Even though the sodas were evil, he wanted one so bad he'd kill for it.

"I suggest you calm yourself down," Mick said, lighting an excessively long specialized cigarette and blowing red smoke in Graham's face. The smoke tickled Graham's eyelashes and made his insides churn even more. He had a vision of swiping the cigarette and shoving it right in

Mick's eye.

"The higher-ups often frequent Red Rum," Mick continued. "You wouldn't want anyone to give a negative report to the Elders tomorrow." He lowered his voice. "It's one thing to act out of character in the Downtown, to let loose there, but it's another to speak ill of the company that is your lifeblood."

"I've been attached to their strings for too long. You better believe I'm ready to snip free if what I think they're doing is true."

The old waiter brought over another Bloody Mary. Mick held it in the air for a pretend toast.

"Chin chin. Good luck with that then."

"You don't think I'm serious? Tonight, I'm going to control my dreams. I'm going to finally get some answers from whoever that girl is."

Mick chuckled and puffed another red cloud.

"It's difficult to get answers from fabrications."

"Fabrications?" Graham squeezed the Bloody Mary, imagining it was Mick's thick neck.

"Many have cracked up in this City before. The boss man wants slogans, and the pressure is getting to you. It seems like you can't handle this new responsibility–"

"I'm cracking up because of what they're doing to me! You know that!"

"Believe whatever helps you sleep at night, but that won't keep you out of the Zones. If they sense you're falling apart, they'll extinguish you without a thought. I've seen it many times."

"I won't go out without a fight."

Mick shrugged his shoulders, bored with the conservation, or at least trying to appear that way. He finished his cigarette with a stream of red puffs and raised his glass again.

"To your quest for sanity then."

Graham held up his own glass, squeezing it harder now as if he was squeezing every last breath from his former friend. Their glasses clinked and burst upon impact, sounding like a gunshot. Splatters of red everywhere. Mick stared in shock as clumps dripped down his face. Graham licked off his own red moustache with a satisfied grin, and then stood.

"This isn't over between us. I would have never burned you, no matter what they promised me. Maybe I would've burned anyone else living in this charade of a place, but I'd rather be sent to the Zones than fuck you over. You piece of shit scum. You try to go to sleep tonight with that over your head...bud-a-roo."

He spit a red glob into Mick's face and walked away, leaving his former friend seated at the table with a loogie dribbling from his nose.

When Graham came home, he punched the wall, leaving a dent, and tore apart a pillow until his apartment looked feather bombed. Three cherry Pow!s made his anger subside momentarily, but a fury still sat in his stomach. It would eventually have to be released again.

He'd been prepping for an awakened dream like the book instructed, worried it could be his last chance to figure out this never-ending nightmare. He set an alarm clock on a low volume in the hopes that he'd hear it while he was asleep but that it wouldn't wake him. The book also stressed to repeat the mantra: *tonight, while I dream, I will look at my hands and realize I am dreaming.* Finally, he ate some jalapeno peppers left over in his fridge because the book said that spicy foods often caused wild dreams. He washed them down with some galantamine with chlorine bitartrate, a chemical he spent a Stipend on that was used to boost memory and awareness. He put on some binaural beats to lower his brain frequencies and trigger relaxation. Slowly, he found himself slipping into a meditative state. He shut out the lights, feeling the binaural beats thump between his cheek and pillow, and drifted off.

At the start of the dream, he was back in a hallway: a red velvet curtain situated at the end which only led to more hallways with other red velvet curtains. The farther he went, the more he had to squint from a harsh red light. He heard a beeping sound and was pulled away from the red hallway. He realized he was back in his bed, blinking at the red numbers on his digital clock. He shut his eyes and concentrated on those red velvet curtains. The binaural beats were pacifying, and he returned easily to the hallway. He followed it into Red Rum's circular grand room. Tense, primal music thumped from speakers. Wax candles were lit around the walls. Everyone was dressed in red, sipping red-colored drinks, draped over one another. His girl was at the bar with her back to him, the angel and devil tattoos beckoning. Cherry earrings dangled from her ears. She stirred the half-finished glass of blood in front of her. He looked down at his hands that were now covered in blood and repeated the mantra that he was awake in a dream. As he walked toward her, he left a streak of red handprints on the wall before placing his slick hand on her shoulder.

"I want to see you," he said, and touched her blurry

face with his bloody palms.

He started rubbing away the blur until her face began to form. Red streaks remained on her cheeks and he stepped back astonished. He expected it to be Marlena, but the face was someone he never imagined. He was too stunned to speak as he stared at Gayle standing in front of him. Next to her, an old hand reached over and caressed her leg. The hand belonged to E, wearing a tuxedo with a red bowtie and red cummerbund. E did a shot of blood and sucked at Gayle's neck. She bit her lip, aroused.

"You were the girl all along," Graham said, honing in on the devil tattoo that had come alive, flicking its slithering tongue at him.

"I've been watching you," she said, a peal of laughter tickling the air. "Every night. In your bed. In your head. To make sure it all went as planned. That's why I was brought here."

"Have a shot," E said, taking a bloody shot glass from the bar and placing it in Graham's hands.

"You made this happen to me," Graham said, ready to attack. "You picked the guy you thought would be easiest to control."

"And weren't we right?" E asked. Gayle laughed louder and E chuckled as well, their abuse pummeling Graham's ears.

"You've made a big mistake. I promise you that."

Their teeth were stained with blood and the laughter wouldn't stop. He was surrounded by their taunts. A part of him wanted to curl up into a ball and give in, but the rest was mad enough to strike.

E put his arm around Graham and pulled him close, his voice a whisper.

"You think you're smart because you were given a book on *Awakened Dreaming*. This is infinitely bigger than you, or me, or any of us, kid. It's not about controlling you. They wanted to see how you'll tick, but after it's done, you're just an insignificant speck."

"A fly to be swatted," Gayle added, slinking up next to him and goosing him from behind.

"The City is just the beginning of a widespread infection," E said. "It's inevitable."

"Nothing is inevitable," Graham said, making a fist around the shot glass.

E and Gayle howled with laughter. They hung on him, their sour breath oppressive. He clutched his shot of blood and thrust it at E's neck. The glass shattered as blood poured to the floor; E gagged while trying to cover the gaping wound. Gayle let out a curdling scream. Graham staggered backward as E fell into Gayle's arms, a pool of dripping blood at their feet.

"I'll see you in reality, motherfuckers," Graham said, shaking with aggression. He looked down at his hands. "It's time to finally wake up."

The morning greeted him with a red sun cracking through the blinds. He was drenched in sweat. He reached over to check the time on his bed stand and knocked a pair of cherry earrings to the floor. The sight of them did not surprise him. Gayle must've been here last night to watch him dissolve. He crushed the earrings in his fist, the sharp plastic cutting his palms.

He dressed haphazardly, his shirt untucked, his hair cowlicked. He wandered into the kitchen, opened the refrigerator, and downed a cherry Pow!, resisting its pull at first but knowing the withdrawal would be worse. Today would be too important. He breathed through his nostrils, a bull waiting to tear into whatever was in his way. The red sun hovered by the kitchen window, the light stinging. Placing the can down, he then opened up a drawer by the sink, and pulled out a serrated knife. He touched the tip; a drop of blood forming on his index finger.

He sucked at the blood and then slipped the knife into his pocket while whistling.

14

Barreling down Warton, Mind & Donovan's hallways, Graham knew he'd drunk enough cherry Pow! to make him explode, but still he craved more. Tell a heroin addict not to take another hit; not as easy as it may seem. A full-blown addiction didn't lend itself to going cold turkey. Also, what better way to explode on everyone than to have it be due to what they'd put him through. The fluorescent lights outlining the entranceways cloaked him in red. He was no longer a meek individual ridiculed by his co-workers; anyone in his way would get a knife in their gut. He passed by a row of mannequin hands along the walls meant to charge people's cell phone gloves. They made him think of Marlena, and he ripped them off in a fury, leaving behind a trail of scattered false limbs.

Some co-worker with a limp passed by in a red skirt. Another one with bad teeth followed wearing a red tie. Down another corridor he saw Shep, who avoided eye contact as he scurried along wearing...could it be...a red shirt under his suit? The sight of that red was so intense and powerful. Red, red, redderific RED. Next was Josephine, turning the corner in a red power suit. He reached into his pocket, the sharpness of the knife comforting. He stepped in front of her so she was unable to pass.

"What a great red suit, Josephine! Really smart looking!"

His eyes were inhuman.

"Uhh...thanks, Graham. Excuse me."

He waited a beat, making her uncomfortable. She bobbed from foot-to-foot, looking down the hallway for anyone else, but they were alone. A thin bead of sweat trickled down her cheek.

"By all means," he finally said, allowing her to pass. "But tell me, what *new* color will you have on tomorrow?"

She was caught off guard but continued walking away as fast as possible.

Andy popped his head from out of a glass cubicle, a red handkerchief stuffed in his front pocket.

"What's the hubbub out here, Graham?"

Graham marched over and swiped Andy's red handkerchief.

"You sheep are all in on it!"

He balled up the red handkerchief and stuffed it in

Andy's mouth. Andy doubled back into his cubicle, gagging.

Graham turned down another corridor where the fluorescent lights were redder than before. A demon wrestled inside him and he sensed it in his blood, circling around, eager to get loose.

Halfway down the hallway, Gayle was tilted over the copier wearing the same red dress from his dreams last night with the same cherry-shaped earrings dangling from her ears.

"Red earrings," he said, once he was close enough. "What a shock."

"Oh, morning, Graham," she said. He could tell she was trying to remain calm. "How's it...going today?"

He flicked at one of the earrings.

"You've got an arsenal of these, don't you? You were fucking with me every night this week, weren't you?"

"I don't know what you mean–"

He grabbed her by the shoulders.

"You stay out of my head, you understand?"

"Graham, you're hurting–"

"Out of my head!"

He let go, and she collapsed back into the copier.

"But you're not the paid spy I'm after."

In the employee lounge, he found Marlena at the counter making coffee. She was wearing a red hoodie, humming to herself. He stalked into the room, his face beet red as sweat poured down his temples. She was focusing on the coffee and glanced back, aware he was behind her but didn't turn to see the state he was in. He fingered the handle of the serrated knife in his pocket.

"Hi, Graham. Want a cup–"

He latched onto her arm. The coffee pot fell out of her hand and shattered on the floor, splashing hot coffee everywhere.

"What are you doing, Graham?"

"WHY THE FUCK ARE YOU WEARING RED?"

He pushed her into the corner. She lost her balance from the slick coffee on the floor. He held her up, pressing into her, still grasping the knife in his pocket. But he couldn't raise it to her; something deep down held him back. She put up her hands, afraid.

"I was–"

"Don't bullshit me! I expected this from the other one, but not from you."

He shook her harder than he'd ever shaken anyone before, a little doll in his arms. Tears flew from her eyes.

"I was...told to."

He pounded his fist into the wall.

"Told to do what?"

"Told...I had to...had to...wear orange...on Tuesday. And green...on Wednesday. Blue yesterday. Red today. We were all told."

"By E?"

She nodded, trying to worm away from him but he was too strong.

"An office-wide notification was emailed to everyone but you. It specified that you couldn't know."

She tried to mouth *I'm sorry*, but it only came out as a spit bubble.

"Did they tell you to try to sleep with me, too?"

He inched closer in her face, their noses touching. She broke down in hysterics.

"Please don't hurt me."

“What did they promise you if you slept with me?”

He was spitting his words, his hand moving toward her throat. She screamed but he covered her mouth, put a finger up to his lips.

“What did they promise you?”

He removed his hand from her mouth.

“I don’t know anything,” she cried. “I’m just an intern. I got to this City and they...and they...I didn’t know what to do.”

He let go of her. She crumpled to the floor, trembling.

“I liked you,” he said, at peace for a moment. An honest emotion in the midst of everything controlled. He blinked it away and let the rage build again.

“Graham,” she mumbled.

“You make me sick.”

She reached out but he swatted her hand away. She hugged her legs to her chest as he stormed out of the employee lounge.

“Graham! What are you gonna do, Graham?”

Her voice faded as he stomped down the hall, the cameras clicking away under him but he could care less. His brain consumed by the walls sprayed with blood until the whole place would smell like destruction.

15

An alarm sounded while he tried to get to into E's office. The door was locked so Graham took a step back and then burst through. Everything inside tainted red, even the sight of E eating from a bowl of prunes by his desk. Graham clenched his fists, the knuckles glaring white.

"What's going on here?" E demanded.

Like a man possessed, Graham leaped at E. The bowl of prunes dropped to the floor. Both of them fell back into the desk, sending papers everywhere. Graham pressed the knife against E's neck.

"WHAT ARE YOU DOING TO ME?"

He started choking E with his other hand.

Gayle rushed in wearing a blue dress. Security was close behind, but she shook her head at them and they backed up. She tried to pull Graham away from E, but he swiveled around, causing her to lose balance and knock her head against a standing lamp.

"Get him off of me," E yelled, reaching up and grabbing Graham by the face. Graham choked him harder, making E wheeze.

"TELL ME! TELL ME, YOU SON-OF-A-FUCKING-BITCH!"

Graham grabbed E by his white hair and started banging his boss's head into the desk.

Gayle nursed the knot forming on her skull. She composed herself and then checked at the door. Security remained close by, but she waved them away and then closed the door.

"Graham, don't do anything else you'll regret." Her tone was professional, as if she dealt with this type of thing every day. She went over to a mini fridge in the corner and took out a blue-raspberry Pow!. The fizz echoed as she cracked it open.

Graham's ear twitched. He slammed E's head into the desk one more time and then looked over at the Pow!. The drink was in his bones, his tongue drier than ever.

"Leave him alone," Gayle commanded. She held the Pow! out as a peace offering.

The knife was still at E's neck, pressing into his jugular.

"Give me the soda," Graham said. His eyes darted back-and-forth from E to Gayle.

Gayle shook her head and took a step back.

"Not until you put the knife away."

"Give him the fucking soda!" E coughed, holding up his hands in defeat. "We're cool, kid. Cool down."

"Put it to my lips," Graham said, to Gayle.

She nodded and raised it to his mouth. He took a big sip, indicating for her to keep it going. He gulped more as the rest spilled down his chin.

"Now hand over the knife," she said.

"No, step away. Start talking."

She looked over at E to see what to do, but Graham positioned the knife so as to place a cut under E's chin.

"Sweetheart, you better start doing what he fucking said," E demanded.

"Okay, we'll talk," she said. "You keep the knife. What do you want to know?"

"You're wearing blue now. Start with that."

She touched the blue satin of her dress and looked at E for help again.

"Goddamn it! Listen, kid, if you let me sit up, I'll explain everything," E said. "Keep the knife on me, whatever you want."

Graham didn't move but nodded. E righted himself slowly, catching his breath until he was sitting up. Graham kept the knife pointed at him.

"How do I know you'll tell me the truth?"

"I think we're in a situation now where not much else is gonna work. If you think I'm lying, slit my fucking throat. Deal?"

Graham breathed through his nostrils.

"Deal."

"All right, well...Pow! is primed for a complete

overhaul, that you know. Their scientists and I have worked for years on a way to make the sodas more addictive."

"They're addictive all right," Graham said, eyeing the half empty can in Gayle's hand. "Give me the rest while I listen."

Gayle passed over the Pow! as E continued.

"A guinea pig was needed to test out the kinks. Obviously, Pow! couldn't use anyone from their own company because their employees knew too much, which would defeat the purposes of getting an honest result. In terms of our own squad at Warton, Mind & Donovan . . . your name came up."

"Why?"

"I recommended you myself. You seemed to be...thirstier than most to make a name for yourself here, but it hadn't happened yet. I thought this might be your opportunity."

Graham sipped the blue Pow!. Serenity took over while the bubbles popped on his tongue and his anger subsided.

"What about the colors?" he said, glancing again at Gayle's blue dress. He became locked in its ocean-colored shade. The sadness overwhelming.

"There used to be prescription pills in The City called Moods," E said. "They were popular before those black-market Levels came around, even before you got here. They were good for when you had a bad day, or became too stressed, or needed to focus, whatever *mood* you felt like having. They worked well for a while, but an influx of citizens soon found a way to use them for narcotics purposes: crushed up, snorted, even injected; we had a little epidemic on our hands a few years back. This was one of the things the Zones were used for, a way to expunge the waste, the cancer from our City, get rid of the useless. But now Pow!'s scientists have re-engineered Moods and discovered an alternative use. I'm guessing that your mood changed based on the flavor of a soda you drank?"

Graham thought back as a tear formed in his eye. "Yeah. I guess it did. It's changing right now."

"As it should. You just had a blue-raspberry Pow!. The Mood filtered into that flavor should evoke calmness."

Graham wiped his eyes with the back of his sleeve.

"Then why am I crying?"

Gayle stepped in with a soothing, motherly tone.

"Graham, you were given sodas with maximum doses of Moods. These would not be for the general public. We needed to see what the side effects were in large doses and then scale back–"

"I almost slit your throat," he said to E.

E covered his neck with his hand.

"That was a surprise we didn't expect. Obviously, cherry has more kinks than the rest."

"I still don't understand the colors," Graham said. He eased his grip on the knife, still locked in on Gayle's blue, blue dress. She swayed in place to keep his eyes focused on her.

"It's actually extraordinary," Gayle continued. "The scientists came to the conclusion that when Moods were mixed with carbonation, and a secret ingredient that neither E or I know, visual stimulation increases. Drink an orange Pow! and suddenly everything orange around you becomes that much more amplified. This in turn triggers the brain to want more orange Pow!. For example, the Moods filtered into that flavor should've made you feel passionate, and when you saw the color orange, that feeling should've intensified, am I right?"

Graham was silent, taking it all in. He looked away from her blue dress.

"It's not that simple."

"What do you mean?" E cut in, gruff and impatient. "Tell us exactly what you're experiencing."

Graham stared at his boss, the man who used to make him quiver time and time again, the man who often reminded him of the prickly evil from his youth who still invaded his dreams and his subconscious. He questioned how much he should tell E now, but his feelings started pouring out after being bottled up for so long. Maybe it was an effect of the Pow!.

"I would have some blue Pow!, just like now, and at first I'd feel calm. The sight of Gayle's blue dress made me that way for a moment, but then this tremendous sadness kicks in. It's like every color has a good and a bad side to it. Yeah, orange made me passionate and excited about things, but then I wasn't able to control myself. With green...I was so jealous of other people when I was on green, but at first, I had profound ideas on it, green even helped me come up with those new ad slogans. Then with red... all I wanted to do was...destroy everything in my path, but when I woke up today and first drank it, I felt alive, full of energy. The crazy thing is that I need all the flavors. I'd get tired of one and crave the next, even now...even after what cherry did, I want it...I...need it. I miss the way it made me feel."

"Fascinating," E said, opening up his desk drawer and

pulling out a cigar. "You really felt a need to switch flavors? That's exactly what Pow! is looking for: a momentary satisfaction like a piece of gum, and then the flavor wanes and you want another and another."

E reached into his pocket. Graham got nervous and pointed the knife back at him.

"Relax, I'm getting a lighter, kid. I think you can drop the knife."

Graham shook his head "no". E shrugged and lit his cigar.

"But the sodas were creating these emotions," Graham said, speaking to Gayle as well. "It's manipulation. I was forced to feel that way."

"I would disagree with that," E said, crossing his arms and puffing toward the ceiling. "The emotions were all there. Nothing is being created. Pow! just helps you decide whatever emotion you want to experience at that moment. An argument could be made that it's better than bottling it all up, no?"

He nodded at Gayle to chime in as well.

"Right," she said. "Think about it, Graham. So many people have come to this City to escape their difficult pasts. The terrible things they did, the terrible things done to them. Peel back the layers of any citizen here and be prepared to see some gruesome things. You felt sad on blue, but maybe after enough Pow!s, you won't feel that sadness anymore. You'll have exorcized it from your body, and only peacefulness will remain."

E jumped in, seemingly tired of the conversation and spitting out his smoke with increasing irritation.

"Again, we're gonna scale back the doses in the Pow!s you tested before it goes out for mass consumption."

"We don't want to create havoc," Gayle continued. "We want to promote a product we think will make The City better, that will make all of us more productive citizens. And admit it, there were times this week that you felt amazing because of the sodas. You even said how alive you were on red, initially, and all of the profound ideas you had on green. I saw that in you. I watched how–"

"I know you were watching me," he said, focusing again on her blue dress as his eyes watered. "The blank documents you carried around. It was all just an excuse to observe me. You never had real work that you were doing. And my dreams, too. You even entered my dreams."

Her mouth opened in shock. She glanced over at E.

"Don't look at him," Graham said. "Why were you in my dreams? What were you doing there?"

"Your dreams? I don't know–"

"You do know." Tears slinked down his cheeks; he was exhausted from crying. He jabbed the knife at her. She stepped back, her hands in the air.

"Put down the knife before I start to get offended," E barked, but Graham wasn't paying attention.

"Let me see your back," he said, indicating for Gayle to turn around.

"Excuse me?"

"You have tattoos. An angel on one shoulder blade, a devil on the other. Show me."

"This charade had gone on long enough," E said. "You were chosen for something very important here and most would be thankful. If the Man is watching this right now, I don't think he'll be pleased."

Graham wanted to scream, *Fuck the Man*, but he held it in.

"You're not telling me everything–"

"Fucking Christ, kid. Get a grip. We're telling you everything!"

"Then let me see what's under your dress," Graham ordered Gayle. His hand holding the knife was shaking. "I am in control right now. I'm tired of being attached to strings."

His eyes were red and raw, the rest of him a blubbering mess. He inched toward her.

"You're not in any kind of control," E said, his voice lowered but still angry. "None of us are. Cameras are documenting all of this, and if you're foolish enough to do something stupid, the Man will put you in the Zones, the worst Zone, too."

"Have my last ten years here really been any better?" he said, to himself.

He touched the knife to her blue dress and slid it around as a tease.

"All right," Gayle said, taking a deep breath.

Graham could tell she was mortified, but she didn't show it because she was not the type of person to let anyone see her as weak. She unbuttoned her dress, revealing the tattoos from his dreams. He rested the cold blade against the devil, the tip touching its slithering tongue.

"Are we done?" she asked, biting her words and buttoning her dress. When she turned back around, she wouldn't look him in the eye.

"Gayle was there to monitor you, Graham," E said. "We gave her your apartment key to watch you at night, to make sure you were all right. Now you need to put that fucking knife down, or there's going to be consequences!"

"I'm sorry," Gayle said, chewing on a fingernail. "Nobody wanted it to come to this."

Graham thought back to the night he assumed they had together at the beginning of the week—what seemed like ages ago. The way her body felt, the way her lips tasted. He'd been alone for so long before that. Was it really even her or a fantasy created by sodas?

"You put the knife down and this all goes away," E said. "Your job stays, your life here stays. Trust me when I say you do not want the alternative."

"We can do so much with the Pow! campaign, Graham," Gayle said, her voice soothing again. "You can be a footnote in its history. Every person here is going to want a Pow! in their hands if we do this right. We need your guidance."

He gripped the knife in response. He could strike them down and go on a rampage, but he was not sure he had it in him anymore. Or, he could lower the knife and fall in line, surely to get some type of promotion from this ordeal. But then what? Granted, he wouldn't be left comatose in the Zones, but one day he'd blink and find that the years have passed by, years full of lukewarm TV dinners and a life that lacked meaning and purpose.

With that thought, the glove on E's desk started ringing.

"I'm going to answer that, Graham," E said. "I have a suspicion that it's regarding what's happening between us right now."

Graham heard the cameras zoom in under his feet. E slipped on the glove, speaking into his palm.

"Yes, sir," E said. "Yes, we do seem to be in a bit of a pickle." He eyed Graham. "I do not know if he will use it, sir. I'm not in his mind. Offer him what? That's quite generous. It is true we haven't cast it yet. A place in the Estates, too? Do I think he'll concede? He's a moron if he doesn't. And all this without even calling the Guards? Oh, they're waiting outside the building. No, I'm not surprised, sir. You are always aware of anything and everything."

E slipped off the glove.

"Who was that?" Graham asked.

"Who it was is none of your concern, but what they have to offer is about to change your life."

"I wouldn't have been afraid to use the knife," he said, still keeping it pointed at both of them.

"Regardless, this is what's on the table. First, an apartment in the Estates. Something I haven't even gotten...yet. And second, you will be the face of the Pow! campaign once it's launched: print, billboards, even the airwaves. In just a matter of time everyone in this City will know who you are."

"Are you serious?" Gayle asked, twisting her face in confusion. "He's getting all of that?"

E shrugged and extinguished his cigar.

"Maybe if more people try to slit their boss's throat, they'll get rewarded as well."

Graham wasn't paying attention to E's displeasure. He was fighting with the depression that had enveloped him since he took a sip of blue. But suddenly he wasn't sad anymore. An apartment in the Estates meant that they'd never send him to the Zones, its looming threat forever eliminated. Even more importantly, he could finally have a purpose here. He thought back to the night he first arrived to this City. Welcomers removed his blindfold as the boat pulled into the Wharf, and The City's glass structures twinkled like colored stars. He believed in his heart that when he stepped onto this island, he'd be beginning again as someone new. He'd be the person he always imagined he could be. Someone able to accomplish all the things he always dreamed of doing. No longer would he feel sorry for himself and the childhood he had as an abused boy hiding under the covers. This new world, this secret City, this oasis in the middle of the sea, would be limitless.

He let the knife fall to the floor.

"Does this mean that you'll take the offer?" E asked.

Graham was crying even more than before, his face masked with tears. He didn't know if he was truly sad or if it had been manufactured, but he no longer cared.

"Throw in an orange Pow! and it's a deal," he said.

E grabbed his hand and shook the hell out of it.

"Glad to hear that, Graham." E nodded over at Gayle. "Gayle, you heard the man; orange him up."

She popped the soda's tab. The sound of Graham's future sparkled. He chugged it down until there wasn't a drop of fizz left.

The X train rocked through the tunnels as Graham headed back home to his apartment on Boxed Lane for the last time. It was crowded and he was sandwiched between other travelers, but an orange Pow! rumbled inside of him so the congestion didn't bother as much. When the X stopped, the commuters maneuvered around to let each other out. The X started up again and he was face-to-face with the lookalike stranger who he'd seen on this line before. The stranger had the same part in his hair, similar glasses and an ill-fitting suit. He stared Graham down as if he was judging him, as if he could possibly know the shady deal that Graham had just accepted.

The train car became hot and stifling. The stranger was still staring him down. Graham jammed his fingers into his collar to let in some air, but the sweat continued to ooze from his brow. He was short of breath. The orange taste had faded, his tongue dry again like always. He'd do anything to get off this train.

Just as he was about to crack, the X came to a halt and the doors flew open at Archipelago Station. He poured out of the train with the rest of the commuters, standing on the platform as everyone flew into a line to head outside. The lookalike stranger watched Graham from the window in the train car, disgusted as if he wanted to lunge at him, until the train zipped into the tunnel and disappeared.

Graham let out a huge breath of relief as he slid in line with the rest of the commuters, shaken for the moment even though he couldn't pinpoint exactly why that man had affected him so strongly. He passed by the ads along the station's wall: Wet-No-More umbrellas, New-U make-up. He expected to see the ad that welcomed him at the start of the week. A girl dressed in orange at the beach with a matching Pow! to her lips and the slogan: *DON'T LET LIFE PASS YOU BY, DRINK UP!* He recalled her toothy smile and the curve of her body drenched in orange with the sun as a soothing backdrop. He shivered now as a whirl of freezing wind blew through the station. The ad had been removed; his orange muse gone forever. He shivered again until his teeth began chattering.

There was an empty space where the ad used to be, waiting for him to take its place.

PART III:

REBELS

1

Power. Having never experienced it before as an abused orphan in the Outside World, and as a drone for the last decade at Warton, Mind & Donovan, no one had ever thought of Graham as someone who could have influence or clout. But no more. Now he headed to the Estates Region where his sparkling, brand-new apartment awaited, a neighborhood that housed the Man's scientists and The Finances, other citizens with important roles in The City. The deal he'd recently made to be the face of the Pow! Soda ad campaigns would finally give him that kind of power he'd always longed for but never imagined possible.

He hopped on the Y train, the only way to get to the Estates, in awe at how different it was from all the other lines. Catering to the more upscale citizens, the Y was filled with an explosion of erudite ads, the ceiling one long video monitor of a man with a monocle hawking Cool Cuban Cigars. Each time the man took a puff, a cool mist poured down on the straphangers. On the floor, a hologram mermaid did the breaststroke with a tin of Cultured Caviar in her porcelain hand. Bubbles escaped from her lips and popped with the brand name. He was mesmerized, soon to become one of these walking, talking ads. The train jerked to a stop, snapping him back to reality. A crowd poured in, and a Wealthy Whiskey commercial started with the sound of a banjo. Old-timey salesmen materialized around the train car.

"Wealthy Whiskey," one image told Graham in a thick, Southern drawl. "This is the wildest, most wondrous whiskey you could've wished for."

Graham felt a hand on his shoulder and swiveled around expecting another hologram salesman. Mick stood there instead, dripping with sweat.

"Hey! Bud? Whew, I almost missed the train," Mick wheezed. "I know it got heated between us the last time we saw each other. Never saw you on this line before."

"I'm headed home," Graham said, smug for the first time in his life. "To my *new* apartment in the Estates."

Mick let out a cough and caught the spittle in a handkerchief.

"Did you say the Estates?"

"I did. I've just been made the new face of Pow! Sodas. The Estates are just a perk."

Another hologram salesman materialized between them, but Mick waved it away.

"The new face?" Mick said, clearly taken aback. "What do you...what do you mean?"

"It's really a concession for the company using me as guinea pig all of last week."

Mick mumbled a response, at a loss for words, most likely wondering why Warton, Mind & Donovan didn't let him know about this major change in events.

"By the way, what were you doing on this line?" Graham asked. "Aren't you a little far away from Boxed Lane?"

The gears visibly turned in Mick's head while he tried to figure out a response. It was obvious Mick had followed Graham on the Y to monitor how he was behaving on Pow!s, like he'd been doing all week.

"This line? Uh, it's funny you should ask cause...I was headed to the Estates, too. Yeah...there's this...Asian-inspired bar in the Dynasty Region near there called Red, Red, Red. They've got this...uh...house drink that's worth getting winded for."

Mick mopped his forehead with his handkerchief and plastered back on his shit-eating grin.

"You can drop the act, Mick. I told you, I'm the face of Pow! now, and I know exactly what's been going on. The colors. The sodas. Everything."

"Sure, yeah," Mick said, flustered and sweating more than before. "Ok, so you know. Fucking surprise, right? Well...why don't you join me then? I think we both could use a drink anyway."

Mick slapped Graham hard on the back, but Graham held firm. He'd downed a cherry Pow! before he got the train, the anger from Mick's betrayal brewing. Despite the mood fluctuations from the sodas, he wasn't quite ready to give them up, especially since they aligned with his new role in The City. His former friend had known exactly what was going on at Warton, Mind & Donovan the whole time, but never said a thing—worthy of being hated. So, he slapped Mick on the back, hard enough for Mick to fall to his knees with a thud.

Mick looked up surprised, never believing Graham had the kind of power to knock him over.

"All right, let's get that drink," Graham said, holding out his hand to help Mick up.

Mick grabbed it, hesitantly.

The Dynasty Region consisted of four blocks: Shang, Zhou, Xin, and Han Street. Red, Red, Red was on Han. The area looked like the set of an old gangster film, used as a backdrop for a lot of the porn shot in The City. A movie trailer had been parked in front of Red, Red, Red. Inside, the bar was lit in a delicate red light. Murals of setting suns were painted on each of the walls. Hostesses in red kimonos shuffled between the *Blowjob* cast celebrating the wrapping of their shoot. A group of men gathered around one table, soaking their napkins with alcohol and then tossing the napkins to the ceiling until they stuck.

"It's an old tradition thought to relieve stress," Graham said, as he and Mick found a table.

Pulsing music came on the speakers. The film's star, Yiyi Yiagi, stepped up onto a quasi-stage in the center of the bar and began shaking her body to the beat. Her lipstick shined bright red; Graham couldn't help but stare.

She looked as though she'd gotten cheek implants, a shaped nose, and bleached teeth. She wore a red tank top and jeans shorts with thigh-high red boots. In her bellybutton sat a ruby stone. She ended the dance with a split and a smile that consumed half her face.

Mick was tearing up his napkin. "Look, Graham, it wasn't like I enjoyed deceiving you."

A waiter brought over two of Red, Red, Red's house drinks, Campari and Tabasco with a chili pepper on the rim. Graham took a sip that tasted like flames. Mick had a sip too and went back to shredding his napkin.

"I had to," Mick continued. "I'm sorry–"

Graham wanted to believe everything E and Gayle told him was true, but a part of him remained wary that life in this City could go from pathetic to stellar in a day. "Tell me exactly what they said to you about using me for their experiments."

"What do you mean, bud? Who...who are you talking about?"

"When I became the guinea pig. What were your orders?"

"Shit, basically to just keep giving you Pow!s and wear the same color you were drinking to enhance its effect."

Graham waited for Mick to look him in the eye, but Mick stayed focused on his shredded napkin.

"When did you find out about this?"

"Fuck, I don't know. A week, two weeks ago."

"And what did they give you to do this?"

"What do you mean? The company made us do it. We didn't have a choice."

"The order came from Warton, Mind, and Donovan?"

Mick started breaking out in a sweat again. He glanced

around as if someone was watching.

"No, the Man."

"*The Man*?"

All orders, in a sense, came from the Man; but it was odd to learn that the Man circumvented Warton, Mind and Donovan entirely. Graham had never personally received a direct order from the Man before. In every major company, the orders always came from higher-ups, who in turn, received these orders from the Heads.

"You know how it is here," Mick said, his neck whipping from side-to-side as he scanned the bar. He lowered his voice. "You don't say no to anything."

"I know."

"I'd be banished to the Zones. Living on a diet of Sloth pills in a matter of days. What would you have done?"

Mick put his fat face in his massive hands and started crying softly, but he was right; Graham would've done the same thing. He'd like to think he'd be nobler, but fear would've kept him silent.

"It's ok," Graham said.

"I'm sorry," Mick said. "I'm weak. I'm a fuck."

"Yeah, you are," Graham said, growing tired of the conversation. He went for another sip of his drink, but it wasn't helping his thirst. He got what he needed from Mick, and now his attention had switched to the thought of Pow!s on his tongue, the craving real bad. Red, Red, Red wouldn't have them here, but back at his new apartment, cartons and cartons awaited. Saliva collected around his molars at the anticipation of all that fizz. He soaked his napkin in his glass, inhaled deeply, and tossed it up to the ceiling.

"So, the face of Pow!" Mick said. "That's a real

promotion. Don't forget us small fish."

The pulsing music stopped and Yiyi Yiagi got on the microphone. She bowed to the crowd.

"I want to thank everyone who worked on my latest movie. It will be on Channel P for only one hundred Stipends to watch as many times as you like."

The bar erupted with applause. Yiyi covered her mouth and giggled.

"And stay tuned for my upcoming movie about a poor waitress who becomes a lucrative hooker on the side. This is guaranteed to be Yiyi's biggest hit yet!"

"I've seen all her movies," Mick said. "Her last film was the most purchased film that week. She's a tiny angel."

Yiyi threw on a red blouse over her tank top. She reapplied her lipstick and cracked open a red can. Graham's body went numb at the sight of it, practically leaping out of his chair to pounce on Yiyi and wrestle the Pow! out of her hand; but when he looked closer, it wasn't a Pow! at all, just a regular can. He swallowed hard, the saliva barely able to go down because his throat was so dry.

"I got to go," he said, getting up.

"What? No, stay for another drink, man. Hey, I wanted to ask you something. Have they told you what Pow!'s secret ingredient is yet?"

Graham put on his coat, not listening at all. His eyes were bugging, and a string of drool dripped down his chin.

"I'll see you tomorrow at work, Mick."

The red lights of the bar became more pronounced. His head was waterlogged now that he stood. He loosened his collar as he pushed in his chair and lumbered away.

"Yeah, I was just curious," Mick shouted. "You know

with Pow!'s 'Guess the Secret' ad about to go out there, I guess I wanted to know the secret."

Graham bolted past Yiyi, who was clapping along to the karaoke being sung on the other side of the bar. But he wasn't paying attention to any of it, only picturing a Pow! against his lips as he bolted out the door.

Outside he bumped into a man by the front door wearing a porkpie hat that covered his eyes. The man opened his palm to reveal a fistful of Levels that ranged from 1 - 5 in intensity.

"Clarity?" the man in the porkpie hat asked.

Graham stared down at the vials of Levels. He hadn't had any in days, barely since he started drinking Pow!. He picked up a vial of 3s.

"Everyone's doing them," the man in the porkpie hat said. "They'll help you focus, focus, focus."

Graham handed back the vial of Levels. As much as he might've wanted them, he thirsted for so much more.

2

Entering his new apartment in the Estates, Graham went straight to the fridge and thankfully found a row of Pow!s cooling. Now that he knew what they did, he believed he could control his moods on them better, the thought of never drinking one again too much to bear. Downing two cherries back-to-back, he staggered out of his white and sparkling kitchen like a shot of adrenaline had been injected in his bloodstream. His gloved cellular blinked on the wall, and he slid it on to check his messages. Gayle's voice came on the other end.

"Hello, Graham, it's Gayle...Hanley. I just wanted to

see how you were settling into everything. I can imagine these last few days have been trying for you. If you need to talk...I'll be up most of the night doing work. All right, take care."

He had a flash of the Gayle he'd been dreaming about all last week in her different colored high heels, which felt so real. A surge of anger tinged through his body. Before he could stop himself, he dialed her number.

"Hello?"

"Hey, Gayle, it's Graham," he said, panting. "I got your message–"

"I'm sorry if it's late. I've been doing work all night, and I'm wide awake. I thought I'd call."

"I'm awake, too."

An awkward silence passed between them. She broke the silence with what sounded like the saddest laugh he'd ever heard.

"I've been an insomniac since I got here," she said. "It's so hard to relax in a strange bed. I guess I better get used to it. Can I see your new place?"

"Tonight?"

"I could use an ear."

He pictured the outline of her ear and those cherry earrings she always wore as the rage in his belly simmered.

"I'll see you in an hour," he said. "And bring some cherry Pow!s."

Gayle arrived in the doorframe wearing a slinky red dress with two cherry Pow!s attached by plastic and dangling from her index finger.

"Aren't you going to ask me inside?" she asked with a seductive smile, swishing past him. He closed the door. "This new apartment is pretty amazing. The Estates are equipped with the latest everything. You've gotten used to the remotes yet?"

"I haven't had a chance."

She placed the sodas down and picked up a remote control from the coffee table. She pushed one button and the shades rose to let the twinkling night in. Another button set the lighting to a dim red. A third turned on some elegant jazz.

"The kitchen remote is really impressive. A machine can make you whatever food you desire. Shall we drink to new beginnings?"

"I'll...get some glasses," he said, wiping away the never-ending sweat from his brow.

"No need."

She pushed another button and two robot hands over the mini-bar put ice into two glasses.

"I've become the other half," he said, biting his knuckle.

She cracked open the cherry Pow!s and poured.

"You know, Graham, what you've done for Pow!, we can't thank you enough."

"What I've been given in return is very generous."

They both looked around. Twenty-foot ceilings. Chic furniture. Gadgets galore. The only possessions he'd taken from his old place were his Rorschach paintings. She stared at one now while resting the glass of red against her lips.

"They look like big bruises to me," she said, shrugging her shoulders. "Was I wrong to come over?"

"No."

"Do you hate me?"

"No."

"I feel terrible about what we've put you through."

"In case you didn't realize, my life wasn't that special before..."

He stopped himself, not wanting to give away too much, not trusting her enough to be candid.

"I'm excited to be the face of Pow!, to have a purpose here...finally."

She took a sip that sent a shiver up her body.

"I've never tried red before. Are we playing with fire?" she asked, as her long red nails tapped a beat against the drink.

"I think I can...handle it all now. Can you?"

Another gulp caused her cheeks to flush. She dabbed the cool drink against her forehead. He knocked back his entire Pow! in a few swallows, instantly regretting his impulsivity, but it was already too late. She let out a gasp that fizzled away and then wobbled over to the wall of windows on the far side of his apartment.

"I've been numb since I got here," she quietly said, setting her drink down on the window seat and pressing her face against the glass. "This place...I don't know what to make of it."

"Is your fiancée coming to The City eventually or..."

He punched his leg, knowing he shouldn't have brought up the Outside World.

"No...he isn't coming, at least not for a while. They're trying to figure out a position for him, or maybe even create one...who knows?"

"And what made you come?"

He stood beside her. The City was a sparkling chasm below, surreal from this height. She picked her glass back up and swallowed the rest, holding her throat as it spilled down.

"I had no other choice." She shivered, the glass falling from her hand and crashing to the floor.

"Watch out," he said, guiding her away from the shards.

"I'm sorry," she said, but there was no life to her words. She meandered over to the couch and collapsed between its massive pillows.

"You don't have to talk about your past," he said, sitting next to her.

She crossed one leg over the other. He became absorbed in her red dress again. All he could focus on–how red she was.

"Graham, I still have a fiancée," she reminded him.

"I know, I would never–"

She inched closer, continuing to rub her dress. "I hate myself sometimes. Most of the time."

"Why?"

"You don't know the things I've done since I've become a part of this City, what I'm willing to do."

"I forgive you."

"I don't want to be forgiven," she mumbled into her palm, embarrassed by her honesty. "I tell myself there are more important things than morals."

"Like?"

"Like helping someone I love back in the Outside World. Giving them a chance..."

She put her hand to her mouth, as if she didn't want to say anything more. Part of him wanted to comfort her, but the Graham filled with cherry Pow! was an entirely different species. He wouldn't be able to find that empathy anymore even if he excavated his entire soul. His eyes glazed over as the shape shifter within imagined tearing her dress down the middle. He quickly shook those thoughts away.

"Those were never just dreams, right?" he asked, angry now at the sight of her red dress, for her duplicity like all the rest. "We really have slept with each other before, right?"

"No..."

"But the orange dress, the red earrings."

"Just markers I left behind. To bolster your dreams."

She wrapped her arms around him, leaving fresh tears on his cheek. A darker rage built inside of him now that the soda had settled.

"Please make me feel something right now," she murmured, starting to unbuckle his belt, leaving heavy lipstick kisses on his cheek.

"No, Gayle, I–"

He tried to unravel her arms, but her hold was a vice grip.

"Numb," she said. "I'm so numb."

"It's not right."

"Fuck right."

She slid onto his lap until he was able to untangle her and scoot away. Her cold cadaver gaze observed him from the other side of the couch.

"You always look like the world is crashing down on you, and I get that," he said. "I've felt that, too. But you have a fiancé and there's someone else."

One of her eyebrows rose, resembling a question mark

tipped on its side.

"Another girl?"

"Yes."

She put her head in her hands and shook it back and forth violently. When she lifted it up, she became an entirely new woman, composed.

"I just don't want to go home tonight. To nothing."

The anger from the cherry Pow!s had to be squelched down to avoid what he might do. Like a stone it festered, but at least it hadn't been released.

"Please, take the couch," he said. She'd already curled up with a pillow, so he tossed the throw blanket over her body and slammed himself inside his bedroom before he could do any more harm.

Later that night in his dreams, he looked down at his hands to find shreds of an orange dress. Lying in his bed was a girl. She ran an orange painted toenail along the recesses of her tan leg. Brown hair covered her face. When she parted her hair, he recognized Marlena. It seemed like years since they'd spent the night together; so much had changed. Immediately consoled from the sight of her, he let the shreds of the orange dress fall to the floor and climbed into bed, but by the time he reached her, she was gone. He was left grasping at the sheets.

He woke up murmuring her name.

"Marlena," he said again, as his eyes blinked away crust. He could still taste last night's sugared hangover. Gayle stood at the doorframe wearing one of his work shirts.

"What did you say?" she asked, stirring a cup of coffee.

He hadn't realized he'd said Marlena's name out loud.

"Just...a dream I was having–"

"Thank you for last night," she said. "I apologize for throwing myself at you. I was pickled." She touched his cheek. He winced, feeling a bruise with his tongue.

"Did I do that to myself?" His body went cold with the thought.

He scrambled out of bed, his stomach turning. Sour cherry bile crept up his throat.

"I do it to myself sometimes, too." A dimple of consternation appeared between her eyes. He had trouble catching his breath. She placed down her coffee.

"What do you mean?"

She bunched up the work shirt until her thighs weren't covered any longer, visibly black and blue.

"What the fuck?"

He turned to the massive windows, but didn't want to look at The City either.

"I need a drink," he said. She picked the coffee back up and held it out. He pushed past her and headed for the kitchen. From the fridge, he swiped an orange Pow! and chugged it down. She followed him into the kitchen.

"What is wrong with you?" he asked.

She ran her fingers across her bruises.

"I felt something! I'm so used to feeling nothing here. I've...forced myself into numbness."

The veins in her neck protruded as she shuddered. She pressed down her wild strands of hair.

"God, I'm a mess," she said.

"You don't need to abuse yourself like that; it's sick."

"It's the only way I know to deal." And then, as if she realized she'd said too much, she paced around, flustered.

"We...need to get ready for work. You have a morning meeting with E, and we're shooting a commercial later today."

She wiped off any emerging tears and started to walk away, but he grabbed her arm, gripping more tightly than he expected.

"Listen to me," he said, lessening his hold. "You don't need to hurt yourself. Understand?"

She laughed him off.

"I'm serious, Gayle. You're better than that."

She opened her mouth as if she was about to argue, but then stopped herself.

"Don't ever let me see you bruised again."

"Enough about me," she said. "This is your big day. Let's get you ready for your debut."

A smile emerged on her face, trembling ever so slightly.

Graham tilted his head to the sky as he walked up to Warton, Mind & Donovan. Its black tower seemed less imposing than usual. Even though he was a bit out of sorts from what had happened with Gayle last night, a great sense of pride rushed through his body as he pushed through its revolving doors. In the elevator, everyone watched the numbers, prepping for another endless day that would bleed into the night, the bags under their eyes puffed and purple. Their faces washed out and gray. Regardless of the Pow!s fucking with his mind, he was better off than them now; his life here at least had some meaning. He'd just have to wean himself off the sodas eventually.

Outside of E's office, GUESS THE SECRET? ads adorned the walls.

"Guess the secret," he said, practicing his delivery.

Marlena turned the corner in a professional orange suit. She hesitated when she noticed him, even started to go back the other way, but then picked up her pace to pass right by.

"Marlena," he said, louder than expected. He reached out for her elbow, but she pulled away too fast. "I didn't mean to grab at you."

"I have to go. I'm covering the front desk–"

"Wait."

She eyed him carefully.

"I owe you a tremendous apology for the other day. I'm so sorry if I scared you."

"Yeah, you did."

"I'm all right now, though," he said, with stutter to his voice. "I know now that I was just the guinea pig for testing out the new Pow!s and...things got out of control. I'm trying to control everything better now."

"They sent an office-wide memo over the weekend. No more color constrictions according to what you're drinking. Operation Graham is officially over."

"Is that what they called it?"

"That's what I called it." She glanced down at the cameras under their feet, monitoring like always. "Anyway, I really do have to go–"

"You know that wasn't me, right? I was on a lot of cherry. I don't even remember most of it."

"Well, I do. Excuse me."

She started to walk away, but he stepped in front of her.

"Did I hurt you?" He flinched, afraid of her answer.

"Look, Mr. Weatherend, I just got to this City. I don't want to cause any more trouble."

"Trouble? Why would you think...? Why are you calling me Mr. Weatherend?"

"I was never told to sleep with you, okay?" she said, swiveling around to see if she'd brought too much attention to herself. A man and a woman were talking at a nearby glass cubicle. They both glanced up briefly but continued with their conversation.

"I did what the memos said. I wore the colors they told me to, but I pursued you because I liked you, okay?"

He wanted to tell her how much he liked her as well, but she spoke again first.

"But that was wrong. I got in the middle of something I shouldn't have. I know better now. I've been told–"

"They're making me the face of Pow! so it doesn't matter. The experiment is over. If you like me...you can like me."

He wanted to kiss Marlena in front of the cameras and whoever might be watching. Her body language told him otherwise: arms crossed and her eyes kept scanning the floor.

"No, I can't let myself like you," she whispered, shaking her head.

"Why not?"

She peeked down at the cameras and then back up to him to indicate why.

"There's nothing to be afraid of," he said. "They want to make me happy now."

She sighed, as if to say 'no' without actually saying the word.

"Don't they want to make me happy?" he asked, as his stomach dropped.

"I...need to go back to my desk. Please."

"Oh...okay," he stammered, and moved aside so she could pass. "You...look great today by the way. All in orange."

"Thank you. I'd already set up an orange outfit before I got the memo. And then I was late this morning–"

"Well, you wear it well."

"You take care, Mr. Weatherend."

She went to turn on her heels but then leaned in close until her breath tickled his ear.

"I hate the way they fucked with you," she whispered. "And I hate that I let myself be a part of it. But I can't be with you anymore. Please understand."

He wet his lips, thinking of the best response, but she was gone before he got the chance. She hurried down the hallway without looking back until she became just a tiny orange speck at the far end.

His stomach dropped even more as he had an upsetting premonition that this would be the last time he'd see her for a while.

3

Throughout the entire morning meeting with E, Graham couldn't stop thinking about Marlena. She had insinuated that the company did not have his best interest at heart, even after offering him an apartment in the Estates and a role as the face of the Pow! campaign. She wanted to make it clear that she hated being a part of the experiments and that she was ordered to keep away from him now...but he had to put it all out of his mind. The Elders were presiding over his meeting with E and he needed to stay focused. The Elders, who had the uncanny ability to see someone's secrets, read their thoughts, and expose any insubordination. So, he removed any hesitation, pondering only another can of orange Pow!. That would help with his focus.

The Elders scribbled away as E laid out the details of Graham's upcoming week. Two commercials were to be shot and aired immediately on The City's two major networks along with a five-page print ad for the *City Gazette*. The word "star" was brought up repeatedly. Finally, E stressed that the Man had requested a videoconference with Graham after the commercial wrapped. The Man rarely granted any videoconferences with any citizens, so E made it clear that Graham should feel very special.

Graham forced himself to appear gracious, especially since the Elders were scrutinizing every facial tic and scribbling away to probably notify the Heads of the company how he responded; but Marlena wouldn't vacate his mind. He was taken back to the time in his bedroom a few days ago when she was cast in blue shadows, peering down at the arms she'd lost. If anything, he could try to use his new fame to get her the most lifelike limbs on the market.

"Gayle will be there at the shoot today to help you with anything you need," E said, wrapping up his lecture.

He had completely forgotten about the odd night with Gayle and how in the morning they'd both awoken after bruising themselves. It seemed like nothing more than a fragmented dream.

"And the Elders will escort you over to the studio in the Dynasty Region."

The Elders each gave a chilling nod before turning back to their notepads.

"Are you ready for your life here to change?" E asked.

"Oh, yes, sir," Graham said, lucky that he had an orange Pow! earlier and wouldn't have to feign enthusiasm, glad that orange always made him energetic, regardless of how he really felt. In a perfect world, he'd bolt out of the door to chase Marlena down, but for now he'd have to bottle up those feelings; at least, until he filmed his commercial and became the "star" they promised he'd be. Then maybe he could call the shots in his own life for the first time since his boat pulled up to the docks.

Graham was sandwiched between the Elders in a private car on the way to the Dynasty Region. Outside a sleeted snow had just been turned on and teemed from the sky. Their decayed faces offered no emotion, wrinkled grooves, eyes saggy but observant. There was something eerily familiar about these faces. Looking deeper, the familiarity became even stronger, a hint of déjà vu from long ago, childhood dreams now thrust into reality. A headache began to form; he tempered it by massaging his temples. A nagging need to talk to them emerged, even though he'd never heard either say an actual word before.

"How about this weather we've been having?" Graham asked, as his sharp headache quieted to a mildly irritating buzz.

The Elders turned to him in unison and then scribbled in their notepads.

"What do you write all day in those notepads?"

Graham peered over, but the words were indecipherable, random squiggles and symbols. The

Elders both snapped their notepads shut and shook their heads over-and-over, admonishing him.

"I'm sorry," Graham said, as the car came to a stop and the Elders exited through separate doors.

He followed them as they slouched into *City Studios* on Zhang Street. Seeing that they had their own private language unnerved him; he wondered the purpose for a secret language. It resembled the Man's own unintelligible language broadcasted over the loudspeakers as a fear mechanism. Usually after the Man spoke, the Elders appeared to do his bidding and banish an unlucky soul to the Empty Zones. Graham always figured that the Heads of the companies were second-in-command to the Man, but he'd never even seen or heard from any of the Heads before, which made him wonder if they were all an illusion. He'd been certain that the Heads were the ones who manned all the cameras to watch every employee's move, but maybe the Man wanted to keep everyone scared that a silent but deadly threat existed right above, and that he had a whole army of powerful underlings besides his Guards, when in fact, he only had the Elders. It was strange that the Man requested a videoconference with him while none of the Heads had, meaning, at least, that the Man had a lot invested in this Pow! campaign and personally wanted Graham to become its star.

He followed the Elders inside the elevators. When they reached the top, he stepped out, but they remained inside. They glared at him until the elevator beeped and then went back to scribbling in their notepads before the doors closed. A sharp pain shot up his skull, but he tempered it again by rubbing his forehead.

Before he could ponder the Elders' role in this City and

whether or not Warton, Mind, and Donovan actually existed, Gayle grabbed his wrist to whisk him off to hair and make-up. He passed by a crew setting up the shot on a stage with an orange question mark for a backdrop.

She put him in a chair and shoved the script into his hand before he could say anything, amazed at how professional she could act after breaking down last night. Who was the real Gayle and what was just a façade?

"There'll be a teleprompter but take a gander at the script beforehand anyway," she said. "You'll start off by looking into camera and saying, 'Nobody likes a secret'. Then we need to you to convey various emotions: strength, intense jubilation, passion, etc. They will be interspersed with shots of you drinking an orange Pow!."

She continued talking but he lost focus when she mentioned an orange Pow!. He hadn't had one since the morning. Everything else in his mind got put aside as his heart slammed into his chest at the thought of a cold one on his lips.

"Could I have a Pow! now?" he asked, while she was mid-sentence. She stopped talking, clearly annoyed, but asked the hairdresser to get him one. They finished his make-up as she continued giving him the rundown of the day. When the Pow! was brought over, he held up his finger to silence her while he gulped it down.

"Did you hear what I just said?" she asked as he wiped his mouth.

He had heard nothing.

A first take was filmed, and then another, and another. The director who shot all the commercials in The City demanded perfection. After a few hours, Graham had gone through a six-pack of orange and was starting to throb.

Gayle asked the director for a minute.

"Is everything okay, Graham?" Gayle asked, plastering on a smile to the rest of the crew.

"Get me a lime."

"This shoot is for orange."

"I'm really...aroused right now. That's what orange does to me after too many. I need to balance."

He tried not thinking of Marlena right now, only focusing on his stomach growling for a lime. He could already taste its tartness in the sweat hanging from his upper lip.

"Can we get a lime here?" Gayle shouted.

This was the first time he saw the kind of power he'd have as a star, because a lime Pow! was rushed over, and like that, the shoot changed from orange to green, the entire set sculpted around his whim.

As Graham traveled back to his Estates apartment with Gayle, it was as if he'd stepped into someone else's life. The lime Pow! made him jealous of the man whose life he'd recently taken, as if he was just biding time in these new shoes.

The apartment was dark when they entered. He had no clue how to work the apartment's remote so Gayle pushed a few buttons until the lights embedded in the ceiling shone brightly and the television spanning across the wall clicked on.

"Your commercial should be on tonight."

"So soon?" he asked, making a beeline for the fridge where he grabbed two lime Pow!s.

"They'll edit it on the spot and air it right away on

Channel A. The new and improved Pow! shipments should be out by next week so the commercials need to whet people's appetites. That also gives us time to wean you off the prototypes."

"Have you ever talked to the Man directly before?" he asked. He'd been thinking about the Man during the whole ride home.

He cracked open a Pow! since he might as well finish the rest of his stash, and waited for her response as she chewed a fingernail.

"Why do you ask?"

"He wants to have a videoconference with me, and I'm not sure what to expect."

"Oh," she said, as if she was relieved it was all he wanted to know about the Man. "Well, I spoke with him very briefly when I was initially hired."

"What about Warton, Mind, and Donovan?"

"What about them?"

"Have you met them before?"

"No."

She gnawed on a different fingernail and then composed herself. "Aren't you going to offer me a Pow! too?"

He cracked open the other lime and handed it over.

"Have you heard any new updates about your fiancé?" he asked, a twinge of jealousy rocking through him because of their possible happiness. Especially since Marlena felt farther away than ever.

"He isn't coming," she said, quietly.

"Since when?"

"Since never!"

Her face became vicious, teeth bared and ready. This

was the real Gayle.

"I made a decision to come here," she said, after taking a swig of Pow!. "And my fiancée wasn't included in that decision. The Man...wouldn't allow it."

"But why did you come then?"

"Why did you come?" she snapped back. "Didn't you have any family back home, people who loved you?"

He closed his eyes and plunged again into those cold waters from his childhood.

"I killed my parents."

He'd never said the words out loud before and they tasted like rancid fruit on his tongue.

"It...it was an accident, but that doesn't change anything I guess."

He swigged some more Pow! with shaky hands but there was nothing left. Gayle passed over the rest of hers.

"I had no idea."

At the moment, he was not sad, just envious of everyone who had parents to pick them up from school and tuck them in with bedtime stories and hugs, who were able to have memories of their folks. When he thought back, he had to create who they were each time.

"You can cry if you want to," she said, rubbing his shoulder.

"No, the past doesn't have to exist here, right?"

He surprised himself by hugging her, squeezing tight, as if holding onto her was the only thing preventing him from remembering what he'd tried so hard to forget. Their moment became broken by a large green question mark appearing on the television.

"It's your ad!"

On the screen, Graham was saying, "Nobody likes a

secret" as he put a finger to his lips. He cracked open another lime Pow! and sipped. There was a flash of him smiling, then a flash of him in ecstasy before he continued by saying: "Pow! has a secret ingredient and they're not telling, so take a sip to figure it out for yourself. Is there something missing in your life? Lack passion? Can't focus? Feel depressed? Let Pow! give you back whatever it is you've been missing. We know you'll want more and more, but we guarantee you'll never guess the secret. Can you prove us wrong?"

On the screen, Graham raised an eyebrow and took a final sip. He let out a satisfied *aaahhhhhhh* as his image faded into the green question mark and the television beamed a green light into the room. It washed over the two of them as they delighted in its glow. The words *Pow! Is Coming* pulsed on the screen.

"I think we have a raging success," she said.

Graham licked his lips and allowed the lime's tang to take over his mind.

"How are things going with your other woman?" she asked.

"Oh...not so good. I mean, it's not gonna work out," he said, wondering if somewhere an alternate City existed that wouldn't be intent on keeping him and Marlena apart.

"What if you pretend I'm her?"

"Gayle..."

"I'm serious." She put her finger to her lips. "I won't tell anyone."

She slid down her dress, naked with green light pouring over. She swiveled around as the angel and devil tattoos gestured for him to follow her into the delusions of his bedroom, where he'd be able to quiet his longings, if just till morning. He could pretend she was someone else, and one day after pretending for long enough, maybe she could become that someone else.

Gayle's body gave him chills throughout the night so he was forced to sleep as far away from her as possible. At one point, he'd opened an eye to see her watching him from the other side of the bed; but then he snapped his eye shut and feigned sleep, hoping to return to a dream where Marlena lay in his bed while he caressed her stubs.

When he woke, no one was in bed with him, no dress dangled from the bedpost. It was enough to make him question if it had been a twisted fantasy. His stomach grumbled. Before he could quench it, his gloved cellular rang.

"Hello?" he said, his mouth still sticky sweet from last night.

"Graham!" E's voice boomed through the phone. "Didn't wake you, did I?"

He rubbed his head, murmuring into the glove.

"Get down to the office immediately. We've gotten the feedback from your commercial."

"How'd you get that so soon–" Graham began to ask, but E had already hung up. The dial tone pulsed in his ear. He slid the cellular glove off and reached for the blue-raspberry Pow! on his nightstand. He took a flat sip, unsure from E's tone whether the feedback had been good or bad and if either outcome would affect the hollow feeling in his stomach.

4

In E's office, Graham found his boss leaning against a bust of Stalin's head and feeding his face from a tin of prunes on the desk.

"You look like you've lost your fucking dog," E said, closing the tin of prunes. "You better shape up when the Man calls."

"I had a blue-raspberry Pow! this morning," Graham said, licking at the tart tear stuck to his cheek. He'd woken up adrift in sadness, punishing himself for what might've happened with Gayle.

"Oh yeah, blue makes you depressed, right? This new

shipment from the scientists should fix those bugs."

Graham rubbed his hands together from the chill in the office. Marlena was the only one who could make him feel warm—he felt like it'd been eons since he'd seen her.

"Who told Marlena to stay away from me?" he mumbled, barely able to get the words out through the tears. "Fucking blue-raspberry..."

E pulled a cigar from out of a humidor on his desk and cut off its head.

"You mean your little intern?" he laughed, lighting the cigar and taking a puff.

"You're not going to control me anymore," Graham said, unable to stop shaking. The blue raspberry Pow!s had never affected him this bad before.

"Kid, I said we'll get you on the improved Pow!s once the shipment comes in."

"You're a puppet." The thought of another sip of Pow! made him want to hurl, even if the scientists could fix the kinks. All he wanted was Marlena, right then, right there. The tears flew from Graham's eyes faster than he could wipe them away. "We all are."

"Get a hold of yourself!"

"Why keep us apart?" He stepped toward E, who backed away, obviously remembering the knife to his throat from a few days ago.

"Jesus Christ, Graham, you're a mess."

"Have you ever had someone taken away from you?" Graham asked, pleading with E to listen and make it all better. "We're powerless."

E eyes softened in a way that Graham had rarely seen before.

"Don't blow your opportunity, kid. Few opportunities

are ever given here. I was given a big one once, too."

He placed his hand on Graham's shoulder. At first, Graham flinched out of instinct, but then E removed a handkerchief from his front pocket to clean Graham's face. From far away, the two of them must've looked like a little bullied kid and a father consoling his child.

Graham accepted the alien comfort and slowly stopped shaking. He blew all of his sadness into the handkerchief and the two of them floated away from the constraints of The City. They left behind the roles they'd been required to play and became human again with one another, if only for a second.

E spoke but hardly moved his lips, not wanting the cameras below to be able to read them.

"When my opportunity came around, I didn't ask questions. And that's served me well here; it can serve you well, too, but you have to be smart." E's voice dropped to a husky whisper, struggling to continue. "The Man sees all, the Man knows all, and he'll come after you if you're causing trouble."

Instinctively, they both faced the Eye Tower hovering outside of the windows. The gloved cellular on E's desk rang and they both started at the sound. E coughed into his fist and regained his composure before sliding on the glove. A woman's voice came on the other end.

"E, *Dobre Utra.* [3] The Man is ready for Mr. Weatherend and wants you to switch on your video monitor."

"Thank you, Shelby."

E took a deep breath and wiped his forehead before turning on the video monitor that spanned one wall of his

---

[3] *Good morning*, translated from Russian.

office. Shelby appeared on the screen, her face bloated, her hair stringy from what looked like stress. In place of the eye the Man had taken from her was a closed zipper the length of her eye socket. Her other eye had a frozen look of fear as if it could be next.

"I'm patching him in," Shelby said, into a headset.

The screen went black for a second.

"Don't react when you see him," E ordered, speaking quickly.

"What do you mean?"

"Most react to his appearance. He doesn't like that. Do not show fear in your eyes. He's sent many to the Zones just for that."

"Thank you," Graham nodded. "I know you didn't have to tell me all this–"

"Never mind that." E waved him off as his eyes hardened. He indulged in a final suck from his cigar. "Here he comes."

The Man materialized on the wall screen. Graham had imagined what the Man might look like up close, but nothing prepared him for the reality. The Man's waist was only a few inches in length and his body had stretched to the point of distortion. Over a dozen arms spilled from his body. The sheer white mask covering his face was pulled so tight that when he breathed, a dark circle of moisture formed around his mouth like he was permanently screaming.

Graham repeated to himself that the Man was normal like everyone else.

"E," the Man said, speaking as if he was chewing on his tongue. "Could you kindly give us some privacy?"

"Oh? Yes...yes of course, sir."

The disappointment in E's voice apparent: an unwanted, unloved treble. His boss slipped out of the office, crestfallen. For once, Graham would've preferred him to stay.

The Man studied Graham without saying a word, long enough for it to be uncomfortable. It was hard to stare back because the Man had no visible eyes to stare into.

"I see that your commercial went well," the Man finally said.

"Yes...that's what I heard."

The Man breathed what looked like a dark scream that sent a chill up Graham's back.

"Hearing about something is unreliable. You will have to *see* the commercial for yourself."

"Yes, I've seen it, too."

"Good, good," the Man breathed, his mouth turning black as coal again. He scratched his chin with three sets of hands.

"I bet you wonder what my interest in Pow! might be?"

"I know that's none of my business," Graham said, thinking quickly.

"Are you scared to be in a conference with me?"

The Man laughed, causing his body to shake as if it was made out of putty.

"No. I'm...honored."

"I wonder if all of those I've sent to the Zones have felt honored as well?"

Graham's stomach turned.

"I am curious, Mr. Weatherend. When you go to bed each night, do you pray that you will not see my face in the morning?"

The Man moved in closer until his phantom image

covered the entire screen.

"Not at all," Graham said, at a loss for words.

"Do you find my face vile, Mr. Weatherend?"

Graham gagged but managed to keep his bile down.

"Most liken my appearance to a nightmare. However, this is the face I present, since the one behind the mask is incomplete. Soon enough, though, I will be wholly realized, as will all of you. But I am aware that even though I have given my citizens new lives like only a God can do, I am not always respected like one. I have to find other ways to garner that respect."

Graham nodded, not knowing what else to do.

"There are those that will always fight authority, which is sad because I am a giver, Mr. Weatherend. I want nothing more than to give you a life far different than the one you came here to get away from."

Upon hearing those words, Graham pictured his parents' car frozen in the sky before they all fell into the ocean. How different his life would've been if they'd never taken that drive.

"But some of my citizens can't let their pasts go. The anger, the sadness, the jealousy they felt in the Outside World, even the passion that possibly put them over the edge and caused them trouble with the law—it is still a part of them here. And of course, they want to take that out on me. I become the focus of their displeasure, but it doesn't have to be that way. They are all about to be given the opportunity to control their emotions better. The new batches of sodas will provide this once my scientists have perfected the chemical equations. My citizens will be able to decide how they want to feel and exactly when they will choose to feel that way. Instead of being sad at work, for example, and having their emotions affect their job, they can purge their sadness by drinking a blue-raspberry on their commute home, or even before they go to bed. A much more productive use of time management. All I've ever wanted to do was help my citizens deal with whatever troubles plagued them. That's why I work you to the bone here. Work is life; work is the present. Your job is your purpose. And then I've even given you the Downtown to let loose, to forget your hardships even more. I've given my children everything, but that isn't enough. The Zones are getting more populated because of insubordination, but I truly believe Pow! will be the solution that keeps everyone on track to make this City greater and greater. When we look back upon our history, this will be the moment of our true birth, when we decided to collectively soar. Because my citizens are all capable of so much, Mr. Weatherend. That's why I Selected them, why I Selected you. Now doesn't that sound like a great vision?"

Still sucked into his past, his parents' car had unfrozen from the sky, plunging deep into the waters below. Graham replayed the image over and over, rewinding and fast-forwarding the film ad nauseam.

"When I look out from my Eye Tower, Mr. Weatherend, I want to like what I see. I want to appreciate what I've created. Most of all, when everyone looks up, I want them to appreciate me for taking that chance on them when no one else would, instead of plotting in the back of their minds on how they will cut me down."

In Graham's mind, he'd emerged from the destructive waters that swallowed his parents. He boarded a boat pulling up to the docks of The City. His blindfold had been taken off and he looked up at the Eye Tower, believing it would watch over him and that he'd stepped upon a rock of salvation.

"I don't think anyone wants to cut you down," Graham said, but he was lying. He'd spent the last decade looking up at that Eye Tower hoping that something would change.

"I've never been a fool, Mr. Weatherend," the Man chuckled in response. "The Elders have told me many things about what goes on down in my City that the cameras are unable to catch. My question for you is what will you do after I've told you all of this?"

"What do you mean?"

"Well, you are essential now in my plan for Pow! Soda and for The City as well. And look at what I've given you in gratitude for your silence. I've upgraded your apartment to the Estates. You are no longer threatened by being sent to the Zones. You are about to become famous. You will have a charmed life here, more than most. But you will know something that they do not—how you are all being controlled. But controlled for your own benefit, don't you see? The question, however, remains: What do you do with this information? Do you go against me and shout it from the rooftops–"

"I...won't tell anyone," Graham said, nervous as to why the Man would be so forthcoming. He had to assure him that he'd remain loyal. "I...know you only want what's best for us."

Deep inside coiled a glimmer of a different Graham who longed to stand up to this multi-armed travesty who thought he was a God, but that Graham was too small, too hidden to show himself. He wiped away a tear.

The Man's mouth trembled at the sight of a delicious

tear falling from Graham's eye. He held out a few of his hands, as if to catch the tear through the screen.

"I hope you mean that, my child," the Man replied, his black smile shrinking back into the image of a scream. "Because if I believe you are being false, if I ever think you will reveal my intentions to my City, that you will ruin this fantasy, I will cut you, I will expunge you, and I will dance on your grave."

Graham shuddered as the Man folded all of his fingers together.

"This is never to be repeated to anyone, *moy malen'kiy pitomets.* [4] My little pet, my little devilish, wind-up toy. You alone are receiving this gift of knowledge as a thank you for weeding out that imbalanced batch of Pow!. Because of you, the perfect combination of ingredients is in our grasp. And I will celebrate with an IV of the sweet stuff when it's ready for show."

"I won't tell anyone," Graham repeated, making sure he believed his own promise.

"Yes, my little pet. You've been a good boy."

The Man touched the screen with a long, slender hand, as if he was petting Graham.

"Such beautiful eyes you have. Maybe one day you could let me get a closer look? I have a collection you know. Sometimes, I hold all of those eyes in my hands and get gooseflesh thinking about what they have seen. I'd love to feel what you've seen, too, *moye osoboye malen'koye domashneye zhivotnoye.* [5]

A black smile took over half of the Man's face before

---

[4] *My little pet*, translated from Russian.

[5] *My special, little pet*, translated from Russian

the screen clicked off. On one hand, the idea of being able to control one's emotions better sounded good, to even forget his traumatic past, which always seemed to be at the forefront of Graham's mind, but the Man hadn't been completely forthcoming with his intentions for Pow!. Regardless, he couldn't show that he had any doubts, for the cameras whirred under him, and the Man could still be watching his facial expressions to make sure he was complying.

As Graham went to leave E's office, he yanked at his collar to let in some air, his neck slick with sweat. He inhaled a few deep breaths, trying to coax himself into thinking he was all right. He opened the door with a thud, smacking Mick, who rubbed his eye.

"Fuck, man, you got me right in the eye."

"Were you listening to our conversation?" Graham asked.

"Trying." Mick knocked on the door, which gave a hollowed metal sound. "Too thick."

Graham moved past him toward the elevators.

"Buddy, yoo-hoo? Earth to Graham-O."

"I've got to go," Graham said.

"You okay, bud?"

Graham nodded as he continued down the hall.

"Where are you going?"

Mick hurried to stay by his side.

"What happened in there?"

The elevator arrived and Graham stepped in without responding. Mick joined him before the doors closed. The sound of the cameras whirring below them cut through the silence.

“You look like you could use a drink,” Mick finally said. “There’s this place in the Downtown called Out to Sea.”

Of all places in The City, the Downtown was the least monitored by the Man. While Mick was the last person he wanted to see and he knew he couldn’t tell Mick anything he’d learned, he could use a moment away from this building, a break from scrutinizing eyes.

“A quick drink,” Graham nodded, his throat drying up.

At Out to Sea, Graham went right for the bathroom to splash some water on his face. He caught his reflection in the mirror, unable to look for long. He’d never see himself differently now that he’d become a stoolie for the Man, but he knew that he had no choice.

When he returned to a table in the shape of a boat, the waitress was arriving. Mick ordered something with the word blue in the name of it.

“That sounds good,” Graham added. “Make it two.”

The sound of the ocean played over the speakers as they sat in an uncomfortable silence until the waitress returned with two enormous blue drinks with tiny umbrellas.

“Damn, that’s a lot of drink.”

“Go on, dig the fuck in and tell your old buddy what’s making you frown?”

If Graham said the tiniest thing about what he’d learned, then all the rest would come rushing out. He shook his head and took a small sip.

“So, you had a conference with the Man?”

“I can’t talk about the videoconference,” Graham

responded curtly. “You have to understand.”

“Sure, sure.”

Graham took another swig of the massive drink. His heartbeat slowed, his body beginning to cool down. The sensation to consume more grew to a massive itch that couldn’t be scratched, but finally, after a third sip, he was quenched. All was right again, at least in this mirage.

“Is there Pow! in this?” he asked, though he already knew the answer. He was too exhausted to care. Let tomorrow be the day he cuts himself off completely.

“Those ads are making everyone wonder like crazy what the secret is. And the damn drinks aren’t even out on the market yet.”

“The power of advertising.” Graham tried to laugh, but he let out a yawn instead.

“You can tell your old buddy, though, right?” Mick nudged. “C’mon, how ’bout a little hint?”

Even though Graham had no idea what the secret might be, he couldn’t see any harm in letting Mick think that he knew. He shrugged his shoulders with a tired grin, getting so sleepy all of a sudden. A sense of calmness washed over his body, but it became hard to hold onto concrete thoughts anymore as his eyes drooped. The next sip tasted different than the rest, a sourness hitting his back molars. Mick was observing him closely now.

“C’mon, tell old Mick. I won’t repeat it to anyone. It’ll be our secret.”

After another sip, Graham became wobbly in his chair. The room pivoted and spun as bile crept up his throat. He pinched the bridge of his nose in pain, his skull burning.

“What’s in this...?” he mumbled.

“You don’t look so hot,” Mick said, matter-of-factly.

"What's...going...on?"

Graham peered down at the floor that was painted like an ocean. He lost all control of his muscles and his jellied body collapsed into the fake waters. One eye remained partially open as Mick glanced around the bar, playing it cool. Mick pulled him to his feet and threw an arm over his shoulder. He was shouting to the bartender that Graham had had too much to drink before they burst through the front doors into a swirling snow that had been switched on outside.

Knowing he'd been drugged, he cursed Mick internally while being dragged toward a taxi on the corner. The flakes nipped at his cheeks, keeping him awake until the taxi sped off and his stubborn eye finally closed out of exhaustion.

5

Opening his eyes, Graham had no clue where he was. A blinding light beamed down from overhead. He could hardly stand up; two men in white coats held him by his arms. The overhead light was too glaring to see their faces. His legs weren't working as he was dragged across the floor. The room so cold, like a thousand needles were prickling his skin. The walls and floor, a sterile, immaculate white. In the corner, a bunch of machines beeped and buzzed. Someone threw him onto a metal table in the center. Looking down at his little dangling legs, he was still a child. Fear gripped his throat. He'd been in this dream before, but it always felt more than just a dream: a real, waking nightmare.

The two men in white coats strapped him down while laughing. He didn't have the energy to struggle. One of them spoke to the other, but he couldn't understand what was being said. The overhead light still burned his eyes, and the two men appeared as hovering shadows. The man to his right removed a long metal object with a sharp end and stuck it into Graham's ear until it punctured his brain. The man on the left clamped his hand over Graham's mouth so he couldn't scream. The sharp metal object released something inside of his head. From his other ear, he heard a rush of water flowing outside of the room. The doors then opened and an endless tidal wave burst inside. The man to his right removed the long metal object. Graham cried out when he saw that it was covered in blood. The water continued to pour into the room at an increasing rate, reaching up to the two men's ankles. The man to his left slowly let go of Graham's mouth, as Graham screamed and screamed until his throat was raw. The overhead light was moved away and Graham stared directly into their faces.

Identical twins. Or he was seeing double. He wasn't sure, but their faces were fraught with wrinkles but still blurred. The water continued to pour in as it filled up to their waists. They spoke to each other with raised voices, and Graham still couldn't understand what they said. He ground his teeth, the pain in his head becoming too much to bear as his little body started convulsing. The water filled up to the men's chests. His eyes rolled to the back of his head as he traveled away from the white room.

He found himself submerged in what seemed to be an

ocean that went on forever. Above the surface came the men's unintelligible voices and their haunting shadows. He floated for a moment before taking a breath into his lungs that caused him to flash back to the white room. The tidal wave now rushed through the doors. It slapped him in the face and sent the table spinning across the room. Just as he was about to crash into a wall, he blinked and left the white room again. Diving back underwater in the ocean, a car plummeted by him into the depths below. A looped scream, which sounded like his parents' voices, spewed from the exhaust pipe, calling out over and over in horror. Once the car disappeared into the darkness below, a new car broke through the surface and repeated the same traumatic plunge. This time, however, there was a glitch—the image not as pure, the whole scene imbued in static. The car froze in place as it swooped by and then rewound a little, receding back to the surface before fast-forwarding at an accelerated pace. Before it disappeared from sight again, another car flew past him and then another, its dramatic impact lessening each time. His parents' screams still spewed from the exhaust pipe, but none of it seemed real anymore, as if the whole scene belonged to someone else's nightmares.

He kicked up to the surface, emerging this time without his mouth frozen in a scream. In the distance, a fisherman's boat tooted its horn and bobbed over. Graham splashed water on his face, but he couldn't feel the water against his skin. It all was make-believe, digitized memories inserted in his skull, an elaborate ruse. He headed in the opposite direction of the boat and hit an imaginary wall. When he turned back around, the boat had vanished, the memory no longer complete, and this time when he woke, he was more awake than ever.

A bucket of water was thrown in his face. He shook the drops out of his eyes, thinking he was still in a dream, but the water dripped down his face and he tasted it in his dry mouth. His head throbbed as if a giant had picked him up and shaken him senseless. He didn't have time to think about what his dreams meant because his hands were tied behind his back and his feet tied to a chair. The bucket got tossed away and then Mick stepped in front of him with a wooden bat.

"When you're out, pal, you are out."

Graham squirmed in his seat, trying to loosen the rope around his wrists, but it was tied too tight.

"Struggling won't do you any good. I was a Boy Scout in another life and those knots are good enough to earn badges."

"What the hell is going on?" Graham shouted. The shouting made his head hurt even more.

"We don't have time to fuck around, so just listen. I need you to tell me what the secret ingredient is."

"Did you drug me?"

"Look, if you fucking tell me, I'll untie you right now. I know you have another commercial to shoot this afternoon."

"You've completely lost your mind."

Mick shook his head and swung the bat into Graham's shin. Graham cried out in agony, his leg throbbing in pain, certain now that Mick meant business.

"Okay...okay, don't hit me again, don't..."

"Are you going to talk?"

"I...have no idea what the secret ingredient is."

"Bullshit, you're Pow!s little golden child right now. There's no way–"

"Moods! They're using Moods. When you mix them with carbonation–"

"Everybody fucking knows that. They've reengineered the Moods that were on the market years ago and added them to the sodas. Haven't you seen your print ads yet? But that ain't the secret. There's one more ingredient that's been kept hush-hush."

"I don't know," Graham cried, getting really nervous now. "I swear I would tell you. Because I don't give a damn and, I don't want to get hit again."

Mick raised the bat. Graham squinted his eyes, trying to shut out the inevitable beating about to occur.

"Are you lying to me?" Mick asked, bending down until his face was at level with Graham's.

"I've known you for ten years, Mick," Graham said. "I've never lied to you. No one has told me anything. I shoot the fucking commercials, that's it."

A gloved cellular hanging from a mannequin hand on the wall started ringing. Mick slid it on.

"Hello...Yes, I still have him here...No... He says he doesn't know...I'm not sure...Yes, I think twenty-four hours is fair... Understood... Good-bye."

Mick removed the gloved cellular and balled it up, tossing it on the floor. It reformed into the shape of a hand.

"Twenty-four hours to do what?" Graham asked.

"Fuck," Mick said, shaking his head. "You need to find out that secret ingredient."

"Or what, you'll kill me?" Graham said, half-joking, but an eerie chill spilled down his spine when Mick nodded solemnly. "Mick?"

"This is serious," Mick said solemnly.

"Is the Man making you do this?" Graham asked. "That doesn't make any sense. Look, I promised the Man I wouldn't be any trouble. I'm planning on doing everything he wants me–"

"It isn't the Man. Just understand that who I'm working for means business. Knowing them, they've already started the countdown on your twenty-four hours."

"What if I told the Man what's going on? I can't see he'd be pleased I'm being threatened like this. He needs me for the commercials."

"That's where you are wrong. You're disposable because the product advertises itself. Your face is the least important part of the equation. It was easier for the company to throw you a bone rather than risk you blab about how Pow! played with your mind. I wondered why they didn't just kill you."

"How would you know whether I'm disposable or not if they didn't even tell you they wanted to make me into the face of the campaign?"

"I did know, Graham, and honestly, you're only wasting time right now."

As Mick's words sunk in, Graham felt his thirst for a Pow! grow, but he tried not to lose focus. He scanned his mind for anything that could help him.

"The Man will see your employers killing me," Graham said, hopeful for a moment. "He'll come after them. He'll find out who they are."

"They'll find you in places the cameras aren't looking. They have their ways."

Graham winced as he tried to formulate another plan. In the midst of angry tears, a smile broke out across his face.

"I'll give you up then, Mick. Whether or not the Man gives a shit about me, you know he doesn't like insubordination. You'll be shipped to the Zones."

"I'll be gone."

"What do you mean gone? Gone where?"

"My job was to deliver you this message. There's a boat waiting at the Wharf for me once this is accomplished."

"You can leave?"

"I wouldn't have done it for anything less."

"You get to leave here?" Graham repeated, in disbelief.

"I'm sorry, bud. You would've done the same thing given the chance."

"No, I wouldn't."

"There are a few key moments in life, Graham. Isn't that what we were told when the Scouts brought us here? Well, I was given a four-leaf clover the day I found out I had a chance to get off this fucking rock in the middle of hell. I'm seizing my opportunity, and trust me, I will not be looking back."

He showed Graham a different gloved cellular.

"There is a direct line on this that leads to my employers. When you find out the secret, just push one and they will tell you where to meet them."

He stuffed the glove in Graham's front pocket, then reached into his own and pulled out a white pill.

"What's that?"

"One-hour Dozers. Can't untie you and risk that you'll attack me."

Graham clamped his mouth shut. Mick shrugged and

pried his mouth open. Graham gagged as the pill was shoved down his throat. Mick held Graham's head back. He tried to resist but couldn't. The pill slowly scraped down, and the room became hazy.

"I'm sorry," Mick said. "I am."

Graham woke up in his apartment with a start. It was mid-afternoon and the Dozer had knocked him out for an hour like Mick promised. His shin hurt badly, and he was thirsting for a Pow!, filled with delirium tremors: shaking, shivering, sweating. He could use a blue-raspberry and then crawl into the shower and cry until he wouldn't be able to feel anything anymore. Life had changed too quickly for him to cope. Even though a Pow! was the last thing he knew he should have, it'd be the best way to deal with this awful reality he'd been thrust into.

He limped to the fridge, but when he opened it there were no Pow!s on any of the shelves. He limped over to the dining room table to check if he'd placed a carton under there, but it was vacant too. The last of the old shipment of Pow!s had been finished. He was forced to sip from empty cans scattered around the apartment, hoping for some swill at the bottom to dictate his emotions while the clock ticked down to his demise.

He stared at a Rorschach painting trying to search the giant ink stain for some sign of what to do, his mind so clogged he could barely think. His gums thirsted for the sweet sizzle. He took a deep breath as the painting began to speak to him. The huge ink stain began taking shape. The body of a girl appearing. She had hair down to her shoulders and smiled so wide, calling out to him. The ink stain was no longer black in this dreamy haze but orange. A beautiful dress wrapped around her tan body. Her lips now puckered for a kiss. She reached out a hand for him to join her in this Rorschach world where anything was possible.

"Marlena," he said, as the empty Pow! cans he held fell to the floor. He was no longer worried about death anymore, or becoming a star here, or the fact that Mick could leave. He only wanted to find Marlena because maybe they would figure out a solution to all this madness; or at least, he could say good-bye. She was the only thing in this City that had ever felt real. The only thing actually worth living for.

With that thought, he bolted out of the door, his legs moving independently, sprinting toward Warton, Mind & Donovan. But he worried that by the time he got there, she'd already be long gone.

The elevator opened on the 31st floor as Graham burst toward the front desk like the tidal wave from his dreams. At the desk, a fresh, young intern filed her nails. Tan and pretty, but inferior to Marlena. Her eyes were in perfect proportion to her face, unlike Marlena's: nothing unique about her.

"Can I help you?" she asked, sweetly. Only a recent Selected could still have that kind of ignorant hopefulness in their voice.

"I'm looking for Marlena!" he said, talking fast. "Marlena Havanderson! Do you know her? She's an intern here. She works this desk. She was wearing an orange suit last."

He was panting so hard, the girl got scared.

"I work this desk now," the girl said, still acting sweet but with a drop more of forcefulness in her tone, as if she was trying to establish her place in this company already.

"Had she been moved? Why don't you know the answer?"

The girl glanced at the cameras below. She put on a pageant grin and shrugged her shoulders.

"Check her name in the computer," he demanded.

The girl pushed a button and an imbedded computer emerged from the desk. She typed in the name and then shrugged her shoulders again.

"There's no record of her."

"Check again!"

"Sir, she's not in the computer–"

Graham slammed his fist against the imbedded computer, which caused the girl to let out one solitary yelp. He heard the cameras zooming in from below. Running his fingers through his hair caused a few clumps to come out. He jetted off, unsure where he was headed, afraid that he was about lose control and do something terrible again as a result.

6

Graham flew into E's office wiping a string of drool from his lips. The need for a Pow! had once again overtaken all thoughts. He tried to keep Marlena on the forefront of his mind, but she kept receding until all he visualized was a Rorschach blob in the shape of Pow! can. He pictured himself cracking it open and taking a long, sugary sip.

"What's going on, kid?" E asked concerned. His hands were already motioning for Graham to calm down.

"Where is she?" he asked, squeezing his fists.

"Who are you talking about?"

"Marlena Havanderson. I need to see her."

"You've got a commercial to shoot in about an hour."

E held out a bowl. "Prune?"

"Nothing else matters," Graham yelled, swatting away the bowl.

E held his palms up again.

"Your commercial does matter. You matter. You're very important here, Graham. The new sodas are being shipped today, and your commercial will be airing during Yiyi Yiagi's latest film on Channel P. It's going to be the biggest audience Pow! has had so far."

"At least tell me where she is."

E picked up a rogue prune that had fallen to the floor.

"She was too much of a distraction for you," he finally said.

"What did you do to her?"

"I...didn't do anything, kid, so don't start pointing fingers my way. There is a lot riding on your commercials, and the Man can't have you losing focus for the time being."

"What does it look like is happening right now?"

"You have to learn to put things out of your mind, Graham–"

"I will never put her out of my mind. She is all that matters!"

Graham pictured the Rorschach blob again, but it was no longer a Pow! can. It had morphed into her. He took a breath and looked straight at E. "I love her. I need to find her."

"Love doesn't exist here," E said, shaking his head at the thought.

"Then what's the point of this place? What are we

living for here?"

E was about to open his mouth to tell him; nothing came out. His face scrunched and he appeared older than he ever had. Graham guessed why someone like him came here. He'd probably hurt someone he loved in the Outside World, now paying the consequences in this purgatory.

"Is she dead? Or in the Zones? Please tell me," Graham begged, trying to appeal to E again as a human. They both acted like humans to one another once before. Maybe they could find that commonality again.

"I can't," E sighed, and lowered his head.

"You're weak, just like everyone else here. One after the other just uses me to do their bidding."

"I'd be careful what you say," E muttered, eyeing the cameras nervously.

"Or what, you'll have me killed? Is that all I have to fear? Well, how about staying alive here and rotting without anyone who gives a shit about me. You tell me what's worse."

The door to the office flung open as Gayle entered. Graham watched E's Adam's apple bob up and down as he struggled to swallow the rest of the prune. A loud gulp echoed through the room. Gayle caught E's eye, trying to read the situation. E nodded as if everything was all right, as if he hadn't had a revelation about his purposeless existence.

"I have been looking for you, mister," Gayle said, plastering on a wide grin and taking Graham by the arm. "We have a commercial to shoot."

As much as he didn't want to follow Gayle, causing an uproar would be foolish. They would physically stop him from trying to find Marlena by any means. He had to be smart if he was planning any deceit. For now, his words had affected E and that would have to be enough. His voice had never had an impact like that before. He was a mute in this City, but now he spoke the truth. A rush of adrenaline coursed through his body, a pure emotion, not chemically produced, not at the whim of fizz. E's sullen face was enough to give him hope. He could have a voice here for those who were too scared to use their own. As the clock to his demise continued to tick down, he no longer had anything to lose.

He closed his eyes for a moment with Gayle on his arm, leading him away, imagining she was Marlena again. He wanted to burst away from their chains and scour The City until it revealed Marlena, but it would have to wait. Even if he found her, they'd just make sure she became lost again. The only way to assure her safety would be to end The City's entire ruse. To take control back. He remembered when he first met Marlena during her entrance interview. She had said that a 'man's mind, once stretched by a new idea, never regains its original dimensions'. And also, that 'advertising was the best forum to spread your ideas as messages and make people feel like they need your words, that it gives them the comfort they're searching for.' He could be that comfort for the citizens. He could find it inside of him to start a revolution, especially if he had her at his side.

The power of advertising saving them all instead of being used for manipulation.

Graham found himself speeding to the Dynasty Region in a private car with Gayle. He could see the back of the driver's head, but the chauffer's cap was pulled too low over his eyes to make out the driver's face. A heavy snow had been switched on like the Man enjoyed doing at times, assaulting their windows and covering The City in a white shroud. Gayle spoke about the new commercial, but he wasn't listening, stuck in the center of two warring factions: the Man and his desire for a City full of controlled citizens, and Mick's new employers who wanted Pow!'s influence for their own gain. This commercial shoot was his only chance to expose Pow! to The City. He needed to make clear how it'd be the citizens' last chance to stand up to the Man and whoever else wanted to constrain them before they turned into soda junkie zombies. He had no idea how he'd get this message across and if anyone would actually listen. The only other people apt to follow him would also have to be so desperate they'd have nothing to lose.

"Are you following what I'm saying?" Gayle asked, as he came back down from his lofty fantasies to her scowls.

"Yes, I got it," he said, turning toward the white streets.

Gayle frowned and pushed a button by her armrest that opened a small refrigerator by her feet. She pulled out a can of orange Pow!. He glanced away from the whiteness, the shiny orange can catching his eye. Its new design had been implemented with an orange question mark and the word *Secret* wrapping around the can.

"Maybe you could use a drink?" she said. "These are the new prototypes that will be sent out to the public tomorrow. Demand has already reached a fever pitch."

The can glistened in the dim light of the car. He sat on his hands that were dying to grab what he'd missed since yesterday, but he had to be strong. This was the first time in over a week that he'd be in charge of his own emotions.

"You don't want it?" she asked, offended.

"Is this all really worth it to you?" he asked her.

She was caught off guard, cocking her head to one side as if she didn't understand.

"Take it, Graham. You might as well start prepping for the orange shoot."

"Why do we just keep *taking* it?" he asked, raising his voice.

"Graham, lower your voice."

She pushed another button on her armrest and a dark partition went up between them and the driver.

"Do you remember who you were before you came here?" he asked, thinking back to the chronic dream of his parents' death. He didn't even know if it was real anymore, if anything he'd ever experienced before he got here was real or just fabricated.

"Graham, we don't have time to get into this–"

"I don't really know who you are. I don't even think you know who you are anymore."

"You know exactly who I am," she said, sliding closer to him, running the cold can up and down his leg. "We fit together, Graham."

"You'd fit with anyone who treats you as bad as you do to yourself."

Her mouth dropped open, as if exhaling a dark cloud.

"And I don't fit with you, Gayle. I never did. You tried to seduce me the other night when you knew I really wanted someone else but couldn't be with her."

She plugged her ears. "Enough!"

"I have no time left. I'll be done in a matter of hours,

and you've never been real to me. You've been hanging around just to keep tabs."

She shoved the orange Pow! into his hand. "You need to drink this because you are a nasty son-of-a-bitch when you haven't gotten your fix."

He pushed a button that lowered a side window and flung the can into the blizzard.

"Graham!"

He grabbed her by the shoulders and pressed her into the side of the car. The snowy air whipped her hair around as her teeth chattered loudly.

"What have they done to Marlena?"

"What are you talking about? Who is Marlena?"

"Don't play dumb with me, Gayle."

She winced, trying to weasel out of his grasp. "You're hurting my shoulders."

"You know you're just a slave to the Man and you'll be a slave until you die. Is that what you want from your life? Just to roll over and take it again and again? Tell me why that's worth it?"

She angled her cheek toward the window as the snow got caught in her eyes. "Please, let go." She shivered in his hands.

"Tell me why it's worth it," he said, releasing her.

"My daughter," she admitted, and then pushed a button by her armrest until the side window closed.

He paused, absorbing the information. "You have a daughter? Where is she?"

"Not here."

"What did the Man promise her?"

She let out a laugh, about to break down.

"What didn't he promise? Arms. Legs. She has none,

never had any. Every few years he'd add a limb as a payment for my services..."

"He preyed on those who were weak, Gayle. Me. You. Your daughter. Everyone here."

Gayle covered her face with her hands. He stroked the back of her neck. She rested her head on his leg, still shivering, it seemed, from the exhaustion of keeping up appearances.

"What other choice do we have?" she whispered.

"Please tell me if you know where Marlena is," he insisted, aware it might be his last chance to find out.

"Is she really that important to you?"

"Yes. For the same reason your daughter is important. She's real. And there are few things I've known in my life that were real."

"I'm sorry," she said quietly.

The car traveled past an Empty Zone. With snow blanketing the ground, the land looked untouched except for a few fires with rings of smoke spiraling to the sky. In the midst of this whitewashed void, a figure fought against the elements. Their car had to slow down to push through the piles of snow. Graham moved Gayle aside and pressed his face against the window, rubbing away the frost to get a better look at the figure with an obvious death wish. He could tell it was a man; the snow had piled up to his waist as he twisted through the rising mounds. He wore a torn business suit that had bunched up around his shoulders because of his slim frame. He had broken glasses and a part in his hair just like Graham's. They were practically twins, except this man's hair had turned metallic silver and his face was scarred. He realized it was the same doppelgänger stranger he'd seen many times before on his commute to Warton, Mind & Donovan.

"I know him," Graham said, opening the side door and jumping out as the car rolled slowly through the snow.

"Graham!" Gayle yelled.

Her cries became muted by the deafening snowstorm. The City must have switched on their blizzard setting.

Graham stood up straight as the snow continued to pummel him. The car had stopped in the distance, but Gayle remained inside. He headed toward the stranger he'd seen before on his train ride who'd always looked beaten by The City, but was worse for the wear now. The stranger collapsed into a mound of snow and struggled to get up, each hand missing a few digits. Graham rushed over and grasped this poor soul by the arm.

"Let me help you," Graham said.

It took a moment for the stranger to seem to register what was going on. He looked up with tired eyes, a dead rat in his arms.

"Where are you coming from?" Graham asked. "Where can I take you?"

With forced effort, the stranger managed to nod over to an abandoned warehouse in the distance. Graham threw the stranger's arm around his neck and started to drag him. The snow had wiped out all the surrounding fires. The icy pellets stinging his face made his eyes water. They arrived at a door made out of cardboard with a pair of holes cut out for someone to peer through. The stranger held up the dead rat and the cardboard door swung open.

Most of the windows in the warehouse were broken and filled with cardboard, barely warmer inside than it was outside. A few dozen people shuffled around like zombies, comatose, all of them missing an arm, or fingers, or hopping around on one leg. The few that were cognizant focused on the dead rat in the stranger's hands and licked their lips.

A big, burly man swiped the rat and took it over to the lone fire in the corner about to die.

"This isn't right," Graham said, wandering past a clearly dead woman starting to rot. Without any arms or legs, she was the smallest corpse he'd ever seen. He'd never taken the time to truly imagine the depravity that went on in the Zones. "How long have you been here?"

"Just a day or so," the stranger coughed. "But this would be the first real meal I've had besides the pills they leave for us." He picked up a dirty Sloth from the floor and slipped it into the pocket of his double-breasted suit.

A rancid smell wafted through the air as the rat got cooked over the fire in the corner. The stranger's nose twitched in delight.

"Thank you for helping me," he wheezed. "But I have to be ready when the meat finishes cooking. We must be strong for when the Guards come to take us down below."

"What do you mean? Why are they taking you down below?"

"For the experiments," he said, holding up his hands. Only four fingers remained in total. Wires hung from the stubs where fingers used to be.

"What experiments?"

"Lifelike Limbs," the stranger said, touching an exposed wire.

"You mean the Zones are used as a testing ground? And they're taking your limbs?"

The stranger nodded solemnly.

"A few days ago, I had all my digits, but once I got to

the Zones they started to fall off. It just happens."

Graham looked around at everyone in the Zones, each of them missing some appendage, all with exposed wires sprouting from where a limb once was.

"Why are you all losing your limbs? What's causing that?"

The stranger shrugged as he stuck his hand in his pocket and pulled out a Sloth pill. He went to put it in his mouth.

"Wait!" Graham yelled, swatting the pill out of the man's hand.

The man desperately searched for the pill on the ground, others crowding around him.

"The Sloths could be what's causing you to lose your limbs."

Graham's twin pushed past the others in his way and grabbed the pill off the floor. He popped it in his mouth.

"It's the only nourishment we have besides an occasional rat. What other choice do we have?"

As the stranger walked away, Graham noticed something orange by the far side of the warehouse. It was hard to tell what it was at first, but his gut urged him to investigate. As he stepped closer, he could see that it was a person wearing orange clothes. His heart started beating fast. He picked up his pace, leaping over bodies until he realized who he feared it might be.

Twitching on the ground beneath him lay Marlena. She had on the orange suit he'd last seen her wearing, her face smudged with dirt and blood, her eyes vacant and glazed. In her lap were her arms.

"Marlena!" he called out, his voice echoing through the warehouse. He scooped her up, careful to keep her arms from spilling. He carried her out of the warehouse with a simmering rage inside of him that he'd never experienced before, worse than when he was on too many cherry Pow!s.

Once he stepped outside, the winter winds greeted him like a thousand daggers puncturing his skin. He trudged on, his limbs straining. Gayle's car appeared as a black dot in a sea of white. His knees were about to give out, but he kept going forward. Marlena murmured something, her eyes rolling to the back of her skull. He kissed her bloody cuts and chapped lips. The taste of death was present on her, but he made sure to say that everything would be okay. He took another slow step, hardly able to hold on.

Just as they reached the car, he collapsed to his knees and lost his grip. As she lay broken in the never-ending snow, he kept whispering that everything would be okay, unsure he even believed those lies anymore. He glanced up at the Eye Tower, hovering like always.

He didn't have it in him to gather Marlena's pieces. He slowly felt himself passing out, his eyes squinting shut. Then, the car door opened and a high heel stepped out into the snow.

"Let me help you," Gayle said, reaching out her hand. He hazily looked up at her. "I'm real, too, Graham," she said, as if she was reiterating those words to herself.

Behind her, the Eye Tower became blocked from his line of sight. She took his hand and pulled him to his feet.

7

"I'm thirsty," Marlena said. Her skin tone had lost its luster, now washed out and pale like the surrounding snow-drenched Cityscape. Her head rested in Graham's lap; her feet dangled off the edge of the seat. Next to him lay her separated arms, folded together as if in prayer. She ran a coarse tongue over her dried lips and pleaded again to be quenched.

Gayle sat across from them as the car crawled through mounds of emerging snow. She radiated jealousy. Graham knew it wasn't because she actually wanted to be with him, but he imagined it was because of the connection that he and Marlena had, something she might never have again.

"There's one more Pow! in the mini-bar," Gayle said.

He glared at her in disbelief.

"She's dehydrated, Graham. She probably hasn't had anything to drink since she got to the Zones."

Gayle cracked open the can from the fridge.

"It's just one," she said.

He hesitated and then took the can. Saliva collected at the back of his tongue, as he put the can to Marlena's lips. The bleached world outside assuaged him, as the can became lighter in his hand and he heard Marlena sipping. Once she finished the Pow!, two orange lines dribbled down her chin. Her eyes fluttered open, and her breathing picked up just a bit.

"Here, let me wipe that for you," Graham whispered.

He smeared the back of his hand along her lips and down her chin. The sugary scent enlivened his senses. He raised the back of his hand up to his mouth to take the tiniest lick but stopped himself.

"Are you okay?" he asked Marlena.

She looked over at her separated arms.

"I never wanted you to see me this way," she said.

"Tell me how to put them back on."

He picked up her arms, holding them out and causing her to blush.

"Marlena, you're beautiful–"

"I'm a hideous creature."

"I don't see that at all. I only see you."

She managed a tiny smile.

"The arms have sockets," she said. "Just line up the sensors in my shoulder with them. It works like a plug."

He touched the sensors that dangled from her

shoulders like pink fingers. She shuddered from his touch, the area ultra-sensitive. He lined up both mechanical arms until they locked in place.

"Thank you for doing that," she said.

"Always."

He leaned down and kissed her, getting a rush from the taste of her orange lips. She caressed his cheek with her robotic fingers.

"Can you sit up?"

Marlena nodded and slowly righted herself.

"My daughter doesn't have any arms either...or legs," Gayle said, as if she was only thinking it and didn't mean to say out loud. "Well, she has one arm and one leg now."

"Is that why you came here?" Marlena asked.

"Ten years ago, I said I would do anything to make her whole again. In the Outside World, children like her are tossed aside. After the War to End All Wars, people have fallen in line with the belief of the current government that her kind don't serve enough of a purpose. Labor is the only means to get Amercyana back on its feet, and no one wants to hire a cripple."

"I understand," Marlena said. "I told myself I'd do anything to be whole again too."

"I'm sorry," Gayle replied, shaking her head. "I knew you had been sent to the Zones. The Man didn't like your relationship with Graham. He gave an order and we–"

"Do you regret coming here for your daughter?" Marlena asked, rubbing the area where her arms had been connected.

Gayle pushed a button that closed the divider between them and the driver.

"I used to be a good person," Gayle said. She then

gnawed at a fingernail and looked at her whittled-down nubs. "I've done bad things, a lot of them...but none of it was selfish; it was all for my little girl. There's still some good in me despite the bad. I repeat that to myself every morning. It's why I marked myself with the tattoos years ago—to remind me."

"Don't you miss your daughter?" Graham asked.

"Not a second goes by that I don't," she said. "But I do it because maybe one day she'll have a shot at a normal life, as normal as anyone could have right now–"

"How do you know the Man will make good with his promise?"

Her eyes grew heavy. She'd clearly asked herself that question before.

"This whole City is an unfulfilled promise," he continued. "That's his game."

"I have to believe his word. Otherwise, all these years have been wasted, and then what was the point?"

"We can take him down," Graham said, passion in his voice for the first time since before he tasted his first Pow! beverage. "People aren't happy here; they're just afraid. They need someone to guide them, but once Pow! has them in its grip, it'll be a lost cause. Their emotions will be controlled and they won't be able to stand up for themselves anymore. Don't you see that's what the Man wants? He's planning something terrible for all of us."

"We shouldn't even be talking like this," Gayle said, with her finger to her lips.

"You didn't see what went on in those Zones. He causes those people to decay and then uses them as experiments for Lifelike Limbs. Who's to say he wouldn't put you there if you did the slightest thing wrong? Who's to say he wouldn't have your daughter brought there just to get back at you?"

Marlena jolted up, her eyes narrowing. "What can we do?" she asked.

"We film the commercial today, Gayle, but you call for a closed set. Say it's an order directly from the Heads; no one will question that. Instead of the normal script, I'll tell the truth about Pow! and the Man's intentions. We'll spread it across the airwaves—we'll show it on hovering ads. The Man won't realize anything is happening until the commercial airs. They're gonna kill me anyway, so why not give it a shot?"

"What are you talking about?" Gayle asked. "Who will kill you?"

"Someone else who wants the secret ingredient in Pow!, probably so they can take control of The City. They said they'll kill me if I don't tell them."

"So, tell them, Graham," Marlena said. "Give them whatever they want."

"I don't know it. They've given me a cellular glove and twenty-four hours to establish contact."

"Oh, Graham," she mumbled, and threw her arms around his neck.

"Our only choice is to start an uprising in The City," Graham continued. "If we all storm the Eye Tower, the Man won't have enough Guards to stop us. We can advertise the right choice for everyone to make."

Gayle turned to the whitewashed streets sweeping by and tugged her lip hard between her teeth.

"I know the secret," she whispered. "Fuck. I do."

Marlena let go of Graham, her eyes wet and fearful.

"You have to tell us. They'll kill him!"

"Hold on," Gayle said. "Everything I've ever done here was for my daughter and if there is the slightest chance that the Man would suspect that I said anything–"

"But the Man doesn't care about you, don't you realize that? After ten years, wouldn't he have already given your daughter all of her limbs if he did?"

"No, this is my last assignment. Graham is my last assignment."

"He'll never let you go, Gayle," Graham said, trying to be sympathetic, reaching across the seats and taking her hand.

"It's in my contract," she insisted.

"But it's *his* contract."

"Tell us," Marlena said, taking her other hand. "You *are* good..."

Gayle stared off again into the whiteness whooshing by, her eyes dizzy and scared. Graham sensed that deep down she knew they were right. She pulled away from them, resting a bloody hand on the frosted window and watching the red streaks blend with the white.

"It's Levels," she said, exhausted, defeated, but with an inkling of a smile.

When they reached the studio, Gayle took charge by ordering people off the set saying that Graham needed minimal interference to create this next commercial. Thankfully, the crew bought her excuse. She had wrapped her bloody hand with a bandage and seemed to be back to her old commanding self.

"Let's do this quick," she said, getting behind a video camera on a tripod after everyone had left.

Graham stared into the red light of the video camera. He had so much he needed to say but the words weren't coming.

"Just let out whatever you're feeling," Marlena said. "People will listen if it's from your heart."

The room grew silent. His hands grew clammy; his throat closing up. Marlena gave an encouraging nod. Once he began, they'd never be able to go back to the way it was. They'd be fugitives.

"Citizens of The City," Graham began while clearing his throat. "You've been duped. The Man had fed you lies ever since you got here and now he wants to control you even more. Every sip of Pow! will take away your ability to feel an honest emotion. You will feel what he wants you to feel. But we can take back this City. Who's to say it isn't ours as much as his? Everything we've done here has been for his benefit. We've blindly followed him because he saved us, or rehabilitated us, or kept us out of prison. Well, this place is a prison anyway and the key was thrown away when you stepped on that boat. But this doesn't have to be. Reject Pow!. Reject the false concept that is being sold to you. You crave Pow! because you were told to crave it. Think for yourself. I know what the secret ingredient is, and we don't have to be slaves anymore. The secret is Levels, the same Levels that have been pushed on us from the black market for the last few years. It was all a way to secretly control us by making us think they are illegal. They promise clarity, but that advertisement is false. This had been the Man's plan for us all along. So if you're questioning your life here, if you live in the Zones and are tired of being experimented on, or if you're just fed up with the Man's lies and deceit, then light a torch, go down to the Pharma Plant by the Wharf, and burn it to the ground. Then let us take out all of the Image Projectors at the borders that keep this City hidden. Let's reveal our horror to the Outside World so we won't have to be imprisoned any longer. Then we'll go after the Eye Tower. We'll cut the Man out of our lives. We will rebuild. We will flourish. We will always remember the history of when we became free. This commercial is probably only going to air once. It will undoubtedly be pulled so spread the word, fight the power, and close that *fucking eye*! Thank you."

Seeing Marlena finally smiling again caused Graham to get choked up. He stepped off the stage to give her a long, slow kiss, glad that her lips no longer tasted like orange Pow!.

Gayle came running over.

"We got it," she said, shutting off the camera and removing the tape. "Now let's get the hell out of here before anyone wises up to what we've done."

A pulsing energy rocked the air when they got back into the car. With the tape in Gayle's hands, they felt powerful. Revolutionary. Like they were about to make a difference here in some way. Graham put his arm around Marlena and held her close. She rubbed his leg. The car started and Gayle raised the divider between them and the driver again.

"All right, this is the plan," she whispered. "Graham, you need to call the people who threatened to kill you and say that you need to meet with them face-to-face. That'll give me enough time to get the commercial on air. I'll go to the control room to make a copy for safe-keeping, and then take it up to the hovering ad machine on the roof."

"Should I have them meet me at Warton, Mind & Donovan then?"

"Yes, that's perfect. The whole place is full of cameras so they won't be able to hurt you."

"What should I say about the tape?"

"We'll use it as leverage. The last thing they'll want is the entire City finding out the secret ingredient at the same time as them. Since the Man has no idea right now what we're planning on doing, he isn't an immediate threat. We'll take care of these threats first and then go after him."

"Okay, I think I'm covered then. I'll tell them that if they kill me, I have someone who will automatically release the tape. They'll have to let me go so I can call it off."

"I should stay in the car," Marlena said. "The Man can't know I've escaped from the Zones."

"That's a good point," Gayle said, rubbing her forehead. "Okay, we'll all give ourselves an hour to take care of everything and then meet back in the car. By then, the commercial should be ready to air and we can drive around and see what the mood of The City is like before we make our next move."

"You can do this, Graham," Marlena told him. "We'll be right here for you."

She rubbed his leg again and he patted her hand. He dialed the glove Mick gave him. A voice came on the other end that sounded like tinfoil crinkling.

"Mr. Weatherend," the voice said, as the hair on the back of his neck stood on end. "We've been waiting for your call."

"I've found out the secret," he said, defiantly.

"Yes, I know you have," the voice crackled. "I was right all along and my colleagues were wrong. One of them bet that you wouldn't come through and the other was undecided, but I knew you would."

"How did you know that I found out?" Graham yelled, confused by this turn of events.

"No need to be so brash, Mr. Weatherend. You might not realize it, but we are not the enemy here."

"I need to trust that you won't still come after me."

"Well, certainly, Mr. Weatherend. We are men of our word."

"You are also men who threatened to kill me."

"Touché."

"I want to meet you in person to tell you," Graham said, trying to keep the upper hand. "To see you face-to-face so I can be sure you're being truthful. We can meet at Warton, Mind & Donovan. It's where I work–"

"What a coincidence; I was about to suggest the same location. Come to E's office."

"E? Are you working with him?"

"Is that fuck in on this?" Gayle said, under her breath.

"Mr. Weatherend, like your friend Mick McKillroy told you, who we are and who we work with should not be your primary concern."

"I need to know," Graham said. "Tell me if E is calling the shots."

"E has nothing to do with us. Currently, he is out at a meeting and therefore his office is vacant."

"How do you know where he is?"

"We can see where everyone is, Mr. Weatherend."

Graham's stomach turned. He squeezed his gloved

hand into a fist and almost hung up on the voice.

"What do you mean you can see everyone?"

"We are truly the eyes in this City," the voice said, rising higher in pitch until it faded into a squeaky laughter. "Right now, we see you very clearly. You are in a black car with your co-worker Gayle Hanley and your former co-worker Marlena Havanderson. Around you the snow is lightly falling. You've just left the Dynasty Region."

"You can see all that?" Graham asked. His eyes caught Marlena and Gayle, who both seemed worried.

"Like I said," the voice crinkled. "We can see all. Don't look so perplexed, Mr. Weatherend. Close your mouth before you let flies in."

Graham closed his mouth and searched the car for any signs of cameras.

"E has a bathroom in his office," the voice continued. "Meet us there in exactly half an hour. And since we can see all, we saw when your co-worker Ms. Hanley revealed the secret ingredient and we also know about the little tape you've created as well. We have larger plans that we want to clue you in on, but we hope you don't plan on playing games with us. We hope there are no other surprises flitting around inside of your head that we were unable to see. Half an hour, Mr. Weatherend. Till then."

The voice clicked off and the dial tone rang in his ear. He crumpled the cellular glove and stuffed it in his pocket.

"The people on the gloved cell are watching us," Graham said. "They know about the tape. They heard you tell me what the secret is."

"There are cameras in this car?" Gayle asked, looking around nervously.

"These people seem to be on our side, though, at least

more than the Man. They could be lying, but since we have nothing else to go on, we have no other choice."

He gave this speech as if he truly meant what he said. Even Gayle and Marlena appeared to believe it, so he could be certain his watchers bought the lies too. But he didn't trust them for anything. The only people he trusted were sitting in the car with him now; everyone else was expendable. He nodded reassuringly at Gayle and Marlena, but his insides were a mess. These people's threats would pale in comparison to the Man, who was bound to release a fury unlike anything ever seen once the tape aired—Graham sure to be his direct target.

The car hurtled through the snow-blanketed streets as he tried to catch his breath and prepare for the war about to begin.

8

E's office was unlocked. The lights were all off. Graham flicked them on, shocked by the bust of Stalin's head on E's desk. He imagined what must have gone through people's minds back in the day when they saw the dictator's salute before they were sent to their deaths. The Man was no different; from purging citizens to the Empty Zones, similar to Stalin's Terror where people were sent into forced labor, to Stalin's crippling paranoia and rule by terror with a totalitarian grip in order to eliminate anyone who might oppose him. This, along with having citizens spy on one another, the Great Purge issued by the Elders, and finally, even the desire for a half man hybrid like Stalin's ape-man capable of great strength, with his own multitude of limbs.

A flush of anger raced through Graham. He knocked the bust to the ground and headed into the bathroom. Inside, he saw writing on the hand towel dispenser that said RIP ME. He yanked a few towel squares as the wall to his left opened to reveal a dimly lit elevator.

"...the fuck?"

He stepped inside the elevator and glanced up just in time to see a spider crawl across the ceiling. Only one button existed, and it went to the 81st floor. He pushed it and the elevator whooshed up, making his ears pop. It opened onto a long metallic hallway. Outside he heard the echo of his feet against the metal floor. At the end, a ladder led up to an opening in the ceiling. He climbed it and hoisted himself through the opening onto another flat metallic surface.

He stood up in a large room. There were no windows; the room entirely made up of television screens showing thousands of images of the company. Every single worker accounted for, every nook in every office filmed. In the center of the room were three men. None of the men had any arms or legs. The ends of their suits were pinned over their stubs. They were propped up in seats that resembled high chairs with placards depicting their names: Warton, Mind, and Donovan. In front of each of them was a large silver box with a ton of metallic straws popping out of their respective boxes. The man in the middle with the placard 'Mind' blew into one of the straws. A camera zoomed in on Graham's face, causing him to appear on all of the television screens.

"I see you've found our abode, Mr. Weatherend," Mind said, in a voice that resembled the one Graham had spoken to earlier on the gloved cellular, raspy and high-pitched.

"You're the voice on the glove?" Graham said.

Each of them looked at the other and managed a silent laugh.

"It would appear so," Mind said. Despite his chubby baby face and an unfortunate comb-over, he exuded an authoritative presence over the other two who seemed to look toward him in awe.

"This room is a base for all the cameras in The City?" Graham asked, peering into the lens of a camera. The screens all showed a close-up of his face.

"We seem to have misled you," Mind said. "We only see everything related to this company. Therefore, we saw what went on in the company's private car."

"Does the Man know I'm here right now?" Graham asked, eyeing a camera in the corner of the room.

"More than likely, no," Mind said, raising an eyebrow. "The Man may think he sees everything that goes on in this City, but that is impossible. In terms of our corporation, the Man believes that we will tell him what he needs to see; however, we keep much hidden."

"Did he promise you limbs too? Is that what brought you all here?"

The three men eyed one another. Warton and Donovan indicated for Mind to continue.

"Many years ago, a group of us Heads began this City with the Man, each of us running a major corporation: the advertising firms, the financial institutions. We had the utmost belief that our City would become a dream world, a place for people to begin anew, but that did not fit into the Man's ultimate vision. He wanted to become a dictator to a land of pawns. He set us up in this tower without a way to ever escape, just like all the other Heads. Kellner and Woods, who ran the other advertising agency in the City, were the last of the originals besides us."

They all glanced down at their missing appendages.

"The Man removed all of our limbs like the sick sadist he is, and his scientists shaped them onto his own wretched body. He believed that we owed him for giving us everything, even spoiling us compared to others in The City. He's gotten us the finest foods, those with mechanical limbs to pleasure us. We are trusted with having ultimate control over our company. We blow on a straw and can lock any door, or turn on any light, or watch the drama of all the employees' lives unfold. After all this time, we know you better than you know yourself."

"And you're fine living like this?"

"We were. We took our lumps and knew we had no other choice. Where could we go? We were trapped."

"How come your colleagues don't speak?"

Warton and Donovan opened their mouths to reveal that their tongues had been cut out.

"Unfortunately, my colleagues did, and the Man did not like what they had to say. E is now the consigliore between us. That is why his bathroom leads to our chambers. We have accepted this life for quite some time, but no more. The *City Gazette* stated that Kellner and Woods flung themselves off their own tower, but we know better. The Man got rid of them just like the other Heads, and unless we act smart, he will eventually get rid of us too, for things are about to change in this City. The Man had a plan we feel he will soon enact. One day, your co-worker Mr. McKillroy was snooping around in E's office and we saw an opportunity. We opened the elevator in the bathroom, waited for him to show up, and made him an offer."

"Do you want the secret ingredient so you can have the power in this City?" Graham asked. "Cut the Man out of the equation and take charge?"

"Look at us, Mr. Weatherend. We are old and feeble creatures. We do not even desire limbs anymore, like so many others who have come to this place. We only want to see our vision for this City come into fruition, one that has been tarnished by a psychopath. We applaud that you've made a tape to broadcast to the citizens."

"Why did you threaten to kill me then?"

"Yes, we regretfully apologize for that. We thought scaring you was the best option to light a fire."

"Why now? Why haven't you tried to stand up to him anytime before?"

"It used to be that everyone was oppressed here, but at least our emotions were our own, not dictated by a beverage. We're headed for even darker times once Pow! becomes widespread."

"The tape is about to go on air." Graham told them. "What do you think the Man's going to do once he sees it?"

Mind blew into a straw and the television screens switched over from a close-up of Graham's face to Gayle making a copy of the tape in the control room. He stretched his lips into a smile and the others followed suit.

"We chose you for a reason, Mr. Weatherend, besides the fact that we thought, or I should say *I* thought that you'd come through with the secret."

"Why was that?"

"The Man needs to be ruined. The only one who could do something so difficult is someone who had been dreadfully wronged by him all of these years, who'd be angry enough to do whatever was necessary to take him down. He has been destroying you since you were a little boy."

"What do you mean?" Graham asked. The room became small as if he was looking at it through the wrong side of a pair of binoculars.

"The Man killed your parents, Mr. Weatherend, not you."

Graham heard this tiny being say those words, but the meaning of the words did not compute. He felt faint; his forehead broke out in sweat and his legs trembled before he collapsed to the floor and everything went dark. He waited to get pulled under by the tide from his dreams, but it never came. In the darkness, a television screen turned on with the image of his parents' car plunging into the ocean. Again and again that image replayed, but he saw now he was never there. Nor were they. The screams he'd heard throughout his life were never theirs either. The sensation of drowning he'd never experienced; his defining moment in life . . . just a ruse. He opened his eyes to the three men hovering over him in their high chairs. He tasted his saliva to see if he'd been drugged again, but he couldn't taste anything abnormal.

He winced from a sharp pain in his ear.

"What happened?"

"We removed the implanted chip. You won't be bothered by those false memories any longer," Mind said.

A pair of robot hands tossed a bloody chip into a chute.

Mind blew into another straw that caused two other

robotic hands to emerge from the floor with a wet facecloth.

"What do you mean?" Graham asked, as a facecloth rubbed across his forehead.

"Here, sit up, Mr. Weatherend," Mind said, as a different pair of robot hands shot over and propped him up.

"When you were a boy, the Man had the Elders kidnap you one night when you were still living in the Middle Territories and plant a chip in your brain with the memory of your parents dying. He wanted to destroy you emotionally."

"It was all a lie?" Graham murmured. "Were my parents a lie, too?"

"No, no, Mr. Weatherend," Mind said. He blew into another straw and the robot hands rubbed Graham's shoulder. "You see, Max and Lana, your parents, were the only ones who had ever escaped from this City. The Man did not like that in the least." Mind blew into another straw; a television to his right showed a picture of a young man and woman. "He used the Scouts Division to locate them so he could kill them. Then he planned to make you pay for their treachery simply because you were their spawn."

Graham looked at the youthful faces of his parents on the screen, who he hardly recognized. His mother and her long hair with a part down the middle and his dad with sideburns licking at his cheeks.

"Your parents started an uprising against him. While it didn't destroy the Man, it was the first time that anyone went against him, and that pissed him off. After that, he trusted no one. He went berserk. Anyone who spoke against him was killed. We watched The City we founded disintegrate, but we couldn't wrap our minds around the fact that he'd steer us wrong. There had to be an ultimate vision for all of this destruction. We thought your parents just couldn't see that, that they were blind. Everything we had ever learned up until then was that the Man had to be followed above all else."

He shook his head, as if in regret. Warton and Donovan did the same.

"Who told you to do that?" Graham asked, trying to process all this information. "Who brought you here?"

"We were employed by a privately funded organization called the Management. The Man ultimately had another Man above him, just like it always is. We believe now that the Man had been ordered to turn this City into the cesspool that it's become. This rotting place was the vision of another evil being who's even more powerful than him. This had to be so because if the Man simply got drunk with power, why would we still be left in this hell? Why had no one at the Management stepped in to correct this travesty that the Man is responsible for? This is because their vision was never for a utopia. Like you, Mr. Weatherend, we all had been duped, too."

Tears spilled from Mind's eyes. He toppled over in his highchair, distraught. Warton and Donovan blew into their straws and a pair of robot hands descended from the ceiling and propped him up again. A tissue floated down that the robot hands used to wipe his eyes.

"Thank you, friends," Mind said, to Warton and Donovan. "Over the years, we've had to become each other's hands."

Warton and Donovan nodded.

"You see, Mr. Weatherend, eleven of us were the elite in the Management's class and were to become the Heads of a new City, but no one was greater than the Man."

He blew into a straw as the image of Max and Lana switched to a picture of a young boy with one grotesquely long arm.

"We know little about his origin except that he was born unnamed and blind in Russia. After being left on the streets by his unknown parents as a child because of his mutant-like features, the Man caught the eye of the Management when he fended off a few thieves who had attacked him."

The image on the screen changed to three dead bodies massacred beyond recognition.

"He had even scooped out their eyes and left them on the side of the road."

Mind blew into another straw as the image zoomed in to depict a horrified crowd pointing at a row of eyes.

"The Management knew they had discovered a machine they could mold."

On the television, a younger version of the Man appeared. He was still thin and wiry, but without his many appendages, just one magnificently long arm. His face was blurry due to the lighting of the shot, but his head at least had substance, unlike the hollow shell of his current form.

"Despite his deformity, the Man always excelled a few percentage units above the rest of the elite. For as long as we could remember, the Management had already decided that once The City they were building was ready, the Man would be the one to lead us. All decisions would be decided between the Heads, but he'd have the final say. This had been drummed into our heads since we were children, so we got used to blindly following anything he said. We all loved him, or wanted to be his best friend, or wanted him to tell us he was proud of our accomplishments.

"For a while, it seemed as if The City was turning into the vision that the Management had predicted, a place that would welcome those who needed a fresh start, and we were ready to spread our uplifting message to the rest of the world. Our Selecteds had done some things in life that they regretted, but we'd turn them around. We put them to work so they could feel good about themselves. That was why we had been in training our whole lives.

"But soon, we saw that the Man had other plans. The work the people did never seemed to be enough. Once we got to The City, he became our only link to the Management. He repeatedly told us how upset they were, that the Sponsors investing in The City weren't satisfied with the output. The idea of Rehabilitation seemed to fall at the feet of capitalism, but we still wholeheartedly believed in what we were doing and pushed our Selecteds as much as we possibly could. Then Moods came on the market and people got addicted so the Man created the Empty Zones to ferret out those who were not contributing to The City's growth. Paranoia grew rampant, but we rationalized that the citizens should be working more, that we needed to make the Sponsors happy. All of our lives we were told of how important the Sponsors of The City were. They were ones investing millions in this idea of Rehabilitation, and if our City wasn't in the black, then we had failed as a collective institution. We didn't want to fail! So, we followed the Man into the depths of what humans were capable of. But not your parents."

Mind paused to take a deep breath and then continued.

"They had been his second and third in command, and I guess that allowed them to see his deplorable actions even more closely. They warned the other Heads, but we wouldn't listen. We were too afraid to think we had been manipulated. So, Max and Lana defected. They found support within the Empty Zones from those who had been discarded and were ready to stand up against the thumb that squashed them. They fought hard. They took out a lot of the Man's Guards, who to this day he's still trying to replace. They showed him that he wasn't as invincible as he thought."

Mind blew into a straw as a video of this uprising came on the screen. The people of the Zones were shown slaughtering Guards, their eyes wild and untamed.

"Unfortunately, they didn't win, but they came close and that was enough to know that the next time they would get him. They'd lay low in the Zones until the threat of their uprising died down and then they'd strike again when the Man least expected it.

"After that, the Man became more delusional than ever. He turned on the rest of the Heads. He took our limbs for his own warped obsessions. He set us up in the towers of his biggest corporations and left us with no choice but follow his lead. We secretly waited for another uprising but it never happened because Lana got pregnant. You became more important than a place like this and so she and Max found a way to escape. To this day I've wondered how they did it, but they were the elite of the elite. He spent years trying to find them until finally they were located on some rural farm out in Iowadana and he personally took them out–"

"Yes, in Iowadana; I remember living there now," Graham said, as the memories came flooding back. "I remember a big farmhouse and a beanbag chair that I'd lay in. I'd watch this huge orange sun set into our cornfields, and then my parents would take me in their hands and swing me on our porch, and..."

"Those were all real memories, Mr. Weatherend."

"I can see them. I can see their faces," Graham said, visualizing himself swinging between them, happier than he ever could remember being.

"The Man had used Pow! to manipulate your mind. He tried to get rid of the girl you love. He's tortured you because of what your parents did. Your life has been his cruelest game."

Anger pulsed from Graham's fingertips until it felt like he couldn't contain it any longer.

"Fuck the Man," Graham shouted, the veins in his neck throbbing, the words echoing off the metallic walls.

"Yes, show some emotion, Mr. Weatherend! Once the Man is able to dictate our feelings, there will be nothing left. The City will be entirely his for whatever he has planned for us next. Your tape is the first step. It's a brilliant idea to force an uprising again, but it's not enough. You need to go up to Eye Tower and kill him face-to face."

"What?" Graham asked, the redness leaving his face as he simmered down. "How can I even get into the Walled Region, let alone the Eye Tower?"

"Over the years we've made contacts throughout The City who we call our Agents. One Agent is the captain of a Scout boat. That was how we were able to promise Mr. McKillroy freedom. Another Agent is a computer whiz who can falsify identification cards. We have a Scout ID to get you into the Eye Tower and then we will have our Agent waiting by the Wharf to grant you freedom. This Agent will be in a boat called *Lemonworld*. All you have to do is take out the Man."

"That's all I'm supposed to do?" Graham asked, a hesitant laugh escaping from his throat.

"His Guards will be focused on policing the citizens once your commercial airs. E keeps a gun in his office. If you unscrew the bust of Stalin on his desk, you'll find it. It should be fully loaded. There will be a few Guards in the Eye Tower that you'll have to contend with, but the Man will have to send most of them out into the streets because there's bound to be chaos."

"And then you'll let me go?"

"We are aware, Mr. Weatherend, that even after the Man has fallen, The City is a long way off from achieving its vision. There is bound to be those that will side with the Man, who will praise him as a martyr, so if you don't want to stick around to deal with this Rehabilitation then we understand. Your life has been sacrificed enough because of his whims, and if you take him out, you more than deserve to be free."

"What about Marlena? I want her to come with me. And Gayle? I want Gayle to be able to return to her daughter."

"Anyone you want, Mr. Weatherend, I'll have their IDs ready for you at the boat. All of our Agents are only a call away."

Mind paused to blow into a straw. Robotic hands emerged from the wall and held out a Scout ID.

"You can do this, Mr. Weatherend. Finish what your

parents started."

The robot hands pinned the ID to Graham's chest.

"My parents," Graham said, as an even stronger rage swelled inside of him. He was out of tears and long past being depressed. He only wanted blood. His cheeks started throbbing as he clenched his fists. An image flashed in his mind of the Man stalking through his parents' cornfields in Iowadana toward their house. From out of a trench coat, one long arm emerged with a shotgun in his hand as the Man broke down their door.

"I'll do it," he said to Warton, Mind, and Donovan, as the gunshots rang in his ears. The three men looked at each other and nodded gratefully. "But that boat better be there."

"Mr. Weatherend, we are men of our word. We have no reason to deceive you."

"I've just always been deceived."

Mind glanced up to the television screens and saw Gayle on the roof readying the hovering ad blimp.

"Go now, Mr. Weatherend. Ms. Hanley is already on the roof. Get the gun from Stalin's bust and head to the Eye Tower. We have faith that our destinies will be so much more than these grim realities. We have faith in you."

Graham heard the echo of the elevator ding from the other end of the metallic hallway. Warton, Mind, and Donovan gave him three supportive smiles but he was aware of a twitch in those smiles after so many years of disappointment. He backed out of the room, climbed through the opening and down the ladder, and held his breath as the elevator zipped him down.

9

Graham repeated the plan in his head as the elevator flew down. All the information he'd learned from Mind was buzzing around but he tried to focus solely on the fact that the Man was responsible for killing his parents and that nothing short of vengeance would suffice. He crammed the fake Scout ID into his pocket and relaxed his shaking hands. When he reached E's bathroom, he stopped for a moment to look in the mirror and convince himself he could do this, that in a few hours he'd be sailing far away from this place.

He left the bathroom after gathering up his courage.

When he stepped into E's office, Stalin's bust lay on the floor with the head cracked open. He heard the sound of a gun being cocked and turned around. By the front door, the driver of their private car had Marlena in a chokehold with the gun to her head.

"Marlena!"

Pure fear reflected in her eyes. She screamed but the driver clamped his liver-spotted hand over her mouth. The movement caused the cap to slip off his head and revealed him to be one of the Elders. This Elder showed no expression on his face, no remorse, his eyes like two dark marbles. He shook his head, warning Graham not to come any closer.

"I'm sorry, Graham," Marlena cried. "He waited until you guys were gone–"

The Elder clamped his hand over her mouth again. She struggled but his grip was too forceful.

"What do you want?" Graham asked, holding up his hands to try and ease the situation.

The Elder nodded at Graham and then indicated toward the Eye Tower out of the window.

"You're taking me to the Man?"

The Elder nodded at Marlena as well.

"What are you going to do to her?"

The Elder ran the gun from one side of his neck to the other.

"She didn't do anything," Graham said, stepping closer. The Elder moved the gun away from Marlena and aimed it at Graham.

"Does the Man know what we're planning?" Graham asked.

The Elder gave a long, slow nod.

"What does he want from me then?"

The Elder pointed the gun at both of Graham's arms and legs.

"My limbs?"

The Elder licked his lips with his old, dry tongue. He then took Marlena by her hair and stuck the gun into the back of her head. She clenched her eyes shut and let out a muffled scream.

"No, no, don't!" Graham cried, closing his eyes. He waited to hear a shot, but instead the door burst open and E entered instead. The entire room froze in place.

"What the fuck is going on here?" E asked.

The Elder stared E down and motioned for him to leave with a flick of his wrist. E took a step back, but then hesitated. The Elder scrunched his face, not pleased.

"None of this matters," Graham said. "The Man is sweating because The City is about to see an uprising. Killing her and dismembering me isn't going to change that."

"What are you talking about?" E asked.

"The commercial I just filmed is about to expose Pow! and all of the Man's deceit."

Fed up, the Elder reached out and whacked Graham on the back of his head and quickly trained the gun on Marlena again. Graham slumped to his knees. The Elder motioned again for E to leave, this time more threateningly.

"The whole City is about to turn on the Man, just watch," Graham continued, feeling a spot of blood on the back of his head and looking up at E. "You better really decide whose side you want to be on."

E rubbed his bloodshot eyes. His face had grown gaunt

and gray since their last interaction, an old man's visage. Graham prayed he'd do the right thing, but E just shook his head, sadly.

"Kid, don't fuck with the Man. Others have tried before. It only makes things worse."

He shrugged his shoulders as if there was nothing else he could do.

"It can't get any worse, don't you see? We've been living for nothing for too long."

The Elder hit Graham on the head again with his gun before pointing it back at Marlena.

"Graham!" Marlena screamed, as Graham fell face first to the floor. His wound expanded and his head became coated with blood.

The Elder snapped his head up like a lizard and warned E with his eyes that if he didn't leave there would be serious consequences. He pressed the gun hard into Marlena's cheek, his thin lips eking out a smile.

"What do you have to show for yourself, E?" Graham said. "If your life ended right here, right now, what would you have to show for it?"

The cameras zoomed in. He pictured Warton, Mind, and Donovan watching all of this play out and biting their fingernails if they had any.

"You're bleeding," E said, reaching out to help but then withdrawing his hand. He lost balance, wobbling around and mumbling over and over how Graham was "bleeding".

"How much blood has been on your hands since you got here?" Graham asked, goading him.

All of a sudden something snapped in E, a twitch in his shoulder. He let out a gasp and ran his fingers through his hair until white tufts spilled to the floor.

"You are bleeding like that the last time I hit you," he said to Graham, his eyes off in another world. He reached out again, as if Graham could pull him back to reality.

"What do you mean?"

"You were just a kid," he said, trembling. "Each night he made me destroy you more and more."

The Elder had his gun on them all, unsure who the target should be.

"And for what?" E asked, his voice barely above a whisper, his head tilted back. He looked toward the ceiling and above for answers, but the only response was the whir of a million cameras. He wiped a sleeve across his eyes. "Fuck, I'm sorry. I'm so sorry."

It took Graham a moment to realize what E was talking about, but then it all came back. Waking up and seeing a dank bedroom through black and blue eyes. Smelling the stench of cigars sizzling in the air. Going to sleep every night on a bloody pillow. He stared at this man who he'd spent his lifetime hating. Somehow, they must have infiltrated his brain and blocked his receptors from recognizing him. In his mind, he leaped at E and dug his thumbs into this monster's eyes until E cried blood. He'd finish what he started when he charged into his office before with a knife. They'd fall back, E wailing as Graham slammed his head into the marble floor for all the cameras to watch. The floor would crack apart, the cameras would stop whirring, and E's head would split open like a coconut leaving Graham to swim in his former boss's blood. That was what he wanted to do every time this man crept into his room as a child. These visions were a part of his dreams every night while sleeping on a wet pillow that smelled from never being washed.

His young, abused self was even yelling at him to attack, to get revenge, but looking at E now, this white-haired man seemed more lost than Graham could ever imagine. Graham's rage started to cool until it was just a tiny ball in his stomach. They'd all been puppets here, and E was never a monster, just too weak to be anything else.

Before Graham could say that he forgave him, E leaped to his feet and rushed at the Elder.

"Fucking kill me. Kill me!"

E grabbed for the gun in a fury.

"Do it!" he screamed. "Put a slug in my brain, you wrinkled raisin. Put me out of my misery!"

He threw his weight onto the Elder as they crashed into the desk. They were both fighting for the gun, hard to tell who had the upper hand. Marlena ran over to help Graham up.

"You son-of-a-bitch, you goddamn–" E yelled, gripping the gun with one hand and grabbing the Elder's throat with the other. The Elder wheezed as his face turned a disturbing red. They fell to the floor as E slammed the Elder's head into the ground while still choking him. A shot went off that caused an imbedded computer on the far wall to explode.

"Where's your twin?" E asked, while still slamming the Elder's head into the ground. "Does he know that you're about to get choked out?"

The Elder gasped as he fought against E's grip. The gun slowly inched toward E's chest.

"Years and years of you fucks scribbling away and tattling to the Man."

He slammed the Elder's head into the floor again. The Elder finally wrestled the gun away and shoved it into E's stomach. He fired.

"AAAARGGGHHHH!" E howled.

Blood spilled from E's guts onto the Elder, but he didn't let up. He choked the Elder even harder as one last shot was fired into his chest.

"Is that all you have?" E roared, his mouth full of blood. He shoved his thumbs into the Elder's throat and choked him until the Elder spit out his last breath of life. The Elder's body flopped around, too weak to fire another shot, his marble eyes receding into his skull.

E rolled off the dead Elder, holding onto his stomach so his guts didn't spill out.

"Oh, fuck me," he said, reaching inside his wounds to feel for the bullets.

"Don't move," Graham said.

Graham went to take off his shirt but E shook his head.

"No, come here, kid, come here."

"You need a tourniquet."

"Kid, sit by me. Just...quick."

Graham knelt down, hesitating but then grasped E's bloody hand. Part of him wanted to shove that hand into E's gaping wound to cause even more pain, but he didn't.

"I deserve to die," E said.

"You saved us," Graham said, the words difficult to get out but true.

"If it's Hell that's waiting for me, so be it." He tilted his head toward the ceiling and cried. "Oh, my bunny, I should've been sent there a long time ago for what I did to you. My bunny, my beautiful sweet girl, broken to pieces on the ground."

He let out a scream from deep inside, a lifetime of haunting regret.

"E, we need to stop your bleeding," Graham said, but E pushed him away.

"Call me, Edmond Edwards. That was my name once."

"Edmond–"

"The bullets are too deep. My guts are on the floor." He indicated to his splattered remains as if no one could tell. "I'm sorry for everything I ever did to you."

"It was the Man–"

"It was me. I had a fucking choice. We all have a fucking choice. Just like you're choosing to stand up against him right now. I've spent my life fucking up other people's lives. The enemy during a long-ago war, my lovely wife at home, using my status here to convince Scout Trainees to sleep with me. And you. Just a kid who'd look up at me wanting nothing but love and I'd respond with a fist."

He coughed up a blob of blood and mucus, his eyes moist with tears. He took Graham's hands.

"Forgive me, forgive me...."

His lips turned blue as he stopped moving. Graham could feel E's cold hands wrapped around his own. He pried them away as if he wanted nothing to do with them anymore. He closed E's eyelids, a final graceful gesture to someone who'd only caused him anguish but saved him when he needed it most. Marlena scooped him up and they hugged out of exhaustion, leaning on each other until their strength returned. Then he picked up the gun and wiped off the blood with his shirt.

"Do you really think we can do this?" Marlena asked. "That we can take the Man down?"

She waited for an answer, but Graham was lost for words. He knew he should nod. Even though he was scared, he should make her feel relieved, if just for a moment, even if it was a lie. He knew that she'd do the same for him, but this was war now, and war was anything but predictable.

"No," he said, looking her dead in the eye.

He stuck the gun in his pants and exited the office. The last thing he needed to worry about was empty promises. After all the empty promises this City gave them, he loved her too much to give her anything less than utmost honesty, however brutal it might be.

When Graham and Marlena reached the street outside, they saw Gayle standing by the car.

"What happened?" Gayle asked, patting the bloodstains on his body in shock.

"You're going to have to take the wheel," he said.

"Is that blood?"

"It's E's blood."

"E is dead?"

"Yeah."

He opened the car door for Marlena and she went inside.

"Oh," Gayle said. She rocked in place, wrapping her arms around her body.

"Did you send out the hovering ad?" Graham asked, but Gayle was still withdrawn and murmuring to herself. "Gayle?"

"Oh? Yes. Yes, I did. I'm just...I've known E for some time now. I don't know how to feel."

Graham massaged her shoulder.

"He died saving us and he apologized for everyone he

hurt."

"Everyone...he hurt?"

"We need to leave because the Man knows about what's going on. Are you okay to drive?"

"Yeah," she said, with the tiniest smile emerging on her lips. "I am."

Gayle jumped behind the wheel as Graham sat in the backseat. Marlena faced a side window, watching the last trickles of snow float down.

"Gayle sent out the hovering ad," he said, inching closer to Marlena, but she was distant. "Did you hear me?"

She nodded with a quivering lip, her head angled so she didn't have to look at him.

"Marlena, did you hear me?"

She didn't respond.

"Is this because I said I didn't think we'd be able to defeat the Man?" he asked. He went to take her hand but she slid it away.

"Marlena, look at me."

She licked away a solitary tear and turned to him.

"I don't want to give you false hope," he said.

"It's better than none."

"That's not true. My whole life has been based on lies. I want to always be one hundred percent truthful with the person I care about the most."

He kissed her robotic shoulder and ran his lips up to her cheek.

"They promised me a boat," he said.

"Who?"

"Warton, Mind, and Donovan. They were the people on the cellular glove. If we take down the Man, we can leave, all three of us. Did you hear that, Gayle?"

He caught Gayle's eyes in the rear-view mirror.

"And we can go anywhere—Marlena, me and you. Back to your hometown in Floraldala if you want, somewhere warm. I'd like somewhere warm, but I know anywhere will be warm if you're there with me. Will you go wherever with me? That is...if we're victorious?"

He felt her nod against him and the tears staining her cheek. He kissed her lips and tasted her breath. Her tongue sweet and probing, her breath revitalizing. If she could believe in him, it was about time he started truly believing in himself.

The small television in the backseat emerged from the floor.

"The commercial should be coming on Channel P," Gayle called out, wiping away her tears and getting back to the business at hand. "Yiyi Yiagi's new film is about to end, and I guarantee most of The City will be watching."

Gayle pushed a few buttons and an image appeared on the television. A distraught Yiyi sat upright in an ornate bed, the room she was in inside a golden palace. She held red dragon sheets up to her neck. An Asian businessman crawled on top of the bed in a pinstripe suit.

"I'm glad I had a hankering for water chestnuts that day at your restaurant, or I never would have met an angel like you," the businessman said.

The camera panned to Yiyi's face as her lips trembled and her eyes filled with delight.

"Oh, Ryu," she cooed, as she stuck her hand down his pants.

"I thought you no longer sleep with men for money," he said.

"I won't. I sleep with you out of love," she said,

removing the red dragon sheets and revealing her naked body as the credits rolled.

Yiyi's porn faded. In its place, an image of Graham came on the screen as the three of them watched him renounce The City. He appeared forceful but genuine; his message direct and clear. Right at the end, the commercial turned to static. The Man had probably noticed it by now and removed it from the airwaves before it played again.

"Now we wait and see what happens next," Graham said, as their car sped toward the Eye Tower.

10

By the time their car pulled up to the Walled Region, the snow had stopped falling and a teeming rain poured from the sky. The gun was jittery in Graham's hand. He stepped outside of the car and walked through frozen puddles until he reached the Wall. Two cameras zoomed in and poked him in the head. He ran the Scout ID across the sensor and the doors opened.

When he entered, the Walled Region appeared different than he imagined. He had always pictured the area packed with Finances: making deals, talking on their gloves, showing off their power suits; but the Region was vacant. He almost expected to see a tumbleweed roll past his feet. An eerie silence filled in the air as if at any moment someone could pop out with a gun.

The Eye Tower stood so tall that he couldn't see the top. He expected Guards to be policing the Tower but there were none. He waved his Scout ID in front of the sensor at the Tower as the door opened to an elevator. Inside, he pushed a button in the shape of an eye, and the elevator whooshed up. Once in the air, he could see a swarm of citizens heading toward the Pharma Plant in the Factory Region. Behind them were all of the Man's Guards, close behind. He inhaled a deep breath, realizing that his voice had been heard.

The elevator reached the top and the door opened. The front office was empty like the rest of the Region. A long receptionist's desk greeted all who entered but no one sat behind that desk.

The silence in the room made him tense. He wiped a glob of sweat from his top lip. His ear twitched. A slight movement echoed from the other side of the room. He swiveled his gun over, no clue what he'd do if someone was there. He continued on toward a massive eye-shaped door, assuming it was the Man's private office. He was about to run his fake Scout ID across the sensor, but a Guard leaped out from behind an Imbedded computer. Without thinking, Graham fired the gun. The Guard twisted to avoid the bullet, but it hit him and he slumped to the floor. Graham caught his breath as he peered over to see the damage done. A visible bullet hole smoked from the Guard's back. He wouldn't let himself feel any remorse for the life he'd taken. If he didn't react, there'd be a smoking bullet hole in his back instead.

He quickly ran the Scout ID across the sensor and the eye door opened. Immediately the fetid odor of urine knocked him in the face. An array of television screens on the walls depicted the goings-on in all the Regions and the uprising that had started. His eye briefly caught an image of a Guard snapping the neck of a regular citizen, but his attention shifted to the gruesome reality of the Man looming over him. Over a dozen arms sprung from the Man's body like black boughs on a tree; his face hollow and vacant like an apparition. Those many arms were wrapped around a large object he held close to his chest. Graham stepped closer as the Man unwound his arms and revealed the large object to be his receptionist Shelby. He kept one hand over her mouth to keep her from screaming. She resembled an abused doll because of the zipper that he used to replace her eye. Her other eye pulsed in fear.

"Mr. Weatherend," the Man said, as a black circle appeared where his mouth would be.

"Let the lady go," Graham replied, pointing the gun.

"If you come any closer, I will kill her."

Graham took a step and the Man reacted, snapping her neck with a few of his hands. She collapsed headfirst to the floor. Graham fired a bullet into one of the Man's arms. The Man simply dislodged the wounded arm and left it discarded on the ground.

"I can feel pain in my appendages, but it is a manageable pain since it is a replaceable arm. I'd like to see you actually hit my real one."

"Don't be so certain that I won't."

The Man let out a laugh that sounded like he was gargling on glass shards.

"Feisty, Mr. Weathered. You're not the same spineless

sap you used to be."

"A lot has changed."

"Certainly has." The Man gestured out of his window. "You're making a bit of a stink in this City."

"It's long overdue."

"So ungrateful–"

"You fucking killed my parents. You took my life!" Graham yelled, disassociating himself from the words spewing out of his mouth. He'd already left his body and was hovering above. Someone else was handling this situation. Someone far different than he ever thought he could be.

"Oh, that," the Man replied in a coy tone. "Yes, your parents were flies, and I came by with my big can of spray."

"Why did you make me believe that I had killed them...?"

"Will you shoot me if I don't give you all the answers you want? I saw the two shots fired into E, the shot that took out my Guard, and the pathetic one that took one of my arms. You only have two left so you better make them count."

"Don't forget, I got your Guard in just one shot."

"Is that a fact?"

The Man clapped his many hands together, and the formerly dead Guard appeared through the eye door.

"Smoke and mirrors, Mr. Weatherend."

Graham didn't know who to aim the gun at, switching back between the Man and the walking corpse of the Guard at the door.

"You may envision yourself as some kind of a hero—a messiah for everyone who is weak. But there is inherent evil in you, Mr. Weatherend. There is inherent evil in everyone."

"Your Guard would have killed me if I didn't shoot him–"

"What makes your life more worthy than his?"

Graham felt himself getting caught up in the Man's twisted games, his psychological poisons. He responded without a second thought by firing the gun at the Guard. This time the bullet hit the Guard square in the head.

"You just proved my point," the Man said. He laughed a glassy laugh and slid toward the window, his many arms swinging with each step.

"I have created a wonderful City," he said, petting the glass, "from a place full of sinners."

"You've sinned more than anyone else here."

The Man shook his head.

"Mr. Weatherend, I've seen you do some terrible things over these past two weeks that would put you on a similar level as me."

"That was because of Pow!"

"Are you entirely sure about that?"

"What do you have planned with the sodas? You used me as a guinea pig to get back at my parents, I get that, but why do you really want to control all of our emotions?"

"I play many games, Mr. Weatherend," the Man chuckled. "I play my own game, and I play the one that others tell me to play."

"You mean the Management?"

The Man went silent for a moment. He tapped dozens of fingers against the windowpane, his black circle of a mouth turning white again.

"I suppose Mind told you everything he knew, but even

he is very much in the dark."

"Who's behind the Management?" Graham asked.

The Man's face whipped around. The closer it got to Graham, the more the smell of urine filled the air. Graham covered his nose.

"I will tell you, Mr. Weatherend, that I have a job, and I also have someone higher up than me, a great Manager. Someone I fear, but who I wholeheartedly respect."

The Man's face tilted toward the ceiling, and Graham could see a tiny camera blinking in the corner, watching them.

"But make no mistake, this City is my kingdom. There are others who rule other Cities. I based mine on the Stalin-influenced Russia of my long-ago youth and then took those seeds to a grander level. Other Cities are ruled in different ways. We all have a common goal, though. A greater purpose that was decided for us long ago."

"Other Cities?" Graham gasped, his head spinning.

"You didn't think you were special, did you?"

"What does the Management plan to do with these other Cities?"

The Man wagged about fifteen fingers.

"I think I've been forthcoming enough. We all know what curiosity did to the cat."

"Well, I'm the one with the gun in my hand, so I'd say my chances are better than yours."

The Man's dark mouth morphed into as much of a smile as he could muster.

"I am a template for what the Management has planned, Mr. Weatherend."

"What are you talking about?"

"I am a Hybrid. Man and machine fused together,

much like Stalin would have liked. I am far from the only one out there and the plan is to create many, many more. Recently our scientists have discovered that goal can be a reality. We will be the future and someone like you with all of your real parts will be obsolete and inferior. Hence my affinity for all my amputees."

"So what if you can control your mechanical limbs; that doesn't make you superior–"

"Mr. Weatherend, not only can I control my appendages, I possess what will eventually lead toward your future apocalypse. I can crush your entire body with any one of my hands, and my lifespan far exceeds that of a human. Soon, I will be able to survive solely from the nutrients I receive from the new batches of Pow!."

The Man indicated the feeding tube he was attached to full of a fizzy orange liquid.

"You've started an uprising here, but that doesn't matter. All food supplies are about to cease, except for Pow! Soda. My citizens will have no other choice."

"Not if I kill you."

"You are so selfish," the Man hissed. "Mind promised you a boat, didn't he? He promised you off this rock. I saw your entire conversation on camera. There is nothing that I don't see in my City. I could have pulled the commercial just as it aired, but I wanted to show you, Mr. Weatherend, that you are no hero. You have been corrupted just like I always knew you would be. You are leaving behind an entire population to deal with the consequences of your actions. If the Pharma Plant is burned to the ground, we'll build another. And if I'm killed, the Management will just ship someone else over in my place. But worst of all, Mr. Weatherend, if you're lucky enough to leave this City today, your addiction will still follow you to the Outside World."

"I can fight it."

The Man chuckled, his many fingers locking together.

"This plan has been in motion for a very long time. Many years ago, I put Moods out on the market to control the citizens, but there were some snags. Then we put the Levels on the black market and it was a raging success. Practically everyone in The City is addicted, just like they will become addicted to Pow!, even more so. So you see, the thirst had already got you, Mr. Weatherend. It's gotten its hooks in you ever since you pulled up to these shores a decade ago, just like I wanted for a despicable spawn like you."

"You'd say anything to make me lose focus. You've been lying to me my whole life. This could all just be more lies."

Graham held up the gun, aiming it right between where he imagined the Man's eyes to be.

"You think you're aiming at my skull, you fool?" the Man scoffed. "How do you even know that this is my head and not just an illusion? I promise you there is no way for one bullet to kill me because I am all smoke and mirrors, *moy malen'kiy pitomets*." [6]

"I'm not selfish," Graham said, focusing on only that accusation. "I've never been able to really live because of you and I'm finally getting that chance–"

"Everyone is selfish! We come into this world alone and we die alone."

"I couldn't have said it any better."

---

[6] *My little pet*, translated from Russian.

Graham fired the last bullet into the Man's skull. The impact threw the Man back. He crashed through the eye window. The Man's many arms grasped at the air as he plummeted to the ground until he was just a tiny ant struggling for a last gasp of breath on the street below. The rain teemed down, forming a giant puddle around his broken body. His limbs cracked off and were carried toward the drains at the corners. The white face staring back at Graham a hundred stories below stuck in a permanent, dark scream.

Out of the corner of his eye, the red light of the camera flashed in the ceiling. The sound of it zooming closer rung in his ears.

"Fuck off," Graham said, giving the camera the finger.

As he exited through the eye door and headed down the elevator, he tried to forget the ominous future that the Management had planned–Cities full of Hybrids at their disposal for whatever plan they have cooked up. Instead, he envisioned a future with a boat sailing to the Outside World, Marlena on his arm, and a flicker of something real waiting for them beyond the horizon.

He told himself this City was not his responsibility anymore and he owed them nothing.

He repeated this over and over until he could hear the sound of the rocking waves leading them far, far away.

11

The car crawled through a smoky haze along the Wharf. The nearby Factory Region an orange blaze, and they could hear the screams from the uprising even though the windows were rolled up. They pulled up to the boat named *Lemonworld*, its name written in a stylish script with two bright yellow lemons in place of the Os. The captain of the boat waited by the dock, a cap pulled low over his eyes causing his face to be cast in shadows. The captain immediately removed two fake Scout IDs from his pockets and thrusted them at Marlena and Gayle. He then swiveled around and proceeded onto the boat without saying a word.

Graham covered his ears to block the roar of the uprising as he followed the captain inside. If he kept listening, his stubborn conscience would prevent him from getting on board.

"Let's get the hell out of here," Gayle said, marching past him.

The sweep of soot and smoke clouded the air. It was hard to see anything besides Marlena smiling right in front of him. He kissed that smile until it warmed him, until a nagging chill dissipated.

"We did it," he said, but there was a hesitation in his voice. Whether she picked up on it or not, he couldn't tell. She took his hand as they stepped onto the boat together.

The boat was small but had a deck below. The captain already started the motor and was at the bow with his back to them. Gayle had also turned her back on The City, quietly looking out into the distance.

As the boat took off, pockets of his former home were visible because of a few destroyed Image Projectors. Smoldering fires surrounding The City in a halo marred its twinkling colored lights. He could barely make out the Eye Tower reaching toward the sky. A blip along the horizon and then it was gone. He exhaled long and hard until a pair of arms wrapped around his torso. Marlena rested her pretty head on his shoulder. He petted her hair but removed himself from her embrace.

"I just need a minute alone," he said. "To process everything...just a minute."

A worried dimple formed between her eyes.

"Is everything–?"

"I'm just going to go down below. My heart is beating

really fast."

She placed her hand over his heart and felt the thumps.

"You're right, it is." She smiled. "Take a moment and then come back up to watch the views with me."

"I love you," he said, meaning every bit of those words.

"I know," she replied, and patted his heart.

Down below, he tried to relax by taking long breaths, but they were still short and quipped. The room had a couple of beds and an enormous closet spanning one wall. He gulped another breath until his breathing started returning to normal. He was overwhelmed by everything that had happened. He just needed a minute to simmer.

A light beamed from the closet. His curiosity got the better of him, and he placed his hand on the doorknob to pull open the doors. Facing him were shelves upon shelves of lemon Pow! Soda cans.

"What the...?"

The sheer amount of Pow!s triggered something unsettling inside of him. His throat became dry. Sweat plagued his forehead. His hands became clammy and he couldn't stand still. He had a quick vision of popping open can after lemon can and drinking them all in a bacchanal frenzy. His tongue craved the sweet and sour taste of this new flavor. Where had these new flavors come from? Where were they being shipped off to? Could the Outside World be the Management's next target? A million scenarios zoomed through his mind as he reached out to touch one.

"Graham?" Marlena called from above deck. He could hear the clacking of her high heels coming down the stairs.

"I'm coming right up," he yelled, peering around the

door of the closet and seeing her tan legs on the stairs, the rest of her body non-existent.

"Are you okay?"

Sweat dribbled from his forehead onto the floor. He went to shut the closet doors but stopped. He stared at the lemon Pow!s, fighting not to grab one, but his hand became independent from his mind, and suddenly he had a cold can in his palm. He closed the closet door and shoved it into his pocket, his eyes flitting left and right as if someone was watching.

"Graham, are you okay?"

By the time he turned around, Marlena had fully come down the stairs. Her orange blouse and skirt were soiled and torn but she was still a dream. He fell into her arms and let those mechanical fingers of hers soothe him. The lemon Pow! shifted in his pocket. He visualized the moment after they'd all go to bed and he could take a taste, just one sip, no more, until they'd reach the shores of the Outside World and he could hope to delude himself into thinking that the nightmare hadn't followed them all.

"I am fine," he said, licking his lips. "I am fine."

THE END

TO BE CONTINUED IN BOOK II: LEMONWORLD

ABOUT ATMOSPHERE PRESS

Atmosphere Press is an independent, full-service publisher for excellent books in all genres and for all audiences. Learn more about what we do at atmospherepress.com.

We encourage you to check out some of Atmosphere's latest releases, which are available at Amazon.com and via order from your local bookstore:

An Expectation of Plenty, a novel by Thomas Bazar
Sink or Swim, Brooklyn, a novel by Ron Kemper
Lost and Found, a novel by Kevin Gardner
Skinny Vanilla Crisis, a novel by Colleen Alles
The Mommy Clique, a novel by Barbara Altamirano
Eaten Alive, a novel by Tim Galati
The Sacrifice Zone, a novel by Roger S. Gottlieb
Olive, a novel by Barbara Braendlein
Itsuki, a novel by Zach MacDonald
A Surprising Measure of Subliminal Sadness,
short stories by Sue Powers
Saint Lazarus Day, short stories by R. Conrad Speer
The Lower Canyons, a novel by John Manuel
Shiftless, a novel by Anthony C. Murphy
Connie Undone, a novel by Kristine Brown
A Cage Called Freedom, a novel by Paul P.S. Berg
The Escapist, a novel by Karahn Washington
Buildings Without Murders, a novel by Dan Gutstein

ABOUT THE AUTHOR

Lee Matthew Goldberg is the author of the novels THE ANCESTOR, THE MENTOR THE DESIRE CARD and SLOW DOWN. He has been published in multiple languages and nominated for the 2018 Prix du Polar. ORANGE CITY is forthcoming in 2021. After graduating with an MFA from the New School, his writing has also appeared in *The Millions, Vol. 1 Brooklyn, LitReactor, Monkeybicycle, Fiction Writers Review, Cagibi, the anthology Dirty Boulevard, The Montreal Review, The Adirondack Review, The New Plains Review, Underwood Press* and others. He is the editor-in-chief and co-founder of *Fringe*, dedicated to publishing fiction that's outside-of-the-box. His pilots and screenplays have been finalists in Script Pipeline, Book Pipeline, Stage 32, We Screenplay, the New York Screenplay, Screencraft, and the Hollywood Screenplay contests. He is the co-curator of The Guerrilla Lit Reading Series and lives in New York City. Follow him at LeeMatthewGoldberg.com

CPSIA information can be obtained
at www.ICGtesting.com
Printed in the USA
LVHW031308300321
682937LV00009B/405

9 781649 218780